RECKLESS
Kiss

D1714643

TIA LOUISE

This book is a work of fiction. Names, characters, places, and incidents are products of the author's imagination or are used fictitiously. Any resemblance to actual events or locales or persons, living or dead, is entirely coincidental.

Reckless Kiss
Copyright © TLM Productions LLC, 2020
Printed in the United States of America.

Cover design by Lori Jackson Design.
Photography by Wander Aguiar.

"Both light and shadow are the dance of love."
—*Rumi*

"I was standing. You were there. Two worlds collided…"
—*INXS*

Prologue

Angelica

MIDNIGHT BLUE SKY OVER MISTY MOUNTAINTOPS, THE MOON PAINTS the edges of the peaks in shimmering, silver light. Mamá would sit for hours gazing at the twilight, changing filters, changing lenses, manipulating the angles. I was little, and I would watch her, thinking she was magical, imagining her a genie or an alchemist.

Only her vision wasn't gold. It was a nightscape of shadow hues, deep and complex, and layered with emotion. I never asked her why the darkness lured her more than the light. I only wanted to follow her.

"La Luna," she would say, as I studied her photograph. "To the moon and back." She'd smooth my hair off my cheek, smiling warmly, tiny laugh lines crinkling her hazel eyes. "What do you see, Carmelita?"

"A lady sleeping, dreaming of a feast." My voice was little-girl quiet, and she'd laugh, holding the small metal camera.

"What kind of feast?" She'd gaze into my eyes as if she were memorizing my soul for the next time we met.

Her hair was stick straight and dark, inky brown spilling down her back. Her olive skin was pale. Mine was tanned by the blazing sun, and my long, coiled curls were tipped in gold.

Sitting under a string of multicolored twinkle lights, I'd hear a click and look up to see the round black lens tracking me, waiting for Mamá to tell it what to capture, what to preserve forever.

"Chilaquiles!" I'd grin, singing out my favorite dish.

"It's not breakfast," she'd playfully complain.

"Flautas with guacamole!"

"Hm… perhaps." She'd nod, returning to her work.

Our home was full of her art hanging from strings along the walls like laundry put out to dry. Georgia O'Keefe was my mother's idol, but where O'Keefe used canvas and acrylics, my mother used photopaper and film.

She was an artist.

She was a wizard.

She was the most beautiful woman I'd ever seen.

We lived in the Villa de Santa María de Aguayo, where the colorful houses rose in layers along the foothills, and I ran barefoot in a thin, cotton sundress on the cobbled streets with the other children.

She taught me how to cook with spices, how to eat fruit sprinkled with chili, how to dance. She had named me in the traditional way, Angelica María del Carmen Treviño, but I was Carmie or Carmelita to my family and friends.

The days passed slow, but the time moved fast.

Every day, death crept closer to our door.

My mother's death was insidious. More than a year passed from the time she was diagnosed to the day she died. She grew thinner, paler, weaker, but she never stopped working, taking photos, capturing the beauty of the mountains.

She was a Buddhist. She told me Death was a wave returning our souls to the sea. She said it was as natural as Life. Still, I clung to her and cried when she said it was time to go.

"You will be an artist, Carmie." Lying in her bed, she held my cheek, her eyes shining with love, her voice breaking with fatigue. "But your path is not mine."

Placing my face against her chest, I soaked her gown with my tears. I breathed her scent of gardenia and grace as I listened to her heart slowly stop beating.

I didn't know how to live without her. I didn't want to live without her.

I wanted our life in the shadow of the Sierra Madre forever.

Instead, she slipped through my fingers like those salty waves on the shore, and I was put on a bus at fifteen years old, sent to Plano, Texas, a huge suburb of Dallas, in the country where I was born, to finish school.

Closing my eyes, I long for our golden paradise, shining and bright with love, so different from this flat, barren land, baked dry by the sun. I taste the dirt on my tongue, put there by the hot wind that never stops.

My eyes are still closed when I slam into what feels like a brick wall.

"Watch it!" A tenor voice cries.

My eyes snap open, and I look up... up... up... as my breath disappears.

He's tall and slim with brown hair that flops attractively over his lowered brow. He studies me with piercing blue eyes that have flecks of gold around the pupils.

His gaze is so intense, my stomach tingles. It's a sensation low in my belly, a feeling I've never had before.

He's the most beautiful boy I've ever seen.

"I-I'm sorry." My voice is soft, and I can feel my eyes are wide like a deer's caught in a spotlight.

"You can't walk around with your eyes closed." His brow relaxes, and when he smiles, my heart skips faster.

His voice is like ripples in velvet, and he's wearing a navy blazer with a golden patch on the pocket. It's a fancy emblem, like he's royalty or something.

Pointing to his jacket, I find my voice. "What's that?"

He looks down, confused, then his brow relaxes. "It's my school uniform. Phillips Academy."

We start to walk slowly, side by side. I feel his eyes on me, and when I glance up, the way he looks at me reignites the heat in my veins.

"Are you lost?" He's so different from the people in my new neighborhood.

"I'm going to my cousin's house."

More steps in silence. I don't know why he's walking with me. "Why were your eyes closed?"

I'm embarrassed, but for whatever reason, I tell him the truth. "I was thinking about my mother."

He studies my expression, the slump of my shoulders.

"Is she sick?"

My lips press together, and I swallow the knot in my throat. "She died."

Again, he's quiet, thinking. "Mine too. A while back."

A connection, a shared injury pulling us closer, a scarlet thread tied from his finger to mine.

"Wanna hear a joke?"

Not really, but I shrug. "Okay."

"A skeleton walks into a bar. He orders a beer and a mop."

I don't laugh, and he tries again. "A horse walks into a bar. Bartender says, 'Why the long face?'"

My nose wrinkles, and he keeps going. "A hamburger walks into a bar. Bartender says, 'We don't serve food here.'"

I stop walking and squint my eyes at this beautiful boy, shining like the sun, doing his best to make me smile.

His head tilts to the side, and he gives it one last try. "The sign outside our service station says, 'Eat here and get gas.'"

Two heartbeats.

A flutter in my tummy, and my lips curl up at the corners.

His jokes aren't funny, but everything about him has me fizzy and alive. I want him to keep talking. I want to hear what he has to say.

He points a finger at me, winking. "Gotcha. I knew I could do it."

"What's your name?"

"Deacon. What's yours?"

"Angelica." I leave off the rest.

"You got a boyfriend, Angel?"

"No." I only have one friend, but he doesn't need to know that.

Full lips part with a smile. White teeth, and a satisfied look. "Good." Lifting my hand, he holds it carefully in his.

The warmth of his touch, the pressure of his grip echoes in my bones. I've never been reckless in my life, and yet...

I take a step closer. Our eyes lock, and we're engulfed in a magnetic field, drawn together. He takes a step forward, causing me to lift my chin. As his face lowers, heat rises in my stomach.

Warm breath ghosts my cheek, mingling with my rapid breathing. *Am I going to do this?*

Blinking my eyes closed, my heart says *Yes...*

My head grows light as warm lips cover mine. My fingers curl on the rich material of his blazer. His fingers tighten, holding my arm.

Our lips part, and I feel the lightest touch of his tongue against mine, so delicate. Energy surges in my belly, and a bird is caught there, fluttering and beating its wings.

He lifts his head, and his blue eyes hold mine. A real smile lifts my cheeks, echoed on his face. We both exhale a little laugh at this powerful thing we just shared, so simple, yet so overwhelming.

His voice is low, as he makes me a promise. "I'll see you again."

Then he turns and leaves me, walking backwards a few steps before waving, confident and graceful.

I'm still watching, my head spinning, my heart flying, when my cousin Valeria's voice breaks the spell. "What did *he* want?"

He's gone, and I turn to face her. "Nothing."

But my heart says different. My heart says, *Everything.* He asked without saying a word, and I said *Yes.*

"Carmie." Her voice is sharp, and she grips my arm, giving me a little shake. I meet her eyes, and she's blinking fast. "You are never to speak to that boy again. You understand?"

No. "Why?"

"Because he's bad." She looks up the way he left. "Promise me."

"Promise you why?" Defiance is in my tone.

Her jaw tightens. "That boy is our enemy."

"Our enemy?" I actually laugh. "What does that mean?"

"That boy's grandfather cheated ours. He stole all his land, he sent our grandfather, Papa Luis to prison. He left us beggars in the street."

She's right. I don't understand. "But we're okay now?"

"You didn't grow up here, Carmie. You don't understand these things."

Valeria is ten years older than me. She takes care of me now that both my parents have passed, and my brother is back in Mexico. I have nowhere else to go if not here.

Still... My throat is tight as I force the words. "Whatever. I promise."

But my fingers are crossed in the pocket of my hoodie.

Valeria is wrong. Deacon is not my enemy.

My heart is full of light, and I can't hate where love is already starting to grow, what my heart already knows. He's going to change my life.

CHAPTER
One

Deacon
Present day

WHEN I STEP INTO THE WARM-BEIGE INTERIOR OF LA FRIDA JAVA coffee shop from the blazing heat of late May in Texas, I have two things on my mind—air conditioning and the girl behind the counter.

Slim and petite, her hair hangs down her back in tight, spiral curls. She moves like a dancer, spinning to fill the coffee dispensers, hitting the brew button, then starting another order. My eyes drink her in, the curve of her cheek, the fullness of her glossy lips, and every second we've been apart aches in my bones.

It's been a month since I've seen her. I went back to Harristown to finish my degree, and now I want to sweep her into my arms, cover her mouth with kisses, plunge into her depths.

"Welcome to La Frida. What can I get…" Her amber eyes blink up, and as soon as they meet mine, she lets out a little gasp. "Deacon!"

Her smile grows so big, the little dimple at the top of her

appears, and my stomach tightens. I love that dimple. I love tracing my lips along it when I hold her body next to mine.

Angelica Treviño is the most beautiful girl I've ever seen. She has been since the day she slammed into me walking on the sidewalk near a park on the south side.

I'll never forget that day. She had the saddest face, and I only wanted to give her a smile. I had no idea when she did, I would also give her my heart.

We never had time to do anything about it back then. I left for Phillips Academy, an exclusive all-boys boarding school on the East Coast, and she stayed here. For four years, our relationship existed in emails and texts, sometimes the occasional handwritten letter. Until the summers, when I'd organize my life around finding her.

I'd "accidentally" bump into her at the park, at the fair, at the baseball field. I'd slide up beside her, and thread my fingers with hers briefly. I'd make her laugh and steal kisses, but she never let it go further… until the summer after we graduated high school, right before I left for college. It was the greatest night of my life, and the worst, as it turned our time apart into torture. Nights lying in bed dreaming of her beautiful body, her soft sighs…

Reaching across the counter, I lace our fingers. "Can you take a break?"

"I wish. Staci called in sick, the new girl never showed up… We're completely short-handed." Her eyes move to the small line forming behind me. "Do you want coffee?"

I'm still holding her hand, sliding my thumb along her soft skin. I've missed her so much. Our eyes hold, and her cheeks flush as if she can read my thoughts.

She smiles, tilting her head to the side. "You're holding up the line."

Tearing my eyes from her gorgeous face, I scan the menu on the wall behind her. "How about… a tall Frida Latte and dip your little finger in it."

She rolls her eyes, and I wait as she quickly starts my order then helps the next person in line. I watch her move, skimming my eyes down her back, over her cute little ass and down her long legs.

When she hands me my coffee, our fingers touch, and she smiles up at me. "Are you working today?"

"Lourdes asked me to stop by New Hope." I provide free financial advice to displaced women at a shelter near Garland. Angel's best friend Lourdes is the administrator there.

Her smile reappears. "I have an art class at four, but I can meet you there before."

"It's a date."

She's gone just as fast, rushing to the next customer in line. I back toward the door, taking one last look at her pretty face before stepping into the heat.

"CATER-WAITER IS GOOD. THE PAY'S DECENT AND YOU'LL GET WORK REFERENCES." The young mother across the table from me bounces her toddler boy on her lap, watching me with worried eyes.

Her dark hair is slicked back in a tight bun with kiss curls above each of her temples. "I need something with better hours."

"You don't have credit card debt, which is great."

"I don't have a credit card." She just looks at me.

"Right." I return to her spreadsheet. "Can you put a little into savings each month? Maybe five percent of your paycheck?"

"Five percent!" Her eyes are round, and you'd think I'd suggested five million.

I give her what I hope is a reassuring smile. "It doesn't have to be five percent. Even five dollars will build over time. Think of it like running a marathon—"

"I can barely cover my bills. I have to feed Chuy." The little boy squirms in her lap.

"Right." I tap my stylus a few times on the screen of my iPad Pro. "You might qualify for a grant…"

"No." Her chin drops.

She doesn't say more, and I drop it. The women here are either running from bad situations or hiding from them, and as much as I want to help, it's not my business to push.

Still, every time I come here I wish I could do more. It's frustrating, but it's a start. I'm giving them the tools they need to have financial security one day. To stand on their own.

I hope.

Angel enters the cafeteria and warmth fills my stomach. She goes to Lourdes, who is bouncing a baby on her hip. The sunlight through the windows creates a halo around her head, and when she takes the fat infant from her best friend, I imagine her holding our baby. It's a thought I like very much.

The woman across from me breaks, her eyes filling with tears, snapping me out of my daydream. "I'll end up a maid like my mamma."

"Juliana..." I reach out to touch her arm lightly. "Is it okay if I call you Juliana?"

Her brow furrows, and she seems confused. "It's my name."

The little boy in her lap arches his back and pushes. Juliana puts him on his feet, and he toddles off to where two other little boys are playing on the floor with a truck.

"You can do this." Swiping several times, I head over to the government aid section of our website. Then I remember... "Could you start working tomorrow?"

Her thin brows furrow. "Maybe?"

"I just heard about an opening at a coffee shop nearby, La Frida Java. If you're interested?"

The tension in her brow eases a notch. "A coffee shop?"

"A... friend of mine works there. I can ask her." I hate calling Angel my friend.

She says it doesn't matter if we're a secret. It doesn't change our feelings. But it matters to me, and I'm back to set the record straight.

"I'll call Lourdes once I know for sure."

I slide my tablet into the leather case, and Juliana stands quickly, reaching out to shake my hand. "Thank you, sir."

"It's Deacon." I shake her slim hand. "We're going to make this happen. Okay?"

She nods, wiping roughly at her eyes before turning to chase after her son. Putting my things in my black messenger bag, I start for where my angel is with her best friend.

"Hey, handsome." Lourdes steps into a hug, pecking a friendly kiss on my cheek. "Did you put that big brain to work for Juliana?"

"Tried to." I pat her back. "She wants to be a florist, but she really needs a steady job."

"They all do." Lourdes bounces the fat baby on her hip, and Angel slides up beside me, wrapping her arms around my waist.

My chest relaxes with her in my arms. "She'll get there. I believe in her."

"Because you're a rich white boy." Lourdes slants her eyes at me. "Of course you do."

I hold up a hand. "Privilege, I know. But she's made good decisions—"

"Financially." Lourdes is blunt, but she's cool. As far as I know, she's the only person in Angel's life who knows we're together. "Anyway, thanks for helping."

"Glad to do it." I lower my nose to the top of Angel's head, inhaling the familiar scent of jasmine. I've missed her so much.

She lifts her chin to kiss my lips. "Why are you so good?"

"I'm not so good." Our eyes meet, and heat filters between us. I want to take her back to my apartment and make up for lost time.

"Jeez-um… Can you two give it a rest?" Lourdes lifts the baby from her hip. "Here, Romeo, try some reality on for size."

She passes the baby boy to me, and I hold him up a second before bringing him to my chest. "Hey, big fella. He's a bruiser."

Angel is beside me, tracing her finger along his arm rolls. "He's adorable—oh!"

We all jump back when Bruiser wobbles and then barfs all over me.

I look down at the white stream running down my Armani. "That's gonna stain."

"Tito!" A young woman rushes up to me, taking the baby. "I'm so sorry!"

"It's her fault." I point at Lourdes. "She shook him up."

"Come with me." Lourdes catches my arm not even hiding her laughter. "I've got a damp cloth in the kitchen."

"Oh no." Angel stiffens and abruptly walks away from us.

"Angel?"

She doesn't reply, but instead goes straight to a man I don't recognize. He's about my height with dark hair and eyes. He looks a few years older than us, and he's standing beside Juliana, looking down at her with a stern expression.

I start to follow when Lourdes grabs my arm. "Hold up, Chief. Don't go over there."

My eyes are on Angel, and when the man sees her, his scowl softens just a bit. He pulls her into a long hug, closing his eyes.

"Who is that guy?"

"That *guy* is Roberto Treviño, also known as Beto Treviño." Lourdes says his name with a deep exhale. "Also known as Carmie's older brother."

"Brother…" I study his face.

Now I see the family resemblance, but where Angel is sweet and light, this guy is dark and angry. He surveys the facility from under a lowered brow, even as he smiles at his sister.

"Is something wrong with him?"

"Like what?" Lourdes pulls me into the kitchen.

"He seems pissed."

She glances over her shoulder once more as the swinging door closes. "That's just his face."

"Well, good. I can go and introduce myself—"

She grabs my arm again. "Give Carmie a minute. Trust me on this one, okay?" I don't like it, but she reaches for my coat. "You're a big mess. Give this to me."

I shrug out of my blazer and hand it over. She dabs it with a damp cloth. "I heard he was moving back from Mexico. Looks like today's the day."

Leaning to the side, I watch as he speaks to Angel. Her hands twist and she pushes her hair back. She drops her chin and nods, and I can see she's nervous around him. I don't like it.

"It's not coming out." She shakes her head, wrapping it in a loose bundle. "I'll have it dry cleaned."

"No way." I slide the garment out of her hands. "I'll take care of it. You guys are on a shoestring budget as it is." My phone starts buzzing, and when I see the face, I frown. "I need to take this."

"You should go. I'll tell Carmie you said goodbye."

"I want to talk to her. I'll just be a second."

"Deacon." She fixes brown eyes on mine. "I'll tell her you said goodbye."

Angel's on the other side of the door, standing at her brother's side, and my jaw tenses. I want to go out there and introduce myself, but Lourdes guides me to the door.

"Just give her some time, okay? You're one of the good guys."

Possession and frustration war in my chest, familiar feelings I've struggled with growing stronger through the years. When we were young and separated so much, I could understand. Not anymore.

"I'll call her later."

"You should probably let her call you."

I take one last look at my angel before pushing out the door.

CHAPTER
Two

Angel

MY ARMS ARE AROUND DEACON'S WAIST, AND I'M HUMMING WITH the thrill of him being here at last. Tall and strong, he smiles, and I watch the muscle in his square jaw move as he banters with Lourdes.

It's been a month since we were together, and I want to kiss him. I want to bury my face in his neck and inhale his clean scent of citrus and soap. I want him to lift me off my feet and take me away from this world like only he can do.

Then the baby barfs all over him.

Then my brother appears.

It's like a bucket of ice water right in my face. Beto's looking around the room, and I say a silent prayer as I step away from the group, going to meet him, hoping to avoid any questions.

When I was little, Mamá would say I had intuition. She would say I could sense things before they happened.

She also said family was the most important thing. She would say we had to love each other, have each other's backs, but after she died and I came here to live with them, I didn't even know them.

My brother was an angry mystery. When I was a little girl, before Mamá took me to Mexico, I remember him carrying me on his hip. I remember him smiling, and twirling my curls around his fingers. I remember him sweet.

Then I came here and he never smiled. He also didn't stay.

I arrived, and a week later he left. I became a guest in my cousin's home. She treated me like family, but I was very aware I was an extra mouth to feed, an extra person to clothe, a potential burden in her life…

I did my best to help with the chores, care for her two daughters, do as I was told, stay out of trouble.

"My little sister." Beto pulls me into a hug, and I'm surrounded by leather and tobacco.

My brother takes after my dad—darkly handsome, with straight black hair that curls around his ears. His eyes are so brown, you can't see the pupils, and his white teeth are straight behind full lips. His body is lean and hard, and he hugs me roughly, almost painfully. "How long has it been?"

"A long time." I smile up at him, hoping he doesn't see the fear in my eyes.

I had hoped his return would mean we could get to know each other again. I had hoped we might be close, like we were all those years ago when I was a little girl.

Now I'm not so sure. Now my intuition is twisting my stomach, and Beto returning to Plano the same day as Deacon feels like a bad omen.

He nods to where Lourdes is hustling Deacon out the door. "What's up with the suit?"

"A local businessman." I step between my brother and my friends. "Lourdes invites them to advise the residents on stuff."

His brow lowers. "Why?"

"What do you mean *why?*" I force a laugh.

"We don't need his kind here."

"His kind?"

"Ivy league assholes. Easing their consciences handing out advice that only works if you're white and privileged."

My stomach is sick at this response, my voice quiet. *Bad omen…* "I know he means well. He does it for free."

He studies me a little too long before easing up. "Nothing is free, *mija*. Somebody always pays."

I don't have time to argue before Lourdes rushes up to us.

"Beto!" She walks straight into a hug. "When did you get in town?"

"How you doing, Lor?" He gives her a one-armed hug.

"Why are you at the women's shelter?"

"I came to get Carmie."

"That's not weird at all, is it Carm?" She makes a face at me and laughs.

My best friend's superpower is diffusing tense situations. It's what makes her perfect for her job here.

"Pot-stirrer." He gives her shoulder a shove. "I'm taking care of Carmie now."

He smiles at me proudly, and dread filters through my stomach.

"As a big brother should." My bestie smiles, but she can sense my shift in mood. "So you're back to stay?"

"I'm back to make things right."

What the hell does that mean?

A strong hand closes over my shoulder. "You ready?"

"Sure… I have to be at my studio class at four—"

"Then we'd better get moving." He starts for the door, speaking under his breath. "I don't like you hanging out in this place."

"I visit the girls and help Lourdes."

He doesn't respond, and I don't know if he's too far to hear me or if he doesn't care.

Whatever. I turn to Lourdes. "Valeria's killing the fatted calf for his homecoming meal. You should come for dinner."

"I'll try." She hugs me, kissing my cheek. "I've got to finish up some paperwork, so I might be late."

Leaning closer, I lower my voice. "What did Deacon say?"

Her worried eyes flicker over my shoulder. "He's going to call you later."

Nodding, I turn my phone to silent. "I'll text him."

"You're going to have to come clean about him. Now that Beto's back, it's not going to be so easy to hide."

"I will… I will." *Timing is everything.*

She's held my hand since the day I arrived in Plano, a sad, scared little orphan. She's always been by my side, protecting me, taking up for me—not that anybody who knew him would mess with Roberto Treviño's sister.

"I'm here if you need me." Lourdes squeezes my hand, and I give her one last hug.

MY PHONE BUZZES A FEW TIMES ON THE WAY TO THE STUDIO, BUT I DON'T take it out of my pocket. Leaning my head against the window, I close my eyes and let the morning wash over me.

After my shift at La Frida Java, I raced to New Hope, desperate to see Deacon, touch him, imagining what it will be like to have him here in the city all the time, just a phone call or text away.

It makes me so happy.

Deacon is a decadent luxury I've kept close to my heart, a precious secret. My one true love.

When we were young, I'd be on edge every summer until I saw him again. My heart would beat so fast, and my chest would ache. I was sure he'd come to me and say it was over—or perhaps he wouldn't come at all. He'd simply find some pretty rich girl, some debutante from his world and realize spending his time with a waif on the south side of town was beneath him.

Every year he proved me wrong.

He'd show up at the park or at baseball games or at the fair. He'd buy me snowballs and trace his finger along my cheek, twirling my crazy curls, squeezing my heart with his smiles.

I'd see him riding his motorcycle, caramel hair moving in the breeze. A crooked grin, a deep dimple in his cheek. He was a cocky rich boy, and when he stopped beside me, my body pulled to his like a magnet.

My hands wrapped around his waist, my cheek pressed to his shoulder, my thighs sliding against his with only thin fabric separating our bodies.

Being with him was deep blue and shining cerulean, it was a blanket of shimmering stars curling in the night sky. It was my mother's portraits of moonshine tipping the edges of the mountains.

Mamá filled me with dreams of a life she hoped I would live. She made me believe I could become anything I wanted, and Deacon swept in like a promise those dreams would come true. He made me laugh, he made me swoon.

He kissed me, and my stomach flew like diving off the tallest cliff into a cloud of wonder and deliciousness. His lips were soft, his taste so sweet. Deacon between my thighs became a drug I couldn't live without, an addiction I would guard with my life.

With Valeria's original warning in my ear, the promise she forced me to make, I decided it was better to ask forgiveness than permission, and I did my dead-level best never, *never* to get caught.

"You've changed since the last time I saw you." Beto's voice rouses me, and I look over to see him studying me from the driver's side of his truck. His window is down, and the wind pushes his collar-length hair around his temples.

"It's been almost four years."

"Yes. A long time."

"You hardly ever called… We rarely saw you. Why?" I'm old enough to know.

He tilts his head to the side. "I was working, taking care of business, protecting our interests."

My eyes fall to the holstered gun on the console.

"Why do you have a gun?"

"Because I live in Texas."

"Jesus said if you live by the sword, you'll die by the sword."

He exhales a chuckle. "I have no intention of dying any time soon, *mija*."

He keeps saying that. No one has called me *mija* since my mother passed.

"Did you visit Mamá's house?"

"Yes." His brow lowers. "I saw the pit you lived in at Villa de Santa María."

"It was not a pit!" I shift in my seat to face him.

Granted, I was only a kid when I left my mother's ranch, but it was a beautiful place full of art and light and happiness.

"It's a broken-down shack with no air conditioning, no Wifi. I'm surprised it had indoor plumbing." Disgust permeates his tone. "Our family are not peasants."

"It was a lovely place. The night breezes kept us cool, and we didn't need the Internet. We talked and sang songs." My eyes go out the open window to the brown, dusty road, and I remember the colors, the joy I felt as a child in Mexico. Everything here is brown and dusty, and the wind never stops blowing.

His nose curls. "You should have lived like queens."

"We're not royals, Beto, no matter how proud you are."

"All that changes now." He pulls into the driveway of the small studio. "Tonight you'll pack your things. You're coming to live with me."

"Live with you where?"

"Lakeside Estates."

My eyebrows shoot up. "Lakeside!" It's one of the richest gated communities in the city. "How?"

"I bought a house there last week." His eyebrows rise, and he looks proud but also a bit smug—like he had something to prove, and he did. "Closed on it this morning before I came to get you. You're not working at that coffee shop anymore, either."

All this new information has my head spinning. "I like working at the coffee shop."

"If you owned it, that would be one thing. You're not working as a waitress. It's beneath you."

"It helps pay my bills. And the schedule is flexible so I can do my art—"

He leans towards me, holding up a finger. "End of discussion."

Fat chance of that.

"I'm not quitting my job." I jerk the door handle and slide out of his truck.

Just before I close the door, our eyes catch. Anger flashes in his, but I flash right back. I'm not afraid of Roberto. He's my brother, and while we might not be close, we're still family. He won't hurt me.

"I'll pick you up in an hour."

"I'll catch a ride like I always do." My heart's beating fast, but I'm doing my best to hold my ground.

"I'll be here in an hour."

"LET YOUR INNER CHILD PLAY." PROFESSOR ROSHAY CIRCLES THE SMALL room, giving feedback as we work. "Relax... Set her free!"

Every year, one of Farrell Roshay's students wins the Arthaus "Artist in Residence" award. It's a massive, twenty-thousand-dollar gift that includes six months to create, culminating in a private show at the Palladium Gallery in downtown Dallas.

Uncle Antonio has helped me pay for these studio classes

since I graduated from community college two years ago, and I want that award so badly, it hurts.

I'm standing in front of my latest piece, a four-foot canvas covered in energetic swirls of red-orange and coral with yellow and white, brown and forest green cast highlights and depth.

Rising above it all is a black charcoal outline of a horse with its tail fanning out. Its mane swirls up and around its powerful, bowed head. In the foreground is the rear and back legs flexing and stomping.

The horse is in a gallop, consumed in the colors like a cyclone.

I'm lost in the movement of the piece, a spiral curl falls onto my cheek, and I push it back, leaving a smudge of paint across my skin. I don't care. My spirit is free, running wild, eating up the miles, chasing the sunset. I've shaken off the scars of my past. My fear is gone, and I can do anything I want. I'm invincible.

"Angelica!" Professor Roshay stops behind me, holding out her arms. "I feel the energy radiating from this piece. Tell me what you've done here."

My breath catches. We have two classes left before graduation, and every piece, every class feeds into consideration for the award. Every interview is a judgement, every answer a step closer or a strike back.

Swallowing my nerves, I ignore the smear of paint on my face, the messiness of my hair, and I speak from my heart. "I'm calling it *Spirit*. The horse is the spirit of the west, but he can also be the spirit of the viewer. He's a mustang, free to run the grasslands, swept up in the fire of the desert, the glow of the setting sun."

"I see it. Now tell me about your technique."

My heart is beating so hard—deep breaths… "I knew the colors and the movement of the sketch would dominate the canvas. For the highlights, I wanted to do something special. I dipped my fingers in the paint and made these smudges, these glows around the nose and jaw with my hands."

"Finger painting?" Her eyebrow arches, and my stomach drops. "A primitive and unexpected choice."

"It felt right."

She nods, taking a few steps, tapping her finger against her lips. "Inventive. I like it."

I swallow the squeal bubbling in my throat, and answer calmly. "Thank you."

She continues down the row, and I close my eyes, fighting tears. *Spirit* is one of my favorite pieces. I can't wait to show it to Deacon. I can't wait for Uncle Antonio to see it. I'll include it in my portfolio when I apply for the award.

"Our time is at an end." Professor Roshay claps, and it's the signal to clean up. "Our last meeting is next week, then the Arthaus application opens online. Good luck."

I float through cleaning and wrapping my brushes, stowing my palette, wiping the paint off my face, and head out the door with a smile on my lips, visions of winning that coveted award in my head. Not even my scowling brother in his truck can dampen my mood. He's on the phone the entire drive to Valeria's small house, so it doesn't matter.

"Beto!" Valeria's happy cry echoes through the tiny house as we enter. "You're here!"

She's in the kitchen holding out her arms for a hug. Valeria is five years older than my brother, ten years older than me, and she's always treated us like her children.

"Hi, Beto." Lola is her oldest daughter. She's at the bar arranging tortillas in baking dishes. "Hey, Carmie."

"Hey." I go to where she's standing. "Need some help?"

"Sure."

"Damn, I'm hungry." Beto steps over and steals a pinch of shredded cheese.

The kitchen smells like sizzling chicken and steak and tomatoes and peppers. The whole place is mouthwatering.

"Get a drink out of the cooler and go see your uncle." Valeria is beside me, pulling down plates. "We'll be ready in ten minutes."

An hour later, we're all on the side patio of my cousin's house, bellies full of enchiladas and guacamole and pico de gallo and so much good food. I'm leaning against the wall of her brick patio under a stream of white twinkle lights. It's beautiful, and I've got to go inside and pack my things and call Deacon. The men sit at the table finishing their drinks, and it's so familiar, a life that brushed past me like an echo.

"At some point, Beto, you have to make peace with the world." Uncle Antonio pulls on his cigar.

Uncle Antonio owns a used car dealership and makes a good living. Valeria owns this house off what her father earns, and she doesn't have to work as a nurse. She just wants to.

Her husband was a Marine who died in Afghanistan. She keeps his American flag in a glass case on her mantle.

"Don't be like your father, driving everyone away."

My uncle's words catch my attention. I barely remember my father. Mamá left him when I was so little, and while they never divorced, they never lived together again. All Mamá ever said was she couldn't be like him, vengeful, bitter.

"I can make peace with a world where justice has been served." My brother's hand is on a tumbler of Mezcal.

"That's not how the world works, my son." My uncle tilts his tumbler of whiskey back and forth. It's the same glass he's had all night. "At least not the real world."

Valeria and Lola have cleared away the plates and serving dishes, and they're inside finalizing plans for Lola's quinceañera on Saturday. I had planned to bring Deacon as my date, so I could introduce him to everyone as more than a friend, show them he's good and not our enemy.

Now I'm worried my brother will cause problems.

"It's how the real world should work." Beto seems relaxed, but his voice has an edge in it. "It's how my world works."

"Such attitudes lead to trouble." My uncle's eyes level on my brother, and anxiety is sticky in my chest. "We've had enough violence to last a lifetime, Roberto."

My phone buzzes in my pocket. It's been buzzing with texts from Deacon all through dinner, and I've been sneaking replies, doing my best to hide my smiles. I'm so happy he's home.

Meet me at the park at ten? His latest text sends a flutter in my stomach. I want to see him. I want to kiss him and hold him.

During the summers, Deacon and I would meet at the park just down from Valeria's house, then he'd drive us to the Yellow Rose lookout tower just outside of town.

It's a beautiful old stone structure on a hill overlooking a lake.

When I don't reply, he texts again, *Park… ten.*

My chest clenches, and I ache for him. I wish I could touch the number and call him, let him hear my voice so he can know how I feel…

Instead, I tell him what's happening, *I'm moving to my brother's tonight.*

Where?

Lakeside. Not sure the address. Will send when I know.

I can only imagine his surprise at this news. I'm still surprised, but I can't linger. In the kitchen, Valeria and Lola are at her laptop looking at photos on Pinterest. Valeria's baby daughter, four-year-old Sofia pushes between them, doing her best to be a part of what's happening.

Lola pushes her back like an annoyed big sister, so I swoop Sofia onto my hip so she can see over them. We watch a minute, then I kiss their heads.

"I'd better get packing." I'm about to put Sofia down when she squeezes me tighter.

"I can help!"

"Okay, little monkey." I've taken care of Sofia since she was a baby, since the day she emerged in the delivery room, and I was there holding Valeria's hand. It's possible I've spoiled her a little… although not enough to be bad.

"I don't want you to go." She puts her light brown head on my shoulder, chewing on her thumb. "I'll miss you, Cee-cee."

"But you'll have your own room. No more sharing with Lola."

"I don't want my own room." Her little voice is so sad, it tugs at my chest, but I know there's no turning back from this.

"You'll love it! You can decorate it however you want. It'll be special."

The small room where I spent the past eight years is not special. It's decorated in the same pale green and pink flowers Valeria put here before I arrived. The twin bed where I slept is covered in a quilt, and the only decorations are my mother's photos. I have two hung on the walls, but the rest are stored away in albums.

I deposit my little cousin on the bed, and she looks up at me with wide eyes. "Are you scared to live with Uncle Beto?"

Beto's not her uncle, but I don't bother correcting her. I'm sure it's what Valeria told her to call him.

"He's my brother." I give her caramel ponytail a gentle tug. "I'm not scared of my brother."

I am annoyed at being passed around like a football. I wish I'd have gotten a little forewarning about his plans, but that's not something I can get into with her. I've made my choices, and my choices have left me with very few options financially.

"Maybe one day soon I can get my own place." If I win that award.

"Mamma says girls shouldn't live alone. She says it's not safe." Sofia watches me pack, and I keep my opinions about Valeria's old-fashioned notions to myself.

Loading my toiletries into a backpack, I heft it onto my

shoulder, catching Sofia's hand and rolling my suitcase to the kitchen. It seems I should have more than one suitcase after eight years, but I grew up simply. I haven't changed.

"I'll come back for the rest of my art supplies tomorrow."

"I'll bring them over in the morning." Valeria smiles up at me from where she sits at the table beside her daughter. "Is that all you have?"

"That's it!" I deposit Sofia into the chair beside them.

My cousin stands, pulling me into a hug. "It's going to be strange not having you here."

"I'll have my own room at last!" Lola bounces in her chair, and Sofia falls back, crossing her arms.

"I will, too." Her voice is pouty.

I turn to Valeria. "I didn't know Beto's arrival would change so many things."

After our short conversations in his truck, I don't know what to expect of living in my brother's house, and while I hope for the best, I don't know if I should be happy or afraid.

Valeria gives me a tight smile. "Try to remember he only wants what's best for you... for his family."

"Apparently what he thinks is best is acting like it's the 1950s."

She laughs, light filling her eyes. "You two are so much alike. You're going to be fine."

My brother takes the suitcase from my hand, inspecting it with a frown. "That's all you have?" I shrug, and he waves me to the truck. "We'll take care of this later."

Whatever Valeria says, I'm not sure this is going to be fine.

CHAPTER
Three

Deacon

"**S**EEING YOU, SITTING THERE... YOU'RE THE SPITTING IMAGE OF your father." My aunt Winnie smiles at me from the head of a long, ranch oak table in the dining room of our family mansion.

She's wearing a sleek, emerald-green dress, and her straight white hair is swept back in a loose bun at the nape of her neck. She's a stern old broad, an elegant beauty, but she's always been sweet to me. Dad would say it's because I'm her only nephew. I'm the only anything, since she never had any children, and they have no other siblings.

A fire is burning in an oversized hearth behind me. She runs the air conditioner so she can have a fire at dinner. It's pretty much the height of old Texas overindulgence.

"That's what everybody says. With my grandmother's eyes."

She lifts a glass of red wine. "Your visits give me such joy. I'm sure you'll never know. I'm so glad you're finished with school. I hope to see you more."

That last bit is a passive-aggressive dig, but I let it pass. One of my late father's last requests was I take care of his sister, so I have dinner with her once a week when I'm in town and do my best to tolerate her outdated notions about life and politics.

I love my aunt, but she'd rather fight than evolve. It's not how I want our relationship to be—if I can help it.

"I'll always make time for our weekly dinners." I return her smile, doing my best to tamp down my frustration over how this day played out.

My plan when I left Harristown this morning was *not* to be having dinner with my aunt. I drove two and a half hours, straight to La Frida Java, in the hopes of being in Angel's arms right now.

Then her brother appeared.

Then it all went to hell.

My jaw tightens. I've wanted to meet Angel's family for years. She always said no. She always had a reason we needed to wait. Now I've been texting her all day, wanting to see her, and she's moving to Lakeside? I'm happy, but I'm confused.

"Do you not like your salad?" Winnie eyes me from above the rim of her heavy crystal goblet.

"It's fine." I stab at the plate of purple and dark green lettuce in front of me. Yellow beets, pecans, and balls of goat cheese adorn the center. "I like this cheese."

"*Chèvre*, Deacon." She shakes her head as if I should know better. "What would your mother say?"

I have no idea. My mother died before I ever had the chance to know her. Winnie doesn't allow for follow-up.

"I must know..." She tilts her head to the side. "Why do you insist on having an apartment downtown? Why not move in right here? There's plenty of room for the two of us."

I glance around our family's one-hundred-year-old estate. Ten bedrooms, eight and a half bathrooms, it's an imposing structure with a grand foyer and a balcony that runs the entire square length. Everything smells of leather and furniture polish and age.

"I'm an adult, Win."

"So what?" She acts offended. "Many of the old families live together in compounds. The house affords plenty of privacy. Besides, who'll look after me if I were to fall or become ill?"

"You're in no danger of that. Even if you were, the butler, the maid—"

"The hired help." Her expression folds like a deck of cards. "How horrifying."

She holds up the bell, giving it one ring, and immediately servers appear to remove our salad plates. They're replaced with dishes of steak and garlic shrimp with potatoes on the side.

My phone buzzes in my pocket, and my stomach tightens. It takes all my willpower not to check Angel's text at dinner.

"I know, you young men need your space to sow your wild oats." She lifts a fresh goblet of dark red Barollo, taking a sip and cutting her eyes at me. "Just remember you can come back home when it's time to settle down."

"I'm more interested in living in a house where I'm the head than being a guest in yours." I'm not going to get into the fact I can't bring Angel home with my aged aunt lurking around the halls.

"Don't be ridiculous, Deacon." She places a slim ivory hand against her chest. "It's our family home. You'd be the head of your own little group just as I'd be responsible for myself."

"Is that how it works?" My eyes drift to the life-sized portrait of my father hanging over the oversized mantle, looking down on us both.

He's standing beside a horse, holding the bridle, but he's not dressed like a cowboy. He's dressed like an English lord. A similar painting of my grandfather is in the great hall, only he's standing in his Texas suit, bolero tie, holding a cowboy hat with oil derricks rising in the background.

"What do you think?" My aunt's voice interrupts my thoughts. She's watching me. "Is it time to commission your portrait to hang in these hallowed halls?"

"No!" My answer bursts out on a laugh. The idea is funnier than I expected.

"What?" Her blue eyes narrow. "False modesty aside. You will be added to the gallery at some point. You're the heir."

"I think it's a little premature for painting my portrait." I lift the heavy crystal goblet and polish off my glass of Barolo. "Who knows what I might do?"

Winnie leans back in her chair, gazing at my father. "I think it's about time we added a female to the mix. What do you think?"

"You're having your portrait made?"

"And why not?"

"I was just making sure." I couldn't care less about these meaningless traditions. "Go for it. I think it's a great idea."

"I think you're right." A rare smile curves her lips. "Will you be attending the Cattlemen's Masque this year? I'd like to tell Haven and Cecilia if so. They'll be thrilled to have you back."

Haven Wells is Rich's mother, and Cecilia Westbrook is one of my aunt's old friends from school. It gives me an idea—one I like very much the more I think about it.

"Yes." It's as good a time as any to introduce them to my girl. "When is it again?"

Winnie laughs, shaking her head. "It's the same date every year, darling. A month from Friday." She leans back with a sigh. "Your mother always loved the ball. She was a rancher at heart. Your father took her away from that life."

"I'll be there." Slipping a bite of steak in my mouth, I nod. "And I'm bringing a date."

"A date?" Her eyes widen with delight. "That's wonderful! Is it someone I know?"

"No." I take a sip of the heavy red wine. "But it's someone very important to me."

"I'm intrigued." Her lips press into a smile, and she flares her eyes. "Someone I don't know who's very important to you? I can hardly wait."

That makes two of us.

AN HOUR LATER, I'M PACING MY BEDROOM ON THE SECOND FLOOR OF THE family home. My aunt has gone to bed, but I stay here because it's closer to Lakeside than my downtown penthouse. My blood is hot, and I must see my angel tonight.

Finally, she texts me back. *I can be at the corner of Lakeside and Greenbriar at midnight if you still want to meet?*

Glancing at my watch, I see that's fifteen minutes from now. *I'll be there.*

I've changed into jeans and a navy tee. Grabbing the black leather jacket off the back of my chair, I dash down the stairs and out into the garage. It's probably eighty degrees out, but the wind and the darkness make it cool. I don't want to wake my aunt, so I roll my Indian FTR motorcycle out to the end of the driveway before pulling on my helmet and kicking it to start.

It's a sleek, black machine, invisible in the night, and it flies across the vacant roads, smooth as silk, eating up the miles separating me from my love. Flying in the dead of night to find her has a romance that matches the heat in my veins. I'm half a mile away when I see her standing in the glow of the streetlight, her dark hair swaying in the breeze along with the thin fabric of her skirt.

Hunger blazes to life in my chest. I want my hands under that skirt. I want her body all over mine. I've waited so long… She's so close.

Pulling up to where she stands, I hop off the bike and whip the helmet off my head. "What a shitty day," I groan, wrapping my arms around her.

"It's definitely been a whirlwind." Her cheek presses to the center of my chest. "I didn't know what might happen next."

She fits so perfectly against my body. I dip my chin to inhale her fresh scent before leaning lower, capturing her velvet lips with mine—something I've wanted to do since I opened my eyes this morning.

I open her mouth with mine, curling my tongue with hers, and a soft noise escapes from her throat. Heat floods below my belt.

"Let's go." Taking the spare helmet out of the back compartment, I hand it to her as I replace my own, kicking the engine to life.

She's at my back, slim arms holding me so tight, and I feel the pressure of her head against my shoulder blade. It's a sensation I've known since we were kids. It's a sensation I've missed so much.

We blaze into the night, gliding over the roads, crossing the miles like water. The Yellow Rose lookout tower is on the other side of town, but at this hour on a Thursday, it's easy to make good time, and I know the back roads to take.

Stars flood the night sky as we travel farther away from town. They form a ripple of glitter curling through the expanse of inky black under a quarter moon. Lifting my hand off the grip, I cover hers clasped at my waist. She fumbles with my fingers, lacing hers with mine, and I lift her hand to my lips.

We're almost there, and I can feel the softness of her skin in my memory. When I was a boy, and I'd leave her to go back to Phillips Academy for the school year, I'd dream of her kisses, sweet like candy.

Now I'm a man, and my dreams are not sweet. They're hot and hungry.

We pull off the road onto the gravel leading to the hill beside the lake. The stone tower rises into the night like a promise of what's to come, and the brown grass and short trees give way to the glow of the lake under the moon.

I park in the shadows behind a scrub bush and help Angel to her feet, taking the helmets and leaving them on the bike. Holding hands, we rush through the narrow black doorway towards the wooden stairs. My back hits the stone wall, and she falls against me, searching for my mouth in the darkness. I kiss her, sweeping my tongue along her lips, and sliding my hands under her breasts, feeling their weight through the thin material.

"You feel so good," I groan.

She gasps softly. "I've missed your touch."

My body is taut and straining for her. "I want to touch you everywhere."

Pushing apart, she takes my hands, leading me higher, all the way to the observation deck overlooking the mirrored lake below.

The wind pushes in strong gusts through the open space. It's less hot and laced with the metallic flavor of water. Dark gray storm clouds are gathering on the horizon, but I've got one thing on my mind.

"It's perfect," she whispers as I turn her back to the wall.

"You're perfect." My hands are on her bare thighs, lifting her against me as I rock my hips forward.

We're shrouded in darkness, and I devour her, kissing, tasting, burning up with the need flaming hotter in my chest, in my pelvis. Our lips pull and slide apart, and a groan breaks the silence. She pulls at the thin cotton of my shirt, ripping it higher, exposing my stomach.

I quickly shrug out of my jacket, whipping the shirt over my head. In the pale moonlight I can see her full bottom lip clutched beneath her teeth as she traces her fingers along the lines of my stomach. It's hot as fuck, and my cock is a steel rod in my jeans.

"Angel," I groan, pulling her to me, capturing her lips again, reaching down to slide my hands along the soft skin of her thighs.

Her body rocks against mine and she moans as my hands rise higher to the apex of her thighs where I discover… "You're not wearing panties."

"Touch me there," she whispers, and my brow collapses.

My fingers slide along the slick wetness of her pussy, and she grips my shoulders, crying out as her head falls back. "Deacon…" It's a breathless plea, and I want to make her come, but I want to be inside her just as badly.

Our hands fumble against each other's, working to unfasten my buttons, lower my jeans, open the front of her dress. Our moves are frantic and fast, trying to rid ourselves of these obstacles to our lust.

My knees almost buckle when cool fingers wrap around my shaft. She slides her grip up and down, speaking in my ear. "So big."

Shit, dirty-talking Angel is so hot.

I turn her facing the stone wall, gripping my cock and sliding it along the back of her thighs.

"Deacon…" She gasps as I find what I'm searching for, thrusting my cock balls deep into her clenching core.

"Fuck." My eyes squeeze shut, and I have to hold steady. It feels too damn good after this day of delayed gratification.

We're panting, and my mind blanks until she backs her hips against me, moving her core up my shaft. "Move," she murmurs.

I fumble with the front of her dress, sliding my fingers into her, tracing them higher to the spot that makes her moan.

"You want this?" My lips are at her ear, and she arches against my chest.

"Yes." Her fingers fumble with mine, threading along her clit, circling the wetness as I rock her body higher, pumping into her faster.

She rises on tiptoes, dropping her head back against my shoulder. I bend my knees, closing my eyes as the pleasure snakes up the back of my legs. It's too good… heat and warmth and pleasure tightening my balls, centering in my cock.

Her other hand grips my neck, and I turn my mouth to find

hers, biting and sucking her tongue as she shivers, circling her fingers faster.

Our mouths break apart. "Don't stop." With one hand on her flat stomach, I knead her breast, pulling her nipple while I trace my mouth along her neck, behind her ear, wanting to taste her everywhere.

She's salty sweat, and she smells like rich jasmine. "Oh," she sighs.

My voice is ragged and gruff, and my instinct is faster... harder...

Her soft ass crashes against my pelvis. Her fingers move faster, I thrust harder. I push her to the wall, and she moans loudly, slamming her palm against it. I feel her insides clench just before she breaks into spasms as she comes.

Fuck me, it feels so good. It's just what I need to let go, driving hard for two more thrusts before holding, balls deep as my cock pulses, my orgasm jetting into her.

I pull her to me, holding her back against my chest as we breathe heavy in time. I slide my hands around her waist, closing my eyes and feeling her body, this woman who owns my soul.

How is it possible to love someone this much? To need her so fiercely, it's an actual, physical pain?

She's the only woman I've ever slept with. It sounds fucking corny, but we taught each other how to move, how to touch... because we were inexperienced kids, we didn't know to be embarrassed by our fumbling mistakes.

Minutes pass as we return to Earth, noticing the sounds of the night. An owl calls, cicadas scree, the water laps on the lake.

"Here." I speak softly, sliding out of her and instantly missing the warmth of her body.

Her skirt falls over her legs, and I pull up my jeans, turning to sit and pulling her onto my lap in a straddle as I hug her close. Her hands are on my neck, and she leans forward, tracing her full lips along mine, kissing and nibbling. It's enough to rouse my sated dick in my pants.

"I should've brought you back to my place." My voice is thick. "I want to fuck you all night."

Her nose curls adorably. "Make love all night. We already fucked."

Damn, this girl.

My girl.

Leaning back, I gaze at the vision in front of me. The top of her dress is still unbuttoned, and moonlight touches her small breasts with silver light. Dreamy amber eyes meet mine, and I shake my head.

"How did this happen to me?" I sound as bewildered as I feel.

"What?" Her head tilts to the side, her brows furrowed.

"You're the most beautiful thing I've ever seen. The sweetest thing I've ever known."

"Deacon." Her chin drops and she hugs her body close against mine. "You're the best thing in my life."

I slide my hands up her back, loving the feel of her in my arms. It's all I ever want, holding her in my arms this way as long as I live.

"It's time, Angel."

She sits back, studying my expression. "Time for what?"

"Time for me to come to your house and meet your family, introduce myself." Sliding a wild curl behind her ear, I grin. "I want to make us official."

She blinks down, almost shyly. "I've been thinking about that. My brother's just getting back in town. I'm just getting to know him—"

"I want to know him, too. I'll pick you up at your house—his new house—and I can meet him, take you on a real date."

"We've been on real dates." Her nose scrunches, teasing me, but I'm serious.

"I want to meet your family. Say yes this time."

She tilts her head to the side, soft curls drifting around her high cheekbones. "Yes."

Our eyes meet, and she smiles. Leaning forward, she wraps her arms around my neck. Her soft breasts press against my bare chest, and I close my eyes at the sensation.

Her voice is quiet. "I don't know what Beto's like or what he'll say."

Sliding my hands under her arms, I hold her back so she can see the smile on my face, feel the confidence I feel. "Whatever he says, we're in this together. I'll take care of you."

She studies me, looking deeply into my eyes, and I wonder what she sees there. I hope she sees what I want her to see—our bright future.

She must, because ultimately her full lips curl into a smile. "I wanted to invite you to Lola's quinceañera on Saturday."

"When and where?"

"It was supposed to be at the Knights of Columbus, but I think Beto is moving it to his house. We'll start at five, so maybe you should arrive around six?"

"An hour late? That seems rude."

"An hour after my brother has been drinking." *When I hope he'll be more relaxed…*

Tracing my finger along the line of her forehead, I kiss her brow. "I'll be there at five thirty. What should I bring?"

"Just yourself."

"I'm bringing her a gift."

She exhales, sliding her nose along my jaw. "We'd better get back. It's late."

The wind is picking up, and the scent of rain is all around us. She straightens her top, buttoning it closed, and I retrieve my shirt, pulling it over my head. I wrap my leather jacket around her, and we hold hands walking down the stairs to my bike.

Rain stings my arms as we retrace the miles, and the warmth of her body presses against my back. We're going to be together forever, and it's going to be amazing.

I won't let it be any other way.

CHAPTER
Four

Angel

WE'RE JUST AHEAD OF THE STORM WHEN WE REACH MY BROTHER'S house. I jump off the bike and give my helmet to Deacon. Smoothing my hair back, he leans down to kiss me again, flooding my body with warmth. "I should walk you to the door."

Reaching up, I thread my fingers in his thick, dark hair. "Soon."

"Saturday." His blue eyes glow in the darkness, and I want to tell him he's the most beautiful thing I've ever seen. He always has been.

Instead I tell him goodnight. "Go now. Before the rains starts. I'll worry until you get home."

He rarely rides a motorcycle. It's too hot most of the year, and his Audi is plush and air conditioned. But tonight, it was perfect for our clandestine affair. Except when I say goodbye at this hour, when it's starting to rain.

I've broken so many rules to love him—I broke my promise

I hid him from my family… I hate feeling like judgment is lurking around the corner, hanging over our heads. Valeria will love him if she gives him a chance. Lourdes does.

Beto should… I can't think about that now.

"I'll text you when I get there." He leans down for another, hot kiss, and my fingers tighten on his slick leather jacket.

He exhales a groan, the muscle in his square jaw flexing attractively. "I hate saying goodbye. I want you in my bed."

He's so damn fine in the darkness, that surge of need filters into my stomach. I swear, he's right. We could be together all night and still not be satisfied.

Reaching out, I place my palm against his warm cheek. "Saturday, right here at this house, everything is going to change." *For the better*, I pray.

It's enough, and he pulls me into one last, consuming kiss. My body is so small against his, covered by him. I want to thread my fingers in his hair again and hold him all night, but I don't dare. He needs to go, and I need to get inside and sleep.

He walks the bike to the end of the driveway, giving me one last wave, one last panty-melting grin before he races off into the darkness.

I've got less than two days to lay the groundwork with my brother. Less than two days to figure out how to tell Valeria I didn't keep the promise I made to her eight years ago… *Did she really think I did?*

Less than two days to try and discern if bringing the love of my life to meet my family is going to lead to World War III… and what I'll do if it does.

THE TINIEST NOISE SEEMS TO ECHO IN THIS ENORMOUS STONE HOUSE. I slip off my sandals to keep from making a sound as I scamper through the grand entryway. When my bare feet touch the smooth stone floors, I think of how proud Beto was when we arrived, telling me they were genuine travertine, beautiful and smooth, and imminently durable.

It's dark as I pick my way through the open floorplan, and the rain grows stronger. I pray Deacon is still running ahead of the storm as I make my way across the first floor.

I'm unfamiliar with the layout of this giant place. I have no idea if my brother's bedroom faces the street or if it faces the lake. Hell, for all I know he could've been looking down at us the whole time... *That's a creepy thought.*

A stairway leads from the kitchen, which is all stainless and stone, and I follow the steps curving up like something out of an old castle.

Chairs covered in cow hide patters, heavy leather sofas with brass studs, and chunky wooden tables fill the rooms. Paintings of horses and cattle drives are on the main walls. It's a beautiful place, if not very warm.

My room is cozier than the rest of the house. Instead of stone, the floors are dark wood with a thick white rug covering the walk from the door to the queen-sized bed. It's made up in red-orange with cream pillows.

"I remember when you were little your favorite colors were the sunrise." Beto had said when he showed me the room.

He was almost hospitable, and I felt guilty for thinking he couldn't be nice. He cares enough to decorate my room in colors I like.

I hung Mamá's black cross photo above my bed. It's the one thing that helps me feel like she's still with me, even after all these years.

Her smaller prints are in the albums, but this image she blew up and stretched like a canvas. It's very similar to an O'Keefe painting, even though it's a photograph. I've spent the last year trying to create something of my own to compliment it.

Mamá worked in intensely dark, cool colors, but my palette is the exact opposite. Eye popping, warm yellows and beaming orange-reds are the spectrum I prefer. I've been experimenting with a technique of adding glaze and baking them to create a thick, glassy coating.

Shedding my dress, I go to the bathroom attached to my room and quickly shower. Restoring my panties and pulling on a long tee, I crawl into my bed, memories of Deacon humming under my skin.

A motorcycle ride, no panties, my arms around his waist, my body pressed against his... It's a potent aphrodisiac. I was practically coming at his first kiss, his first touch. After all the weeks of separation, I couldn't get enough of him. I thought, *This is what freedom feels like—this glorious man in my arms. This is pure joy.*

My phone buzzes under my pillow and I pull it out to see his text. *Home... dreaming of your beautiful smile, soft lips...*

Smiling, I slide my finger over the face. *Dreaming of your ethereal eyes.*

Ethereal... Good one.

I exhale a laugh as I tap my reply. *Thank you for rescuing me, handsome prince.*

Goodnight, beautiful Angel.

Closing my eyes, I drift into a relaxed sleep, the scent of Deacon in my hair, the memory of his kiss warming my lips. Dreams of my mother's place float in my mind, the trees full of dark green leaves, the black-gray mountains rising in the distance, the little cottages dotted along the slopes... so beautiful, so colorful. I long to take him there, to live there with my love in the place where I knew so much love.

It's going to work out.

It's got to.

"ANYBODY HOME?" VALERIA'S VOICE ECHOES THROUGH THE HOUSE, AND I hear the scuffling of little feet on the stone stairs.

"Carmie?" Sofia's voice bounces off the stone walls of the second-floor hall.

Rolling onto my back, I groan, rubbing my eyes and trying to hold onto the last remnants of a dream. I was wrapped in Deacon's arms, lying in a warm blanket in my mother's home.

"Carmie!" She grows more insistent, her tone touched with worry.

"In here Soph!" I throw the blanket back and walk over to pull on my black yoga pants.

Swift scuffling precedes the rattling of my doorknob. I've just dropped a long-sleeved tee over my head as she opens the door. She's dressed in purple leggings and a white shirt with a mermaid on the front. On top of all of it is a green, purple, and white tulle skirt.

Her dark brown hair is up in two ponytails that hang in ringlets on each side of her head. She's the cutest thing. Wide brown eyes meet mine before looking around my impressive new bedroom. It's twice the size of the one I had at her house.

She walks in slowly. "Is Uncle Beto a king?"

"He thinks he is." I can't keep the sarcasm out of my voice as I go into the attached bathroom to wash my face.

It's the same beige travertine as the rest of the house, and Sofia is right behind me.

"Does that mean you're a princess?" She slides an empty drawer open before going to the next empty one. Looking up at me, her nose wrinkles. "You don't have any stuff."

"You know what that means?" I pull a knock-off brand Neutrogena wipe from a package.

"You need to go to the store." She nods, rolling her eyes like, *duh.*

"It means I'm just the same as I always was." I tap her nose lightly, tossing the wipe into the trash can under the sink. "Only the house has changed."

She walks into my bedroom again and climbs onto my big bed. "It's a nice house."

"It's just a house." I know as well as anyone how fast circumstances change.

She's perched on my bed thinking, her cute little head tilted to the side. "But don't you like Uncle Beto?"

"I want to like him." Walking into the room, I hold out my arms and she stands so I can bounce her onto my hip.

"Don't you have to like him? Cause he's your brother?" She shakes her head when she talks, causing her ponytails to sway.

"Well... I haven't seen him in almost four years. And just because someone is your brother doesn't mean he's a nice person."

She presses her rosebud lips together and nods slowly as if she understands completely. I trot down the landing with her on my hip, straight into Valeria's waiting hug.

"It was so weird not having you at the house this morning. Beto might have to let you sleep over a few nights until we get used to it."

The idea we have to ask my brother's permission like he's my dad or something bristles my skin, but I let it go. "Did you bring the rest of my stuff?"

"I put your art there." She gestures to the tall canvases and paper-covered items leaning against the wall in the foyer. "I wasn't sure where you wanted it. Beto says we're not having Lo's Quince at the KOC. We're having it right here."

I expected as much, but I think my brother is probably right on this one. "It's better this way. We have plenty of room, people can stay as long as they want, and best of all?"

"It's free." We both say it together and laugh.

"Not entirely free. We still have to buy all the decorations, the food, drinks..." Her voice trails off, and I know she's worried about money.

Growing up in her house, we were always worried about money.

"I'm pretty sure if my brother told you to move the party here, he's planning to help with everything."

"How do you know that?"

"Trust me. I've been around Beto less than twenty-four hours, and I have a pretty good idea how his ego runs. Now where's the dress?" I follow her across the large entrance to the dining room where my younger cousin's elaborate ballgown is spread over a table.

Lola saved a pin on Pinterest of a dark red gown with a gold-embellished bodice and a tiered, floor-length skirt made of layers of dark red tulle.

Valeria complained loudly a thousand dollars for a dress is too expensive. Lola almost burst into tears, but I secretly ordered the pattern with Valeria's help, and I've been sewing it in my spare time. It's almost done, and it's spectacular.

It's almost finished, but we still have some beading to do and the final tier of tulle in the skirt. I spread the fabric and thread on the table.

"I hope I measured correctly. I wish we could have her try it on."

Valeria makes a sad face. "It would ruin the surprise."

"Yeah…" I exhale, fluffing the enormous skirt over and over. "It'll be more ruined if it doesn't fit."

That pulls her up short. "You make a point."

"Ah, good morning, Valeria, good morning, Carmelita." Beto's deep voice interrupts everything. "What's this?"

He's dressed in black jeans and a white undershirt. His arms are covered in tattoos of snakes and skulls and an eagle crushing bones in its talons.

"I'm finishing Lola's Quince dress." Lifting it by the hanger, I shake it so the skirt moves in all its queenly glory.

Looking at it now, I can't believe I did it myself, and a rush of sentimental pride warms my chest. Smiling over at my brother, all I see is his disapproving face.

"Why are you sewing her dress?" He says it like it's distasteful, and my smile melts.

"Beto!" Valeria scolds. "Carmie has been working on this dress for weeks! It's a wonderful thing she's doing for Lo."

"Poor people make their own clothes. Why didn't you buy something from a store?"

"This dress would be more than a thousand dollars in a store." I don't even try to hide my annoyance.

"I'll buy her dress. Where should she go? Neiman's?"

"She is not going to a store." Valeria's wide eyes meet mine, and she shakes her head. "She will wear this beautiful dress. Carme has worked hard… Lola will wear this, and it will be something to treasure. An heirloom."

"Whatever." My brother waves his hand before going out the kitchen door to the garage. "Just remember I offered to buy her a real dress."

"Don't worry." I won't forget it. I have to fight every instinct in my body not to grab the oversized pepper grinder off the table and throw it at him.

"What's his problem?" I say under my breath, blinking back a tear. "Why is he so… awful?"

Valeria puts her arm around me, pulling me in for a hug. "Just ignore him. Men doesn't understand these things. Having you make this dress is so much more special than buying it from a store."

"I'm glad you think so. It's my gift to Lo." A knot is in my throat. "But if you think she'd prefer a dress from the store, from a real designer, and not something homemade—"

"She's going to love this dress." Val gives me another firm squeeze then releases me and takes out her tape measure. "Your brother is proud and a little arrogant. He's like your father… and your grandfather."

I watch as she trails the tape along the waist of the gown, making a note of the measurement.

Leaning forward, I lower my voice to a whisper. "How does he afford it all?"

She shrugs, not meeting my eyes. "Apparently he did well in Mexico."

"Did well in Mexico?" I can't hide the surprise in my voice. "What does that mean?"

"Not what you're thinking, I'm sure." Dark eyes cut up at me, and I feel my cheeks heat at the scold in her voice. "Your brother is an honest man, Carmelita."

"I didn't mean that. I don't know him very well. I don't know what he does for a living. It's like he's a big mystery to me."

"Beto's no mystery." She takes out one of Lo's old dresses and lays it on top of the one I've made, holding the seams to see if they match. "He's just caught up in the past."

"What past?"

She shrugs, tossing the dress over her arm. "Things that don't matter now. Your mamá took you to Mexico to get away from the drama."

"What drama? Why do I feel like everyone's keeping secrets from me?"

"No one's keeping secrets!" She waves her hand as she pushes out of her chair. "I'm just not repeating gossip. Anyway, you're right. I need to get Lo to try this on. It would be awful if it didn't fit. Especially after all your hard work."

My curiosity is on overdrive, and I want to stop her, make her tell me what she is clearly hiding from me. Front and center in my brain is the promise she demanded I make all those years ago.

But Valeria is out the door before I can stop her. "Watch Sofia for me, okay?"

"Yay!" My little cousin climbs into my lap, and Val is gone before I can say another word.

"They can't keep me in the dark forever." My eyes are on the mahogany front door, but my thoughts are miles away.

"I don't like the dark." Sofia is on my lap tracing her little fingers through the tiers of her sister's skirt. "Lo's going to be a princess."

I wrap my arms around her and give her a squeeze. "She should be a princess. A girl only gets one quinceañera."

Although, I never had one—not that I'm bitter or complaining. Mamá was too sick, and by the time she died, my birthday had already passed. Even if it hadn't, I wouldn't have felt like celebrating without her.

Sofia nods quickly. "Like Princess Aurora."

I lean to the side to catch her brown eyes. "You sure know a lot about the princesses all of a sudden."

She tilts her head like a little expert. "Mamma put Disney plus in my bedroom to help me sleep."

"Is that so?" I bite back a grin.

"Yes. I know all the princesses."

I pinch her little chin. "Who's your favorite?"

"Well…" She exhales heavily. "Elena looks the most like me. She likes the ocean and adventures and she has a sister named Isabel… but she doesn't have a movie."

Not going to lie, I'm not familiar with Elena, but I wasn't a princess type of girl. "I bet she gets one."

"You're babysitting now?" Beto's return interrupts our conversation. "Where's Valeria?"

Sofia shrinks against my chest, and I cut my eyes at him. "Spending time with family isn't babysitting."

"Seamstress… babysitter… waitress…" He shakes his head. "My sister doesn't do these things."

My littlest cousin's arm goes around my waist as if she's trying to hide, which pisses me off. "Your sister does what she wants. Don't you have anything better to do than stalk around here insulting people?"

"I haven't insulted anyone. Where's Valeria?"

"She went to get Lola to try on her dress. Why?"

"We need to discuss parking for the party, food, drinks. What is this?" He's at the front door inspecting my bags of supplies and the large canvasses leaning against the wall.

"It's my art." My tone is sharp, and I brace for his next rude remark.

To my surprise, his chin rises—apparently this is acceptable to Mr. Proud Treviño. "I'll take these to the cottage in the garden. You can use it for a studio."

My anger cools a fraction, and I watch him gathering my stuff. I really don't know my brother at all.

"Thanks."

"You can park in the garage…" He looks around as if just realizing. "Where is your car?"

I pick at the hem of Lo's skirt. "I don't have one."

"What? How do you get around?"

"I catch a ride with friends or I call a Lyft or Uber. If it's late or I want to save money, I ride the bus."

Black eyes flash, and he stalks over to where I'm sitting with Sofia in my lap. "My sister does not ride the bus."

"You know, for someone who just got back in town, you sure have a lot of ideas about what your sister does and doesn't do." Sofia squirms, and I let her down. "Cars cost money. Car insurance is expensive. Driving is dangerous—"

He starts for the door. "I'll get you a car."

"I don't like to drive."

Pausing at the doorway, he fixes me with a dark gaze. "Do you have a license?"

"Yes, but I haven't driven in… weeks."

"I'll pick something for you." It's the last thing he says before he's gone, carrying my art out the back door.

I stand, exhaling a frustrated noise. "Of all the pig-headed, stubborn…"

"Uncle Beto is like King Triton."

"What's he like?"

Her eyes widen. "Grumpy."

Catching her hand, I start for the door, following my brother. "Well, your Uncle Beto's got another thing coming if he thinks he's going to keep this up. Let's check out this garden cottage."

I don't like secrets and I don't like being treated like a child. More importantly, I'm frustrated I haven't had a chance to mention my date for Saturday. It's time King Triton and I had a sit-down.

CHAPTER
Five

Deacon

"**D**AMN, IT'S BEEN A WHILE SINCE WE'VE DONE THIS." RICH GRIPS my shoulder as he leans back on the leather barstool, a whiskey in front of him.

He's wearing jeans and a plaid button-down, and his dark blond hair is a shaggy mess. A ball cap sits on the polished-wooden bar beside him. I'm in my usual, custom suit, but my tie is in my pocket. We're having drinks at the Fillmore, a historic, wood-paneled pub in the heart of downtown.

"So you're back for good?"

"For now." I'm nursing a vodka, and my mind is miles away, wondering what Angel did today, missing her. Last night wasn't enough. I want to see her again. "You must've been in the field."

"Yeah, had to meet with a rookie BP head in Arlington. He wants me to research some land out past El Paso for them to drill. It could take a month."

Rich's job as a landman sends him all over the state research-ing mineral leases, working for the big oil guys. He's damn good at his job and set up to make a killing, and the better he gets, the longer he's gone.

"How does Maggie feel about that?"

He tosses back the rest of his whiskey and signals for a refill. "She's working on her journalism career." A hint of bitterness is in his voice.

"Give me a break." I exhale a laugh before sipping my vodka. "You two love each other."

Richland Wells, Maggie Cox, Lincoln Beale, and I grew up in the same exclusive, gated community, the children of too-rich parents who spent most of their time socializing.

While the three of them attended private school here, I was the lone wolf of the pack, shipped off to boarding school every fall.

After my mom died, my dad threw himself into his work, and when I was home, my family was maids and gardeners, the cooks who rotated through our kitchen.

"What about you?" Rich grins, and I shake off the dark mood trying to creep into our happy hour. "Still giving away all your time to charity cases?"

He loves giving me shit about my pro bono work. "There's more to life than making money. Remember?"

"Because you never had to worry about it."

"Like you did."

He cuts his eyes, and I regret my casual jab. All our families depended on the oil industry in one way or another, but when the embargoes hit and the market flooded, Rich's family bore the brunt. It was so long ago, I tend to forget them living in that big, empty mansion, making weekly stops at the food bank, and pretending like nothing had changed.

Poverty, like loneliness, leaves a mark, even now, when everything comes quick and easy for us.

"You shouldn't give those people charity." He takes another sip. "They'll only resent you for it later."

"Those people." I huff before taking a hit of vodka. "What do you know about it, Ross Perot?"

"I know what I hear."

My eyebrows quirk, but I'm not listening to his arguments against doing good. It's the same logic that keeps any progress from being made, that keeps old grudges alive. "It's the same as I do for my friends in Harristown."

"They're your people. They get it."

"You're too young to talk so old."

"Why?" Blue eyes cut up to mine, and I see sincerity there. He really wants to know. "Why waste your valuable time helping people who don't like you?"

I think about my answer. I have a clear memory of the Christmases I spent alone with only a maid to open presents with me. She said I reminded her of her son, who she lost after her divorce. Even when she smiled, her eyes were sad.

"I guess it's for Erin."

His chin jerks back with a frown. "Who's Erin?"

Shifting uncomfortably, I confess something I've never told anyone. "Our last housekeeper."

"What?"

"She got married right out of high school, never went to college." I think about the fragments of her past I managed to uncover. "After her divorce, she couldn't bounce back. She left after Dad died and Winnie moved in full-time. I never saw her again. I found out later she killed herself."

"Jesus." His lips press into a frown. He reaches out and grips my shoulder. "Hey, it wasn't your fault. Life sucks. Some people can't hack it."

"Maybe…" My brow furrows. "Or maybe she just needed someone to care. Someone to point her in the right direction."

He releases me, standing and fishing out his wallet. "Sounds like she needed more than that, my friend."

"I don't know." I stand, reaching for my wallet, thinking about his words.

"Water under the bridge."

My mind is far away as I remember searching for her years later, the devastation I felt when I found out she died alone, by her own hand. She'd been kind to me, and I wished I'd been able to help her. I felt so powerless. I hated it.

Now I have money and power, and dammit, I help them. It's not charity, it's taking a minute to care. Even small changes can make a big difference, and some people just need a road map. They need the tools we've been given since we were kids.

"So I'm headed to El Paso for a few weeks." Rich's hands are in the pockets of his jeans.

We're out on the sidewalk, strolling toward the Foster building, a twenty-story high rise where I occupy the top floor. It's almost eight, but the sky is light. Heat simmers from the concrete, and the nonstop wind flaps my blazer open.

It smells like dry air and brown brush and dirt.

It smells like Texas.

"Doesn't your uncle still live out there?" I squint up at the sun winking past the high rises. I remember spending a weekend in the desert with Rich's family when we were kids.

"Yeah, Skeeter's in Sunset. Close to the river, view of the mountains."

"Sounds nice. So you'll stay with him?"

"I'll probably crash there a few nights. His place is big enough so we won't see each other. He doesn't like to be around people." We stop at his Tahoe, and he props an arm on the side. "What about Angel? Are you ever going to put a ring on it?"

My conversation with her last night is on my mind. "I'm ready, but she's hesitant."

He adjusts his cap, hazel eyes teasing. "She heard about that incident with the furries?"

"Idiot." I shake my head.

"What's the matter? Cold feet?"

"I don't know. I'm meeting her family tomorrow."

"Hey!" He holds up his fist for a bump. "That's progress. Why didn't you say so?"

"Your big mouth never gave me a chance."

He makes a lunge like he might pull me into a head-lock, and I throw up an elbow, which he blocks. "Let me know how it goes."

"I will."

Our fake tussle turns into a bro-hug, and we say goodnight. I continue up the street, wrestling with my one-track mind. Pulling out my phone, I shoot her a text. *A horse walks into a bar...*

It doesn't take a second for the gray bubble to appear with the little dots floating in it as she types a reply. *Bartender says why the long face?*

The warmth in my stomach makes me smile. Yeah, it's time to make this girl my wife.

I push through the door of my building. *My place tonight?*

A few seconds pass, dots floating on my phone screen. I'm in the elevator thinking about taking out my car and driving to her.

I can sneak away for an hour.

It's like I've won the lottery. *I'll pick you up.*

I'll get a ride. See you in a few.

My jaw tightens, and I'm pretty sure when she says she'll get a ride, it means she'll ride the bus. *I'll order you an Uber.*

No need, rich boy. I've got it covered.

I don't like it, but I trust her. *See you soon, beautiful.*

Stepping into my apartment, I look out the west-facing wall of windows at the purple, red, and golden sunset. It's gorgeous, and I wish she were here now so I could wrap my arms around her small body, kiss her neck, trace my lips along the line of her hair.

From this height, I can see far across the expanse of flat, brown Texas prairie, and while part of me loves my home deeply, another part of me fell in love with the lush greenery of Harristown, the tiny hamlet where I attended college.

I first discovered it as a boy. My dad would take me there in the summer for the annual peach festival, and I want to take Angel there to see if she likes it.

It's a painfully small town in the middle of the piney woods, but the people are friendly, and the peach orchards are beautiful. The truth is, I'd be willing to live anywhere as long as I've got my girl at my side.

I'm showered and waiting on a pot of water to boil in the kitchen when the intercom at my door buzzes.

"I'm here." Angel's voice is clear, and I hit the button, allowing her to access to the penthouse floor.

Opening my door, I watch the numbers on the elevator, waiting for it to ding before stepping into the hallway in my bare feet. Three apartments share this foyer, but I never see my neighbors. Finally, it stops, and the black doors silently swish apart.

Angel stands in front of me looking like the best thing in the world, and I can't help a smile. She's wearing a light blue sundress so short her silky legs are on full display. Her long hair hangs in golden brown spirals behind her shoulder, with one lock curling perfectly over her small breast.

She takes my breath away, just like she did that very first day years ago. I'd just turned fifteen, I was leaving for my first year at boarding school. I thought I was happy to go, and instead it turned into the longest year of my life.

I lean against the open elevator doors, holding them apart. "Hey, gorgeous."

Her pillow lips part in a smile, amber eyes crinkling at the corners. "Hey, handsome."

The tip of her pink tongue touches perfectly white teeth, and the cutest dimple appears at the top of her cheek. Reaching out, I catch her upper arms, pulling her against my chest.

"Come here to me."

I lean down and press my lips to that little spot just below her eye. What the hell are dimples anyway, and why are they so damn adorable?

Her lips are on my cheek, and I feel her nose wrinkle. "So possessive."

"Longest day of my life." I kiss her closed eyes, the top of her brow, then I press my lips to her hairline, taking a deep breath of jasmine. "You smell so good."

"Something smells good. What is that?"

"Oh, shit." I spin on my heel and holding her hand, I drag her into my apartment, leaving her in the living room while I kill the fire under the pot of water boiling over.

"Are you making me dinner?" She walks to the bar separating the cooktop from the rest of the dining area.

"Yes." Holding out my arm, I drop a handful macaroni into the pot with a flourish. "I'm making you my signature dish."

"Is that so?" She laughs, and her eyes sparkle. She has the most beautiful eyes, light brown and perfectly clear like good whiskey. "It looks like mac and cheese."

"Not just any mac and cheese." Grabbing another handful of noodles, I drop them in and turn down the fire so it doesn't boil over again. "It has a special ingredient."

"Love?"

"Two special ingredients."

I break an egg in a saucepan and add a bit of milk before stirring in cheese and the rest of the items.

"You're adding eggs and cream to the cheese?" Her eyebrows rise, and she pokes out her lips. "That's interesting."

I wink and point to the bottle of white burgundy I uncorked shortly before she arrived. "Have some wine."

"Aren't you full of surprises." She pours two glasses, leaning on the bar. "Who taught you to make this special mac and cheese?"

"Actually… it was my aunt." I hate to tell her.

We had an unfortunate incident once a while back where I was out with my aunt and we ran into Angel and her cousin at a Rally's hamburger place. We both wanted to rush together and hold hands, but Angel held back—I guess because of her cousin. I'm ashamed to say I held back, too, because what happened next embarrassed me to the core.

Winnie looked around the restaurant and took my arm. "We've got to go somewhere else, Deacon. This place is crawling with *Mexicans*."

Looking back, the word *Mexicans* wasn't the problem. There's nothing wrong with being a Mexican—I've never believed that, and I sure as hell don't think that way now. It was the way my aunt said it that made me want to crawl in a hole. So much disgust in her voice, like the presence of my beautiful friend and her family was shameful. In that instant, I hated that I'd held back from going to my girl. It was like I agreed with my aunt.

We've never talked about it. I never knew if she even heard Winnie's statement, but any time my aunt's name comes up, I feel a sting of shame over that moment. I wish I'd told my aunt to shut up that day. I wish I'd walked right up and taken Angel's hand in mine, aligning myself with her family.

I've grown up a lot since then, and history will not repeat itself.

"I can't wait to taste this." Angel smiles at me, and she's so purely beautiful. I only want to take care of her, protect her for the rest of my days.

"What's happening with your art class?"

"One left, and I graduate." Her eyes widen with excitement. "Then they announce the award winners."

"Oh, you'll definitely win awards." I sprinkle salt in the pot and lift a noodle for testing. A few minutes longer.

"There's one I really want… It's twenty thousand dollars, a six-month residence, and a private show at the Palladium."

My brow rises. "The Arthaus. That's a big one."

"I know!" She clasps her hands. "Want to see my last piece?"

"Yes."

She types quickly on her phone while I take the pot off the fire, stepping over to give the noodles a quick rinse and let them drain in the colander. Angel always texts me pictures of her favorite works, and every time I'm blown away by her talent.

"I call it *Spirit*." She hands me the phone, and I lean back against the sink.

"Wow." It's a magnificent horse swirled in a storm of brilliant color like a whirlwind. "I wish I could see it in real life."

Tearing my eyes away from the photo, I catch hers and the light in them is so bright. "You like it?"

"It's the best thing you've ever shown me."

Bouncing to me, she laughs catching my forearm and kissing my lips. "Thank you!"

Warmth filters through my chest at her happy, shy response. She's so amazing, yet she's so cautious about it. "You get better every piece."

Picking up the pot of noodles, I pour them into the buttered glass dish followed by the egg, cheese, and cream mixture on top. I'm about to cover it all with parmesan cheese and slip it into the oven when she stops me.

"You're not finished, are you?" She's frowning, and I hesitate.

"That's the recipe."

"No no no." She shakes her head, shooing me to the side. "That's no good!"

Turning to my refrigerator, she opens the door and pushes the few items I have around. While I've got a great view of her cute little butt, my curiosity is winning.

"What are you looking for?" I lean to the side trying to see.

"Don't you have any peppers? Tomatoes?"

Chewing my lips, I look around the kitchen. "I don't have peppers, but I've got this."

I hold out a bottle of Tabasco, and she frowns. "Where are your spices?"

"You haven't even tried my signature dish—"

"I haven't tried it, but I know how to cook for babies. You're a grown man! You need some spice in your life."

"I've got some spice in my life." Catching her by the hips, I pull her to me and plant a kiss on the side of her neck right below her ear.

That gets me a little squeal, and she wiggles out of my arms. "Here." She grabs some chili powder and shakes it over the dish followed by a few hits of Tabasco, gives it a stir, and steps back. "Now continue. And remind me to take you to the grocery store. You're missing some staples."

Shaking my head, I cover the mixture with parmesan cheese and pop it in the preheated oven, setting the timer and pulling her into my arms. "What can we do with twenty minutes?"

Her teeth press against her bottom lip when she grins, and her hands are on my chest. "Only twenty minutes?"

Leaning down, I capture her lips with mine. They're soft and taste faintly of the dry wine she's been sipping. Our tongues slide together, and heat floods the lower half of my body. I want to sit her up on the bar and slip between her thighs.

My hands are on her legs, rising higher when she catches my wrists, and I stop. I take another nip of her lips, one last kiss, and I lean back, arching an eyebrow. "What's wrong?"

Her eyes are on my mouth and she shakes her head, sliding her thumb along my cheek. "Tomorrow's a religious ceremony as well as a birthday. It starts with a special mass for Lola."

"I'm okay with that." Catching her hand, I kiss her thumb.

"It just makes me think how... I'm not very religious when I'm with you."

"What are you trying to say, Miss Treviño? I'm a bad influence?"

"Yes." She leans forward and laughs, kissing my cheek. "You're a terrible influence. I forget all of my religion when you're around."

"I guess I should make an honest woman of you."

She rests her elbow on my shoulder, looking into my eyes. "How are you going to do that?"

"Easy. I'll make you my wife."

Her pretty eyes light up, and she laughs. "You haven't even met my family, and you think you want to join it?"

"I want to be wherever you are."

"We should probably wait to see how tomorrow goes."

"Nothing is going to change my mind about you."

Her head tilts to the side, sending a cascade of curls rippling over her arm. "What if I'm not ready to settle down and start having babies?"

"We can wait a year or two on the babies."

Her nose wrinkles, and she laughs. "And what does a big, rich financial adviser like you want with a little country girl like me?"

I love her flirting. I love answering her questions. I can answer all of them. "Well, let me see... For starters, you're incredibly talented. You're funny... smart—"

"How do you know I'm smart?"

"You're going out with me."

"Ah!" She pushes against my chest. "Such a big head to go with your big..." Her voice trails off, and my eyebrows rise. Her eyes drift around the room as I wait to see how she'll finish that sentence. "Apartment."

"My apartment's not so big, but something else is." Diving forward, I press my lips against the warmth of her neck, making her laugh.

Her warm, soft body, her lips, the scent of jasmine, and the trace of her fingers along my collar has my cock growing thick. Turning my head, I find her lips again, parting them and sweeping my tongue inside. She sighs, and I know she's feeling the heat between us. It's always this way with us.

I'm about to lift her into my arms and carry her to my bedroom when the bell rings. Our shoulders drop, and our eyes meet.

She makes a teasing little sad face. "It smells really good."

Stepping back, I slide my hand over the bulge in my slacks. "I'm having second thoughts about cooking." I'd rather be fucking.

She hops off the bar, going to the cabinet and pulling down two plates. "But I can't wait to taste your signature dish!"

Grabbing it with oven mitts, I place the glass dish on the top of the stove. It's bubbling and golden, and it actually does smell good. She hands me a knife and spatula, and I cut out a large square, placing it between the two of us.

Angel freshens her wine and pours me a glass, and I lean on the bar where she's sitting, holding a forkful of golden pasta in the air as she blows on it. Her pink lips pucker, and I do my best to tamp down my dirty thoughts.

"Ready?" She grins, holding it carefully towards my mouth.

"I made this for you."

"But I helped make it better."

I take a small bite, leaving the rest on the fork. Immediately my mouth is filled with cheesy goodness with a nice kick of spicy heat in the background. She puts the rest in her mouth, and covers it with her hand, widening her eyes and nodding.

"Damn, that's good." I reach for my own fork, cutting off another bite as she finishes hers.

"We made it better together." A note of triumph is in her voice, and I like it.

It's a good omen. It's like us—I'm the raw ingredients, and

she's the color, the music and the flavor. Her phone buzzes, and she jumps off the stool fast.

"Oh, I lost track of time." Running to the living room, she slings her purse onto her shoulder before stepping back to give me a kiss.

"Wait a minute." I catch her arms, stopping her progress. "Where are you going, Cinderella?"

"That's my car. I've got to get back before... anybody notices."

"I thought you had an hour—"

"Including drive time." She's practically running out the door and pressing the button on the elevator. "I'll see you tomorrow, yes?"

It opens quickly, and we step inside. She presses the button for the lobby while I stand beside her, tracing my fingers along hers as we descend. I consider pushing her against the wall and devouring her. She's watching the numbers, her lips pressed together. They're swollen and pink from my kisses and her hair is messy from my fingers in it. She looks amazing.

"I've decided to come early tomorrow."

That catches her attention, and she rises on her tiptoes to kiss me as the door dings open. "Five thirty. No earlier."

My hands are on her waist and I pull her back for a better kiss, a better taste of her mouth, like it's a decadent dessert. "Five twenty-nine."

With a touch of her hand, she skips out the glass doors to the waiting Lyft. I lean against the window watching as she speeds away.

Tomorrow everything changes.

CHAPTER
Six

Angel

BETO SLIDES A CAST IRON SKILLET WITH TOMATOES, CHOPPED ONIONS, chilis, and cilantro over the fire, and as usual, he's wearing a white tank and dark jeans. His feet are bare on the beige stone floor, and my thoughts slip to Deacon last night. Both of them are strong and stubborn, but my sexy man treats me with respect.

"I think we got off on the wrong foot." My brother stands at a stainless-steel Viking range with a spatula in his hand, the morning sun streaming through an open window. "Grab some coffee, and we'll talk over breakfast."

He still isn't asking.

He's still giving me orders like he's some drill sergeant, and I involuntarily enlisted in his army. Still, the delicious aroma makes my stomach growl. I decide to accept his olive branch, despite how it's offered. He is my oldest and only sibling after all. I guess he's used to bossing people around.

"Need any help?" I step over to the coffee machine, putting a mug on the tray and dropping a pod in the slot before hitting go.

He grins, nodding toward the counter. "You could hand me two tortillas."

A plastic bag of flour tortillas sits beside a toaster oven, and I take out two while he slides the red sauce to the side of his large skillet and cracks two eggs, frying them quickly.

I'm on guard, but I welcome a chance to sit down and chat with King Triton. Maybe it'll shed some light on what he's doing here.

Coffee made, I wait as he assembles two tortillas on plates followed by the eggs and the tomato sauce.

"One for you." He hands me a plate sprinkling cilantro over it before letting go. "And one for me. Let's eat."

I follow him to the small table situated before a set of open bay windows. Birds chirp, and we have a beautiful view across his massive back yard, leading down to the lake.

The small cottage is toward the back. A gardenia bush is planted at the southern corner, and when I went yesterday to set up my art supplies, it smelled familiar, like my mother's spirit was there. I wanted to spend the afternoon painting, but I had to finish Lo's dress.

Beto places a mug of coffee on the table beside his dish before sitting. His knees are spread wide, and he attacks his food like he hasn't eaten in weeks. I watch him a moment before taking a bite of my breakfast. It's really delicious.

"So I'm not a seamstress or a babysitter or a waitress, but you're a cook?" I can't resist after the way he acted yesterday.

He lifts his chin after shoveling a large bite of eggs into his mouth. "It's possible I spoke too fast. You're right. Family is different."

My eyebrows almost meet my hairline. Did he just say I was right? This is not how I expected the day to begin.

Last night I went to bed with my insides all twisted. Between Deacon's enthusiasm about meeting my family and the unpredictability of my brother, I barely slept a wink. I planned to at least open the subject of my boyfriend with him before tonight, before Lo's party.

Hunger deserts me, and I push my eggs around on my plate. No time like the present.

"After Mamá died, she wanted me to come here to be with you. She wanted us to be a family."

Beto shoves the remainder of his eggs onto his fork. He exhales a noise before putting it all in his mouth, and I continue.

"But you left less than a month after I arrived." I'm holding my mug of coffee, watching him. "We never got to know each other."

Leaning back in his chair, he glances out the window. The muscle in his jaw moves as he finishes his breakfast. Then he clears his throat and cuts those black eyes at me. "You were just a kid when you came here. I had to work and establish myself. Valeria was in a better position to take care of you than I was."

"I was fifteen…" I hold my voice steady. I'm not trying to fight or shame him. I'm simply stating the facts. "You left, and I haven't seen you in years."

"I've been working."

"Doing what?"

He shrugs, his gaze drifting to the window again. "Our uncle has many connections in Mexico. I helped him export produce, coffee, cocoa, furniture…"

"Exports." I nod, trying not to prejudge my brother. "You made enough money to buy this house on exports? And now you don't have to work?"

"Who says I don't have to work?" He laughs. "Just because I don't keep regular hours doesn't mean I don't work. And yes, the level of trade our family does provides a nice living. Our uncle works in high-end goods, not that cheap shit you see on the streets."

My eyes narrow, and I don't know what to make of this. Valeria says he's an honest man, but how much does she even know?

"You never visited us when Mamá was alive. Why did you go there after she died?"

"Mamá left me with our father. She made her decision." He stands, taking our plates from the table. "She didn't want me there."

I don't miss the injury in his voice. I study his back as he carries our dishes to the sink, broad shoulders, muscled arms. My brother is strong, but I just got a big peek under his armor at the boy who was wounded by her decision. The idea softens me towards him.

"She didn't mean to hurt you, Beto." Standing, I carry my mug to where he's clearing off the cooking utensils. "She talked about you all the time."

He hesitates, and our eyes meet. This time his black gaze is fathomless. My brother and I have spent so little time with each other, but we still share a familial bond. I might not know exactly what he's thinking, but I recognize sadness, a sense of loss.

I carefully place my hand on his forearm. "She loved you."

"Our mother loved her freedom and her art—"

"And her family and her son."

He studies my face a moment then his eyes narrow. He leans a hip against the counter and crosses his arms. "You've grown up a lot while I was in Mexico. You are very beautiful, little sister."

This change of topic confuses me. "Thank you?"

"I'll introduce you to my friend Mateo."

Of all the… "No, thank you."

"Mateo is a good man." His eyes flicker to me again. "It's time."

"Time for what?" *If he says for me to get married, I swear to baby Jesus.*

"A good man will keep you out of trouble."

Trouble. The code word for getting pregnant. "What makes you think I don't already know a good man?"

His cheeks split with his grin. "Valeria says you never date."

"Valeria doesn't know everything about me."

Pushing off the counter, he walks back to the table to retrieve his coffee mug. "Why do you act like a servant to them? You're a grown woman."

"I owe Valeria a lot. She took care of me, she paid for everything. Why, if it weren't for Uncle Antonio—"

"You owe them nothing. I paid him back for your classes."

Heat flashes in my cheeks. "So I owe you now?" The last thing I want is to be indebted to Beto.

"I told you, I'm taking care of you now." Finishing his coffee, he puts the mug in the sink. "You grew up in a pretty fairytale, Carmelita, a bubble. You know nothing of your family. You don't know what our life was here." His smile doesn't reach his eyes. "You have to trust me to know what's best for you."

"How can you know what's best for me? You know nothing about my life since you've been gone." My voice rises, and I hate that I sound small next to him. "You can't come back here and start ordering me around."

"One day when we are old, you can tell me what to do." He touches my chin and winks. "For now, I tell you."

I'm hot all over and ready to fight this out, but he's headed for the door. "Valeria wants me at the church with her and the girls." He pauses, looking back. "Someone needs to be here to supervise the workers, the food, decorations… Would you be willing to do it?"

"Of course."

He nods, and with that, he leaves me standing in the kitchen, with all of my arguments still in my mouth… I wasn't finished! And I never told him about Deacon.

ALL MY ARGUMENTS AND ANGER ARE LOST ONCE THE PARTY CREW ARRIVES. I spend the afternoon flying, directing cater-waiters, movers, florists, bakers… Beto's shiny new mansion really is far superior to the Knights of Columbus community center for Lo's party. Japanese magnolias and Bradford pear trees line the path down to the pristine lake, and the weather is pleasant, despite being almost June in Texas.

In addition to our small family, all of Lola's friends will be here, along with their families. I leave space between the tables for the traditional dances and rituals. It's odd to think at fifteen our culture says Lo is no longer a girl. She's only a sophomore in high school. Still, it's a beautiful tradition I'm only a little sad I missed out on celebrating.

Shaking that memory away, I return to directing the florist on where to put Lo's oversized bouquet, and how to arrange all the smaller bunches on each table.

An enormous five-tiered birthday cake, decorated in burgundy roses to match Lo's dress is in the center of a large table in the back, and a specialty boutique organized the pillow and the last doll. My cousin already has her tiara.

My phone is blowing up with texts from Deacon, starting with his usual, million-year-old, lame-assed jokes, which he completely used to steal my heart the first day we met. What can I say? I'm a sucker for a funny, sexy guy.

A skeleton walks into a bar, he sends me around four.

I'm in the middle of arranging candles under chafing dishes on the long tables lining the dining room walls, but I can't resist. I type back quickly, *Orders a beer and a mop.*

I want to see you now.

My tummy squeezes when I picture the wicked light in his eyes, his crooked grin, his full lips. Then I look down at my cutoffs and dirty tee, my wild hair piled on my head in a messy bun.

You really don't want to see me. I'm a hot mess.

You're always hot. I'm coming early.

FIVE THIRTY!!! I reply, shouty caps and exclamation points intentional.

So grumpy for a party day.

Can't talk, setting up.

It's the last text we exchange before my cousin twirls in an hour later just ahead of her family. She looks like a lady in her ball gown, which fits her perfectly. I'm so proud of her. My eyes heat, and I dab a tear from the corner of my eye. I arrived when Lo was only seven, and now she's a young woman in a beautiful dress I made for her.

"It's a dream come true!" Lo clasps her gloved hands beneath her chin. "I imagined how my party would be, but it's so much more. Thank you, Uncle Beto!"

Her eyes are shining, and even if she's being a little extra, I go to her, pulling her into a hug. Every girl deserves to feel special at least once in her life.

Her friends file in behind her, giggling like the teenage girls they are and eating the party mix and nuts, doing their best to keep their white gloves clean. They're all wearing matching champagne-colored silk dresses with their hair styled in matching updos.

"Are there any special boys in your *chambelanes*?" I give Lo an elbow to the ribs.

One part of her special day is an entourage of fifteen-year-old boys dressed in suits who will lead her and her court through traditional dances.

"No!" Her eyes widen, and she answers a little too fast.

My eyebrow arches in suspicion, and Sofia taps me on the waist, holding up her arms. I lean down to hop my youngest cousin onto my hip.

"Steve." She whispers in my ear like a good little informant. "She's got a crush on Steve Peterson."

My eyebrows rise, and I look over to where Lo is promenading with her friends. "Is he a nice boy?" I ask my cousin, who's also wearing a champagne silk dress, but hers is short with a flouncy skirt—more appropriate for a four-year-old.

She thinks a minute, then pokes out her bottom lip and nods. "I think so."

Her pretend-adult behavior is too cute, and I give her a squeeze. "You know, Lo's giving you her last doll tonight."

It's a tradition where the Quince gets a beautiful doll symbolizing the end of her childhood, which she passes on to a younger family member.

"I know!" Sofia's eyes light up, and she bounces on my hip. "It's Elena of Avalor. She's even got the ruby dress!"

The doll is actually styled to match Lo, but Sofia can think it's Elena. I'm trying to quiet my own nerves about how my brother will react to Deacon, not to mention Valeria.

"I've got to get ready. I'll be back." I kiss Sofia's cheek and put her on her feet.

I'm about to dash up the stone staircase to my bedroom when a strong hand grasps my upper arm.

"Carmelita, I have someone I want you to meet." Beto's authoritative voice fans my nerves.

I try to pull away. "I'm not really dressed to meet anyone…"

"It'll only take a moment."

My argument trails off as a man about my brother's age steps into my path. He has hazel eyes and wavy dark hair that hangs in one length to his collar. His face is clean-shaven, and he's wearing a slim-cut tan suit with a black shirt underneath.

"This is Mateo. Mateo, my sister Angelica." I can tell by the way Beto introduces us it's important to him. My insides squirm at the thought.

"How do you do." I reach out to shake his hand.

"Angelica." He lifts my hand and kisses my knuckles lightly. "Beto never told me how beautiful his sister was."

Our eyes meet, and he smiles. One eyebrow arches, and he has a devilish look. He's handsome, but I'm not interested.

I'm standing here in cutoffs and a smudged tee with my wild hair piled on top of my head in a messy bun. I'm not wearing any makeup, and I'm pretty sure I have burgundy frosting on my face from when I moved Lo's cake earlier.

"You're too kind, Mister…" I look from him to Beto, and they both grin.

"You can call me Mateo." My brother's friend smooths his thumb across my fingers, and my stomach tightens unpleasantly.

"Mr. Mateo, it's nice to meet you." My tone is cool, not engaging.

"Just Mateo."

"Well, just Mateo, I need to get changed before the party. If you'll excuse me."

"I'll be here when you're ready." Mateo makes a face like he tastes something sweet as I walk away.

I immediately think of Lando Calrissian in *The Empire Strikes Back*. I'm waiting for him to say, *Well, well…*

Rushing up the stairs, I've got zero time to worry about my brother's intentions. I've got to fly if I'm going to be ready in time. I quickly brush my wild curls back into a sleek, tight bun and step into a dress I bought at the vintage store. It's floor-length, olive-green silk with a low V-neck, and it has a slit that stops at the top of my thigh. The color makes my tanned skin glow, and the neckline shows off the soft curves at the tops of my breasts. Deacon is going to love it, and my heart beats a little faster at the thought. I imagine his blue eyes darkening, his full lips pulling into a smile…

I dust brown shadow in the creases of my eyes and paint a slick cat-eye with black liquid eyeliner. Lashes on, I fill my lips with red lipstick. The result is a stunning, yet classic look. Holding up my phone, I take a selfie and send it to him with the text, *So you can find me in the crowd.*

Taking a deep breath, I slide my hands down my sides and straighten my shoulders before going to the door. My phone buzzes just as I'm reaching for the handle, and I look down at the face. *You are the most beautiful thing I've ever seen.* It's Deacon. *I'm at the front door.*

My breath catches, and I quickly text back. *WAIT. I'll meet you.*

Grabbing the side of my skirt, I hold my shoes in my hand as I run down the stairs, through the kitchen, and out the door to the garage. Stopping at the exit to the driveway, I catch my breath, placing my hand on my stomach. Thankfully, my brother's house is so new, my feet aren't really dirty. I dust them off quickly and step into my heels.

When I pull the door open, I'm glad I have something to hold onto. Deacon standing on the walk, tall in a navy suit with the moonlight glancing off his full lips, his thick dark hair, streamer lights twinkling in his blue eyes... He takes my breath away. His eyes sweep up and down my body, and his grin is pure sex.

My thoughts trip back to the first time I saw him, floppy dark hair over blue eyes, doing his best to make me smile. Our first, reckless kiss...

I didn't fall in love with him when I was fifteen, but he activated feelings in me I never knew existed. I didn't know much, but I sure as shit knew this boy would change my life.

"Angel..." It's a hot whisper as he closes the space between us, slipping his arm around my lower back.

I lift my chin, smiling up at him. "Hey, handsome."

He leans down as if he's about to kiss me, but I put up my hand. "Wait. My lipstick..." Blue eyes flicker to my mouth, and my stomach tingles. "I want you to meet my family before you ruin my makeup."

That makes him laugh, and I know he doesn't give a shit about smudged lipstick. Our love is nothing if not ravenous.

"Lead the way." He takes my hand, and we walk to the front door. "This place is really nice. It's your brother's?"

"He just bought it." My stomach is flying and falling as I do this. It's so ridiculous, but it's the first time I've ever brought a boy to meet my family, and Deacon's not exactly a traditional boy. For starters, he's a man. A rich man. A rich, white man…

He's not one of us.

"I always thought your family didn't have money."

"So did I." Reaching out, my fingers tremble, and he sees it. He puts his hand over mine, and lifts it to his lips. "Why are you afraid?"

"I'm not." It's a total lie. "It's a big night for my cousin." My voice is quiet, and I'm not sure I can say the words. "Promise me…"

His brow furrows. "What?"

"If things get weird, will you trust me? Will you do whatever I ask?" I don't know what to expect when we walk through this door, and I can't shake a sense of foreboding.

Deacon pulls me against his chest, wrapping strong arms around me. "I'll do whatever you ask, my love."

A quick kiss to my nose, and he releases me.

I square my shoulders and walk through the door. I'm bringing the enemy to make peace.

CHAPTER
Seven

Deacon

BETO'S HOUSE IS LIKE SOMETHING OUT OF MY WORLD, A STONE McMansion in a wealthy, gated community north of town. The joyful blast of culture that greets us as we walk through the door is very different, but I like it.

A lot.

Inside the vast, open downstairs, white twinkle lights wrap around indoor trees and over the curtains, and a DJ plays dance music at the far end of the great room.

A group of teens cluster in a circle on a makeshift dance floor. The girls are wearing floor-length gowns in vibrant colors, and they clap and laugh at the tuxedo-clad boys showing off their moves. When a familiar pop song starts, they erupt into cheers.

Everyone is smiling and talking, hugging and dancing, eating cake, drinking drinks. It puts me at ease, and my fingers tighten around Angel's. I give her a gentle tug, pulling her against my chest and sliding my hand along her lower back

"We should dance." My lips brush the shell of her ear and her shoulder rises.

Leaning down, I brush the tip of my nose along her neck, giving her a brief kiss, wanting to pull her lips to mine.

She looks like a walking wet dream in her long green silk dress. The neck exposes the curve of her soft breasts making me hungry, possessive, and ready to fight off anybody who looks at her. Not to mention the slit up the front, exposing her gorgeous legs.

"Carmie!"

Her body tenses and steps away from me. "Hey, baby!"

I'm confused, looking around when Angel sweeps a little girl onto her hip. She looks a lot like my girl, with large amber eyes and soft wavy hair hanging down her back. She's wearing a dress like the teens on the dance floor, but hers is fluffy and little-girlie.

"I've been waiting for you all night." The little girl crosses her arms and a rosebud lip pokes out in a pout. She's adorable.

Angel leans closer, kissing her small nose. "I just walked through the door, sugar puss. I think you're getting sleepy."

"I am not!" The little girl shoots her arm up, pumping a fist over her head. "I'm ready to dance all night!"

That makes Angel laugh, and I step closer, tapping her on the shoulder. "Who do we have here?"

Angel looks up at me, adoration shining in her eyes. "This is Sofia, my littlest cousin."

"I'm not little." Sofia's brows pull together. "I'm four."

"Wow." I step back, putting my hand on my chest. "Think you might dance with me after while?"

Her eyes widen, and she looks to the side like she's considering my request. I think I might adore her, too. "I don't know. You're a stranger."

"Sorry. My name is Deacon. I'm a friend of Angel's."

"Who's Angel?" Her nose scrunches, and she looks around.

Angel leans close, pretending to whisper. "Deacon calls me Angel. It's short for Angelica."

"Oh…" Sofia leans towards me like she's telling me a secret. "We all call her Carmie. Except sometimes mamma calls her Carmelita."

"I've heard that." I make a face like of course she's right. Then I hold out my hands. "What do you say? Will you spare me a dance?"

"I guess so." She reaches for my hands, and I put her on my hip, swaying to the beat of the song. Angel watches us with shining eyes, and I lean towards my little partner. "I think you look like Angel."

"Her hair's more curly. I wish mine was more curly."

"You're beautiful." Angel puts her hand on Sofia's back.

The song ends, and we hear a woman's voice calling her name. We all look around, and Sofia's head drops back.

She exhales dramatically. "Mamma's taking *another* picture."

She hops down and runs across the floor in the direction of the teens, and I step closer to Angel, putting my hand on her waist. "She's a doll. She looks like she could be yours."

"Well, I was in the room when she was born." Angel's chin lifts, and she smiles up at me. "That's one relative down…"

"The rest of the party to go." I'm about to kiss her, when a friendly voice interrupts us. "What do we have here?"

Lourdes trots up in a filmy black pantsuit that swishes around her legs and arms when she moves. She gives Angel a hug and a kiss on the cheek before holding out her arm to me.

"You are wearing that suit, sir. You know that?" She rises on tiptoes to give me a hug, and I shake my head.

"Great party."

She holds Angel's hand, giving it a squeeze. "Our girl here did pretty much all the heavy lifting. She even made the quince's dress."

My eyebrows rise, and I quickly scan the room. "Which one is that?"

Lourdes steps closer pointing at the group of teens. "The one in the middle. Tiara, burgundy ball gown."

I see a girl in an elaborate dress with a tiered skirt and gold embellishment from the waist to the strapless top. "You made that?" Angel's cheeks flush as she looks down. I pull her against my chest, kissing her nose. "Is there anything you can't do?"

"It's nothing." Angel blinks away, glancing over her shoulder again.

Her eyes flicker around the room, and I wish she wasn't so edgy. I'm ready to meet her family and turn on all the charm, tell them the extent of my feelings for this girl at my side, all the things I have planned for us.

"You picked a good time to spring the gringo on the family." Lourdes gives her a playful elbow to the side. "Nobody's going to cause a scene at Lo's party."

"I hope you're right." Angel's lips tighten, and I don't really like being the fly in the buttermilk. Or however that goes.

"Hey, I thought I was one of the good guys."

"I'm just saying. I'm on your side." Lourdes slips her hands in the crooks of our arms. "Let's get something to drink. Alcohol always helps the medicine go down."

"I thought that was sugar." Angel laughs, but I can tell she's nervous.

We're halfway to the small bar in the opposite corner of the room when a stocky woman in a floor-length navy dress rushes up to us. "Carmie? Who is your guest?"

The woman has dark hair wrapped up in a loose bun. Her dress is strapless and full, and I'm guessing she's connected to the birthday girl somehow.

Angel visibly swallows and blinks fast. "Valeria, this is my date. Deacon."

Valeria smiles, holding out her hand. "How do you do, Deacon?"

"It's really nice to meet you at last." I take her hand and smile. "I've wanted to meet you a long time."

Her head tilts to the side. "Did you go to school with Carmie?"

"No."

"Do I know your parents?"

"I don't think so. My family is Dring. I'm Deacon Dring."

Valeria's face pales, and she pulls her hand away. "Dring?" She cuts an angry glare at Angel, and everything seems to stop.

"You promised me—"

"It was eight years ago, Val."

"You *promised*." Valeria's voice is a hiss. "I said you were not to talk to him."

"I'm confused—" I step forward, hoping to diffuse the tension. "Do you know my family?"

Her expression is furious, and I'm ready to assure her I come in peace when a stern male voice from behind me interrupts.

"Carmelita?" Both Angel and Valeria stiffen. "What's happening here? Who is this?"

Stepping to the side, I recognize Angel's brother from New Hope. He's dressed in a suit, and his dark brown hair is slicked back. His hands are on his waist.

I smile and hold out my hand, ready to make friends. "It's Beto, right? Deacon Dring. I've been looking forward to meeting you."

For a moment, his expression is stone. Then his nostrils flare. "Deacon *Dring*?" His glance flickers from me to Angel and back. He assesses my outstretched hand like I'm holding out a giant cockroach. "What is a *Dring* doing in my home? Tell me, boy, what are you doing at our *Treviño* family gathering?"

My smile fades, and I lower my hand, standing straighter. It helps I'm taller than he is. "I'm not a boy, and I'm here with your sister. She's my date."

"Your date?" His eyes scan me up and down.

"Deacon is my friend." Angel's voice is firm, but I don't like her calling me her friend. "I invited him here. We've known each other a long time. Am I not allowed to have guests in your home?"

Her brother's eyes narrow on me again. "Not him."

"You don't even know him!" Her voice grows louder. "You can't censor who I spend time with!"

"Mateo!" Beto flicks his wrist, and a dark-haired guy in a tan suit appears at his side. "My sister is tired. Take her to her room."

The guy catches Angel's arm, and she falls back, trying to pull away. "I am not a child!"

"Hang on just a minute." I try to stop him, but Beto grabs me roughly by the lapels of my coat.

"You're leaving now, *Dring*."

I don't like the way he says my last name, but I especially don't like how tan suit is half-leading, half-carrying my girl to the curved staircase at the back of the room. Angel struggles to escape, and I'm ready to start throwing punches.

"Get off me." My jaw is clenched.

Grabbing his wrists, I shove him back, but he's strong and ready for a fight. Just as fast, he grabs me again, clutching my arms and shoving me towards the door.

"I said, get out of my house." His voice is a snarl, and our faces are close.

Black eyes clash with mine. I don't know why this is happening, but I'll be damned if I let him come at me or treat his sister this way.

"I came here to make friends," I grunt out the words, pushing against his grip. "But if your guy doesn't take his hands off Angel, I'm going to kill him."

"I'd expect nothing less of you," Beto snaps, reminding me of a Doberman pinscher.

Our altercation is drifting through the room, and the kids on the dance floor have started to notice the commotion as well as the guests lining the walls. The music keeps playing, but nobody's dancing. They're forming a ring around us, and I can feel their eyes watching.

In my peripheral, I see Angel struggling against Mateo, and red fills my vision. "If you don't call off that asshole—"

"Mateo is following my orders, which is what you're about to do."

"Beto, stop!" Angel makes a lunge to get past Mateo, but he catches her clumsily, causing her to fall to the floor.

She goes down hard against the polished stone, letting out a little cry of pain. Fire blazes in my chest, and I shove Beto off me with all my strength. He crashes against the wall, and I'm across the room, grabbing Mateo by the shoulder from where he's bent over, trying to help her up.

I haul him up, landing a solid punch to his cheek.

"Fuck!" He falls back against the wall, crushing a small table and sending a vase of flowers flying.

Pain blasts through my hand, but I don't care. I've got one focus, and it's my girl. "Are you hurt?" Leaning down, I scoop her up.

She's trembling, and her skirt is torn. Her eyeliner is smudged from her tears, and a knife twists in my stomach at the sight.

Now I'm fucking furious.

"Carmie!" A small voice wails from the opposite side of the room, and rapid footsteps close the distance as Sofia runs to her.

Angel leans down to pick up her niece, who's also crying. "What's happening Carmie? Why is everybody fighting?"

"Beto, for lord's sake!" Valeria rushes to where we are, and she looks on the verge of tears herself. "Stop this now! You're ruining Lo's quinceañeara."

Beto's gaze flickers to where my hands are on his sister's waist. He's breathing hard, and I know he doesn't give a shit if anyone's crying or if he's ruining the party.

"Get your hands off my sister." It's a menacing sound, low and cold.

Angel steps up beside me, putting her hand on my arm. "I brought Deacon here to meet you. To make friends. If you talk to him, you'll see he's good. You'll like him."

Her voice is pleading, but I see the ice in her brother's eyes. Everything inside me tenses, preparing to fight.

"We do not make friends with Drings." He's breathing fast, his voice gravelly. "He is not welcome here."

Mateo is beside him, glaring at me with hatred in his eyes. I see what looks like the start of a shiner at the top of his cheek, and it makes me smile. I'm ready to give them a matching set.

"Then I'm not welcome here." Angel's voice turns hard, and I glance down at her. Her amber eyes flicker with golden fire, and the strength I've always known she possessed rises in her posture.

Sofia's arm tightens around her cousin's neck, and Angel's pretty eyes meet mine. I see the tears threatening to reappear, and I take her wrist, leading her towards the stairs. "Listen…" My voice is low and gentle. "I'm going to go now. Take Sofia upstairs, and I'll call you later."

Her slim hand touches the front of my chest, and she inhales sharply. "No. Deacon—"

"It's going to be okay." My insides are churning, but I don't want her to cry.

I know how important her family is to her, and I feel like I'm starting to understand why she tried to put off this meeting for so long. Not that I understand what the hell's going on here, but it doesn't matter. What matters is her cousin's party and Sofia's fear, and I don't want to be the cause of her pain.

"I don't want you to go."

"I'll be back." I give her a smile, hoping it comforts her. "Trust me."

"I trust you." She stretches up to kiss my cheek before giving her brother a withering look and going up the stairs.

My shoulders drop, and I turn, ready to end this shit show. I'm at the door when Beto catches me by the shoulder.

"I know all about you, Dring."

"You don't know anything about me." My voice matches his tone. I'm not afraid of this guy. The only thing holding me back is Angel.

"Oh, yes. I know you." He smiles coldly.

Mateo steps closer, as if he's waiting for a signal. Valeria makes a scolding noise behind us, and I glance over to see the teens all watching with wide eyes. My stomach tenses, and I know I'd better go before I forget my promise to my girl. I'm ready to smash this guy to bits.

"If I ever see you with my sister…" He points two fingers, aiming them slowly like a gun to my face. "I'll put a bullet… right there."

My hand is on the door, but before I leave, I step back, speaking quietly. "My feelings for Angel are real."

"Her name is Carmen." He steps closer, putting us almost chest to chest.

My breath ticks higher. "What's your problem?"

"I'm correcting past wrongs." Light flashes in his eyes. "I'd better not see you with my sister again."

CHAPTER
Eight

Angel

I'M SITTING ON MY BED WITH MY BACK AGAINST THE PILLOWS. SOFIA IS ON my lap, hugged against my chest, and I slide my fingers through her soft hair, soothing her as well as me.

Thinking about tonight reminds me of that ancient, black and white clip of the Hindenburg, engulfed in flames and burning up everyone with it.

My brother acted like a total jackass, and I will not be treated like a prisoner in his home… like I have much choice in the matter at this point.

A fact that makes me really, really frustrated and angry.

Sofia lifts her little head, looking at me with tearful eyes. "I wish we were at Mamma's house. I wish you were making me monkey bread and tucking me in for stories."

Monkey bread… It's been a long time since I made my improvised version of that cinnamon-bun delicacy. I would use canned biscuits and a melted butter-cinnamon drizzle.

"I can tell you a story, Snicklefritz. We don't need monkey bread."

"I wish we had some." Her voice is small and sad and I pull her tighter against my waist.

I know what she means. Warm, buttery cinnamon bread makes everything a little more bearable.

"I wish we had some, too." I'm quiet, thinking of cold nights and warm bread and old movies.

"Uncle Beto was like King Triton breaking all of Ariel's treasures." She sniffs, looking up at me. "Ariel runs away to Ursula after that. Are you going to run away?"

The wobble in her voice aches my throat, and I squeeze her tighter. "No…" I exhale heavily. I want to leave. I want to cry and throw things.

"I'm an adult. Adults don't run away from their problems. We face them."

Not that I wasn't ready to walk out that door if Deacon hadn't stopped me. I guess Sofia was the one who stopped me, crying and asking me to hold her. I hadn't expected to find my phone smashed to bits. I guess it happened when I tried to push past Mateo and we both hit the floor. My hip is still aching from that misstep.

A soft tap on my door makes me tense. "Who is it?" My voice is sharp.

It opens, and Lourdes steps inside. Her dark eyes are wide, and worry covers her face. "Holy… crap." She glances down at Sofia hugged tight in my lap. "That was crazy. Did you know that was going to happen?"

"No."

"Beto kept saying his name… What is it? Some kind of family feud? Are y'all the Hatfields and McCoys?"

"How would I know?" My brows are tight, and my jaw is set. "Mamá never talked about our family history." I only know the little bit Valeria told me. "Clearly she sheltered me from stuff I ought to know. Some ugly stuff."

"Hey, goober-nut, you okay?" Lourdes pokes Sofia on the leg, and my little sidekick shrugs at her.

"Carmie is like Ariel. King Triton doesn't want her to fall in love with our enemies."

"What do you know about enemies?" I reach down to goose her ribs. She makes a noise near a squeal, and I pull her up so I'm hugging her close. "Deacon isn't your enemy. He's a good guy."

I look down at my demolished phone in my lap and over to Lourdes. "Can I borrow your phone to text him?" Her brows furrow, and I show her mine. "He's going to worry."

She smiles, reaching for her device when another tap starts on the door.

Valeria doesn't wait for me to invite her in. "We need to talk."

"Welcome to Grand Central." Lourdes reaches for Sofia. My little cousin looks at me, and I give her a nudge before she walks across the bed into my bestie's arms. "I'll have peanut downstairs." She pauses at the door. "And I'll let Prince Eric know what happened."

I'm confused for a moment, but then I remember. Ariel's prince is Eric. "Thanks."

Valeria watches them go before she walks over to where I'm sitting on the bed, nursing my wounds.

"I'm sorry things went this way, Carmie." Her hand is heavy on my leg. "I thought we dealt with this a long time ago."

"You said he was my enemy, but you didn't even know him. You made me promise, but you didn't ask how I felt about it."

"Would it have mattered?" Valeria studies my eyes, and I know she knows.

It wouldn't have mattered.

It was already too late.

I drop my head back against the headboard, doing my best not to be completely selfish. "Is Lo okay? Is she still having fun? Did we ruin the party?"

"She's okay." Valeria exhales a shaky laugh. "They think it's very Quinten Tarantino to have a fight break out at Lo's party. Apparently, that makes her cool."

The way my cousin says cool is decidedly not cool. Still...

"I'm glad. I wouldn't want to be the reason she had a bad time." We're quiet for what feels like a long time.

I listen to the wind outside my window. I think it's starting to rain. I listen to the clock on my nightstand. After a while, I hear the cicadas scree, and I realize it isn't raining. It's only the never-ending wind. I look down at the shattered face of my phone and decide I'm tired of waiting.

"Are you going to tell me what really happened now? Why he's our *enemy*?" It sounds so foolish to my ears.

Her eyes meet mine, and her shoulders drop. "It's not something I like digging into..."

I'm not in the mood to beg. "Tell me what happened."

Valeria settles back on the bed like she's about to reveal a deep, dark truth. The air around her seems to still as I wait. I can't decide if I'm impatient or annoyed.

"Back before you were born, our grandfathers worked together in the oil fields." She speaks like she's telling a bedtime story. "Rogers Western Dring and Manuel Luis Treviño, Papa Luis. They were best friends. Traveled together through the western territories. Both of them were committed to finding a better life, making it rich."

"What happened?"

Valeria shrugs. "That's the part no one knows for sure. Deacon's grandfather accused ours of stealing. Our grandfather claimed he was innocent." Her voice trails off. "Papa Luis was thrown in jail, and we lost everything."

"What's everything?" I'm still skeptical.

"All the land around Fate."

"Fate, Texas?"

"It was our family's land before the Drings sold it to the developers." She heaves a sigh. "There's more, but that's the gist of it."

"I think you'd better tell me everything."

Dark eyes flicker to mine, and my heart beats faster. "Some things are better left unsaid, Carm. Maybe you don't want to know everything."

"No." I exhale a heavy laugh. "I definitely want to know everything."

"Well… Rumor has it…" She looks down at her hands clasped in her lap. "The story everyone believes is Rogers Dring shot your grandfather down."

The ticking of my cat clock is the only sound in the room for several seconds as her words settle around me.

I'm having a hard time believing this. "You're saying he murdered our grandfather? But why?"

Val shrugs, looking up at the ceiling before returning her eyes to mine. "Why does anything happen? Love… Money."

"Love?" my eyes are really wide now. "What are you saying?"

"See? This is why I didn't want to go down this path." Valeria shifts in her seat, tugging on the bodice of her navy gown and acting self-righteous. "There's no proof of anything. It's all gossip and hearsay. I'm not one to repeat gossip."

Reaching out fast, I catch her wrist in a tight grip. "This is important, Val. I need to know if it's true or not."

"It's true." The deep voice I know cuts through my room. Beto stands at the door with his fingers hooked in the loops of his belt. "His grandfather shot yours in cold blood. It's a truth you can never escape."

Heat flares in my chest at the sight of him. "I'll tell you a truth. I'm not spending another night in this house. I'm finding my own place."

"You're not moving out." His tone is grave. "I'm your brother. You'll stay here with me."

"You can't make me stay." After how he acted tonight, I can barely even look at him.

"No, I can't make you stay. But I can make you listen."

"Technically, you can't do that either." I've had enough of his bullying. Still, this is a story I need to know. "I will listen, because I want to know my family's history. I want to know what no one has ever told me."

My brother straightens, crossing his arms over his chest. "I'm not your enemy, *mija*."

"And I'm not your child."

He steps forward, heels clicking on the dark wood floor. "You dishonor our family by giving yourself to that man. Rogers Dring murdered your grandfather in cold blood."

"Valeria said there was no proof. How could you possibly know?"

"Because our father told me." His voice is stony, and he looks out my window at the limbs swirling on the trees. "He was there when it happened. It would be a slap in his face for you to ignore the truth."

My heart freezes at his words. At the same time, everything inside of me fights against them. It's the past. This isn't our story. Deacon and I didn't play a role in these events. We shouldn't be made to pay for them. None of this matters to Deacon and me.

Beto stands over me, surveying my lack of response. Finally, after another minute ticks by he goes to my door, pausing before he exits. "Now you know."

He's gone, closing the door behind him, leaving me sitting on the bed facing Valeria. We're both breathing quickly. She's watching me just like my brother, like I'm as much of a mystery to them as they are to me.

Only Valeria should know me better. We've lived in the same house for so long.

"Your brother is certain, but your father was just a boy." She stands heavily, exhaling deeply. "It's like I said, no one was in the room when it happened. No one could verify the events."

Blinking up at her, I frown. "So it's not true?"

"I don't know." She shrugs. "I'm sorry, Carm. I tried to protect you."

"Protect me from what? Gossip and hearsay? That's what you called it, not me. You said that."

"All I know is you can't keep your family and this man." Her voice is sad but kind, tender and motherly. "You have to decide."

"But *he* didn't do anything. I love him."

Her dark eyes press closed and she shakes her head. "I asked you to promise—"

"Well, I'm sorry. It's too late for that." I stand off the bed and pace my room. "I'm not a part of this. I'm not carrying on this feud. It has nothing to do with him—or me."

"It has everything to do with you. It's your family." She leans down and places her hands on my upper arms, giving me a gentle squeeze. "Rest. Drink some water and try to sleep. Things might look different in the morning."

I don't know how anything is going to look different. From where I'm standing I see my family on one side of the Grand Canyon and my love on the other, and it's not a hard choice. They're the ones putting him on the other side of the chasm for no reason.

As much as I want to hold my family together, my heart is with Deacon.

I won't walk away from him.

CHAPTER
Nine

Deacon

"**B**UT SHE'S OKAY?" RAIN BEATS ON THE ROOF OF MY CAR, AND I'M parked in the empty lot of a Best Buy outside a strip mall in Plano.

Adrenaline pulses in my veins, and my chest is tight. It's a mixture of too much information and too little all at once.

Lourdes is on the other line reassuring me. "She wanted to call you, but her phone got smashed in that tussle with Mateo. It must've been under her when she hit the floor."

My eyes squeeze shut, and I can't get that image out of my head. Fucking Mateo with his fucking hands on her. Her cry of pain; the tears in her eyes. I've never felt more helpless. I hate it.

"I need to talk to her, Lor."

"I know." It sounds like Lourdes is walking fast as she speaks. "I can't do anything. She's in the room with Val and Beto."

"What are they telling her?" Scrubbing my forehead with my fingers, I'm trying to get a grip on what happened tonight.

Beto said the past couldn't be undone and he kept saying my

family name. Would Winnie know what he's talking about? Hell, I don't even know how to approach this with her.

"Not sure. I took Poogie out of the room before it got too heated."

Frowning at my phone, I try to understand. "Angel has a dog?"

"She has a four-year-old cousin." Lourdes says it like I should know Sofia's million nicknames.

"Sofia, right. Is she okay?"

"She's a trooper." I hear the small voice in the background, and I realize Lourdes has her.

Leaning my head against the headrest, I think about how I left. How much I hated walking away from her. Angel was angry and helpless, and I told her to trust me. "I need to see her tonight, Lor. I need to talk to her and decide what to do."

"I'll keep you in the loop, don't worry. Just hang tight for a little while. The party's still going, but it should be winding down before too long."

We disconnect, and I watch the large drops of rain coating the outside of my windshield in a glassy sheen. I'm amazed the party didn't end with the fight, but I guess teenagers are more resilient these days.

I grip the steering wheel, tightening my fists over and over. This is worse than being at school. I can only trust she's okay, trust she's not crying or starting to believe bad things about me. I don't even know what I'm being accused of doing, other than having the wrong last name.

How could I not know about a connection between our families? Has Angel known all this time? Is that why she kept putting off our meeting? I want to be pissed at her, but the tears in her eyes make it impossible.

Turning the key in the ignition, I decide I have to fill this space of time with something. I hit the gas and head in the direction of our family's estate.

"My goodness, Deacon, it's almost eleven. What in the world are you doing here? You'll spoil my beauty rest."

The kitchen is dim-lit, and she stands on the other side of a dark granite bar from me. Winnie's hair is in a cream satin turban, and she's wearing a blue velvet robe. She looks like something out of an old movie.

"It's Saturday, Win. You can sleep late in the morning."

"I absolutely cannot. I'm expected to be in our family pew at the Presbyterian church at eleven." She flicks her hand as if I'm being obtuse and goes to a small wet bar in the opposite corner of the large, updated room. "I would think you might deign to join me sometimes."

"I'll see what I can do. First, I need some information."

"Information?" She wraps her robe tighter around her neck and turns the tap on the small hot water faucet, filling a teacup. I watch as she adds a slice of lemon and returns to me, looking up expectantly. "About what?"

"What's the connection between Grandpa Dring and Manuel Treviño?"

If I hadn't been watching her so closely, I might've missed the flinch in her eyes. She blinks down, taking a sip of hot water to cover it. "I have no idea who you're talking about."

I cross my arms and lean my hip against the granite countertop. "Tell me, Win. Who was Manuel Treviño?"

"Honestly, Deacon. It's very late, and I'm very tired. I can't possibly be expected to dig through the forgotten details of your grandfather's past at this hour."

"So he *is* connected to my grandfather's history?"

"*Connected* is probably too generous a term." She takes another sip of hot lemon water. "From what I remember, he was your grandfather's hired man. He helped with his horses and helped him prospect. Carried supplies or whatever those old men did. Honestly, love, I have no idea what all he did for your grandfather. They believed that was men's business."

"Did something happen to him?"

She frowns, exhaling deeply and lifting her chin as if the answer is written on the ceiling somewhere. I can't help looking up as well, and I notice the stained-glass window above the sink is a Thomas Grey quote, *The paths of glory lead but to the grave*. Not the most optimistic sentiment for a prospector.

"Well? Did something happen?" Pushing off the bar, I step a little closer.

"Oh, I remember there was some confusion. Father never talked much about the past. Hell, he never talked much at all. I think the most I heard him say as a child was *Heya* to a horse once."

My memory of my grandfather is very faint, but I know this is true. He stood back silently observing us, arms crossed over his chest, jaw set. Once he offered me chewing tobacco, but I was only seven. I didn't try it.

"What happened, Win?" My voice is calmly urging.

She puts her cup into the sink with a heavy sigh. "What does it matter? It was a million years ago. It's ancient history."

"It matters to me." I reach out and catch her slim upper arm.

Her brows pull together over her blue eyes, and she lifts her elbow, pulling out of my grasp. "It's the same story with all those people. He was a drunk and a liar, and he tried to make his problems your grandfather's."

"I don't want to hear racist polemics. Tell me what you know."

"I know he stole from your grandfather. The Treviño man went to jail, so it must have been of some significance. I was just a child at the time." She exhales heavily. "Anyway, they're all gone now."

"Gone where?" I already know the answer to this question, but I'm curious how much she knows.

"Wherever those people go, darling. They have legions of family. For all I know they're back in Mexico now."

"But they were Texans."

"Then I imagine they're around somewhere." She puts a hand on my shoulder and rises to kiss my cheek. "You don't need to worry yourself about all that. Like I said, it's ancient history."

She puts her teacup in the sink and starts for the door. "Are you sleeping here tonight? I'll make a note for cook to fix you breakfast, and maybe you'll consider joining me at church?"

My lips are tight. I'm not happy with her version of events, but my phone vibrates in my pocket, and I need to go. "I'll sleep here, but don't worry about breakfast."

I head for the door. She calls after me, something about night owls and eagles, but I've got to get to my girl.

THE CATERING VAN IS THE LAST TO LEAVE. I SIT UNDER A PAVILION JUST down from Beto's house, watching as they load up, slam the back doors, and finally drive away into the damp night.

It's been raining since I left, and I traded my car for my bike, which means I'm soaked. The Apple store was closed, so I picked up a burner phone at Best Buy for now. I haven't heard from Angel, but Lourdes texted me a basic description of where her room is located in the house.

According to the description, Angel's window looks out over the lake, just above a small cottage with an oak tree that has low branches. I walk my bike to the end of a separate driveway and leave it parked. In this neighborhood, for as long as I'll be here, it should be fine.

As soon as the last light in the downstairs area is extinguished, I stroll up the sidewalk then dash across the dark lawn to the line of trees surrounding the back yard, hoping Beto doesn't have a security system filming the perimeter.

Voices on the patio pull me up quick, and I press my back to a large crepe myrtle near the side porch.

"She didn't grow up here." I recognize Valeria's voice, and

my ears strain to hear what she's saying. "She doesn't understand the way things work."

"She knows to respect her family." Beto's angry voice is unmistakable. "How could she have done this right under your nose?"

"Your sister is a grown woman, Roberto. I don't follow her everywhere she goes. I have two children to raise and a full-time job."

"Ah." Beto makes a dismissive sound. "Then I came back at the right time. I'm willing to keep an eye on her. I'll guide her in the right direction."

Anger tightens my chest. So much for making friends. My jaw clenches, and I scan the area, looking for the tree Lourdes described. I'll have to cross the back yard to get to it, and with these two on the patio, I have to wait.

The noise of a chair scraping on stone catches my attention. "It's late," Valeria sighs. "The party was a success in spite of it all. I'm going to bed."

"We'll discuss this with her in the morning…" Beto's follows her inside, and I lean forward, peeking carefully to see the door close before I streak across the yard to the giant oak tree behind the cottage.

It's an easy climb to her balconette. I have no way of calling her, and I can only hope Lourdes told her I was coming as I swing a leg over the balustrade and tap lightly on her window.

Misty rain settles in the air around me, and I'm glad for my leather jacket, even on this warm night. It keeps me somewhat dry underneath, and it's black. A few moments pass, and I'm about to tap again when I hear her soft voice. "Deacon?"

The curtain swishes away, and bright eyes meet mine. The glass double-doors wobble and open, and I cross into her room, closing them quickly behind me.

"You're here." Her voice breaks, and I cup her cheeks in my hands, lifting her pretty face.

Her eyes are glassy with unshed tears, and I lean down to cover her lips with mine. Hers part, our tongues lightly touch. It's a gentle kiss, soft and warm, and emotion squeezes my chest. I want to wrap her in my arms, take her away from this mess, but she stops me.

"You're all wet." She holds the lapels of my jacket, pushing it off my shoulders. "Were you riding in the rain?"

Shrugging out of the soaked garment, I put it at the base of her window. "I didn't want anyone to recognize my car."

She goes to a large, stone bathroom, returning with a plush, white towel. "Here. Give me your shirt."

Catching the hem, I whip it over my head, and when our eyes meet, she blinks quickly as if she's stunned.

Her cheeks flush, and I'm acutely aware we've only been together once since my homecoming. The memory of our white-hot reunion in the tower has my cock rising to attention.

"It's not the first time you've seen me without a shirt, beautiful." I can't help teasing her.

She shakes her head and goes to her bedroom door. "I'll put this in the sink to dry. Give me your pants, too."

The smooth click of the lock changes the temperature in the room. My body aches for hers. I'm ready to pull her to me and devour her.

"I haven't been here five minutes, and you've already got me naked." I hold out my hand as she returns. "Come here."

She walks straight into my arms, and I hug her tightly against my chest. Rubbing her back, I take a long inhale of her jasmine scented hair. "Are you okay?"

"I'm much better now that you're here." She looks up at me, and I can almost make out her soft breasts beneath the thin material of her long-sleeved tee. She's so damn sexy.

I scan her shapely legs in short white shorts, searching for any sign of bruising or injury. "Did that guy hurt you?"

"No." A sad little smile touches her lips. "I'm so sorry, Deacon. For tonight, for not telling you—"

"Don't." Reaching up, I place my finger lightly against her lips, pulling her to me again. "It doesn't matter. I'm sorry I had to leave you that way. I didn't want to ruin the party—"

"I understood."

"But I had to come here tonight. I needed to see you, to know you're okay."

"I'm okay." She lifts her chin, and I lean down to kiss her again.

Her lips part, and our tongues curl together. It's electric and need shoots straight to my cock. My hands go under the hem of her shirt, finding the smooth, warm skin of her lower back, pressing her hips to mine.

She exhales a soft noise, and I break the kiss, looking around the room. "This is a nice place."

"The bed's big enough for both of us." Her palms slide against mine, threading our fingers, and she takes a step backwards, drawing me towards the bed with her. "Everyone's sleeping over. You might as well, too."

"Sounds risky."

"I'm not afraid." She lifts her shirt over her head, and her soft breasts are bare, tipped with pale light. My mouth waters. "I want you to stay."

"I'll do whatever you want."

She slides the terry fabric of her shorts down her shapely legs, and it's my turn to be stunned by her beauty. Delicate lace rises over the soft curve of her hips leading to her narrow waist and full, round breasts. They rise and fall with her rapid breathing.

"I want you inside me."

I close the space between us, ready to devour her.

I want her all over me.

I want her skin against mine.

She pushes the towel off my hips just as I reach her. It hits the floor with a soft thump, and my erection springs hard and thick between us.

"Deacon…" She wraps her fingers around me, stroking my shaft, making me groan.

I cover her mouth with mine, pulling and kissing, hungry and needy. We move quickly, and I can't think of anything but loving this woman in my arms. She's the girl I fell in love with before I ever knew what that meant.

Turning, I sit on the bed, scooting back so she can straddle my lap. I want her to ride me. I want to see her beautiful body getting off on mine, breasts bouncing, hair cascading around us.

She rises over my cock and drops, sheathing me completely in her warm depths. Closing my eyes, I swallow a loud groan as my mind blanks.

The house is filled with people who hate me. It does nothing to kill my desire, but I have to be quiet.

"You feel so good." My jaw is tight and I grind out the words, holding back.

"Yes…" She gasps, holding my face as she kisses me.

Our lips seal, quieting our moans as she rocks faster.

"Angel… Jesus." My body is on fire with the things she's doing to me.

Her insides clench and pull, massage and tug. It's hot and slippery and so damn wet. I want to yell as my orgasm tightens my ass. Her head drops back and she bites her lip. Her soft breasts are at my chin, and she's better than every centerfold. Angel getting off on my cock is fucking nirvana.

Palming her breasts, I suck a hardened nipple into my mouth, and her body responds. My lips move to her neck, and I pull a nip of skin between my teeth, moving higher, behind her ear.

She breaks with a moan, spasms rippling and clenching her core, and I relax my brow and let go. My balls tense, and my cock pulses as I fill her, holding her, loving her.

We hold each other, eyes closed as our breathing drifts to normal, as I have these thoughts about merging our lives together permanently.

"I have an idea." My beautiful, sated girl props an elbow on my shoulder, smoothing her hand in the side of her gorgeous, wild hair. "We'll pretend they don't matter. They don't exist. We'll go on with our plans, and fuck them."

A smile lifts my cheeks. "You're adorable when you cuss."

"I'm serious!" Her whiskey eyes widen at me. "If they don't want to be a part of our happiness, who needs them?"

Damn, I love this girl, but I know better. "You do."

"I do not. Especially not some absentee brother, who suddenly appears trying to push me around and ruin my life."

Sliding down into the bed beside her, I pull her back against my chest. "I hate to say it… Your brother's kind of a dick."

"Kind of?" Her voice is sarcastic, and I chuckle.

"But a dick with a point. Something happened. We can't just ignore it."

Her fingers thread with mine. "I don't care what happened. It's the past. We're here now. It doesn't change us."

"Life is long, Ang." I squeeze her hand in mine.

She pushes up on her forearm turning to meet my eyes. "Nothing changes us, Deacon. Promise me."

Exhaling a smile, I slide my hand along the side of her neck. "I promise."

She settles in again, nestling close against me. I wrap my arms around her, burying my face in her softly scented hair. This is right, us together, forever. She's all I've ever wanted. She's mine…

But uneasiness is in my chest.

Late night promises are one thing, but when the morning comes, we're facing a lifetime of warring with our families. Angel doesn't want that, and neither do I.

I will fix this. I've just got to find the truth.

CHAPTER
Ten

Angel

I'M FLOATING ON BUTTERFLY WINGS THROUGH CLOUDS OF SPARKLING BLISS. At some point I mount a unicorn and ride his horn to an orgasmic Eden where a lion curls up with a lamb, giving me a knowing look. I smile shyly, warm bands of iron wrap around my waist, and a woodpecker starts tapping against my tree of happiness...

The annoying tapping grows louder.

My misty mountaintop begins to melt.

The pesky woodpecker learns to speak, and it's shouting outside my door. "Ceecee, wake up! Waaaaake up!"

It's not a woodpecker. It's Sofia.

"Oh shit!" I sit up fast, looking at the window then at Deacon asleep beside me.

My shoulders drop at the sight of him. He's so damn sexy in my bed. Full lips rest gently together, thick dark hair curls right around his ears... Muscles ripple down his arms, his abs... My insides clench at the memory of his cock. I'm pretty sure I know whose horn I was riding, and it was thick and delicious.

"Carmieeee!" Sofia's voice grows louder, effectively killing my love buzz.

Locked doors did not exist in Valeria's house. As soon as the girls were old enough to walk, they'd get up every morning at dawn looking for company.

"Give me a minute, Soph!" I jump out of bed, grabbing my discarded clothing and pulling it on.

The sun is only just brightening the horizon, thank God. Everyone was drinking and celebrating last night, and I don't expect anyone to be awake at this hour—anyone older than four.

"Deacon." I gently nudge my sleeping Adonis. "Wake up, babe. It's morning."

"What?" His blue eyes blink open, and when he sees me, he smiles. "Hey."

My heart melts, and I lean down to kiss him slow.

The rapid banging on my door starts again.

He hears it and pulls back. "Who's that?"

"Carmie! You're missing it!"

My eyes narrow. "That's a four-year-old child."

Deacon is out of my bed in a flash. "I forgot to set my alarm."

He's in the bathroom pulling on his jeans and tee. I'm sitting on the foot of my bed, my heart breaking at the thought of him leaving me. Returning to my bedroom, he looks my way and pauses.

"Damn, girl." His eyes are hot as he surveys me, sitting in my short shorts and nearly transparent tee. Crossing the room, he cups my cheeks and kisses me, looking deep into my eyes. "You are so beautiful."

Could I love this guy more? Sofia starts to whine, and panic tightens my chest. She's going to wake up the whole house if I don't let her in, but I'll be damned if I let her see Deacon here. That girl can*not* keep a secret.

I stand, catching his arms and leading him to the window.

"This is so risky." My throat is tight as I watch him throw a leg over the balustrade. "What's going to happen now?"

His lips press together as he looks out across the yard. "This isn't how I wanted things to go."

"I know. I'm sorry—"

"Sh…" He lightly touches my lips. "I told you no more of that."

"I can't help it."

His finger slides to my cheek, moving a curl behind my ear. "I've got to go to Harristown and check in with my clients there. I'd wanted to take you with me, see if you liked the town."

"I want to go…" I'm half listening, half worrying about Sofia's ongoing noise.

"I'll only be gone a day, maybe two. Will you be okay here?"

"Oh, sure. As long as I do what I'm told." Like a child. *I've got to get my own place.*

Deacon's lips tighten, and he pulls me close, kissing me firmly. "I'll be back soon, and we'll work this out. You have the burner phone I got you?"

"I've got it." The box is on my vanity.

"If anything happens, call me. I'll drop everything and come to you." His hands are firm on my arms.

"Can I call you now?"

He traces his thumb along my jaw, resting his hand on my shoulder. "We're going to fix this, Angel. I won't let you give up your family for me."

"Maybe they're the ones giving me up…"

Exhaling slowly, he looks into my room. "Your brother obviously loves you. Look at this beautiful place—"

"It's a beautiful cage."

"Just give me some time. We'll find a solution."

Lourdes would say my boyfriend is so privileged, but I don't want to be cynical. I was raised to believe. "We can try, I guess."

One more kiss, one more longing look, and he's gone, dropping fast behind the cottage and pausing to look back. We extend our hands in a wave… or maybe a wistful grasp… before he dashes across the tree line and off my brother's property.

A feeling of dread tightens my chest. Deacon is so optimistic, and I wish I could be the same way. I'm afraid this is not going to end well. Sofia's voice pulls me from my troubled thoughts, and when I open my bedroom door, she's sitting with her back to it.

"Good morning, sunshine." I reach down for her hand.

She pops up and marches into my room. "Watch *Moana* with me!"

Climbing into the middle of my bed, she props her little body against the pillows. The remote is in her hand, and she turns on the oversized, flat screen television hanging on the opposite wall to the channel she needs.

"I didn't know Beto had Disney plus." I climb in beside her, curling into the blankets and pulling Deacon's pillow to my chest.

"He has all the channels." Sofia's tone is very *duh*, and she immediately starts singing. "You're welcome!"

I bury my face in the down, inhaling deeply of rich citrus and sage. It's almost like he's still here, and I hug the pillow tighter, fighting my sadness, dreaming of his hard body, his soft kisses, his expert touch. His impossible dreams.

"I'M SORRY YOU WERE HURT." MY BROTHER STANDS IN THE KITCHEN WITH his arms crossed. As always, he's in jeans and a white tank, feet bare, brow lowered.

"I'm fine." I finish my coffee, ready to go.

Valeria reaches for my hand across the table. "We don't have to discuss it right now."

"There's nothing to discuss." Beto walks away from where we're sitting. "It's settled."

I'm not in the mood for him. "How's Lo feeling today? All grown up?" I wonder if anybody catches the irony in my question.

"Who knows?" Valeria sits back, lifting her coffee. "I don't understand half the stuff she says anymore. It's all YouTube quotes and video game references."

My brother returns, placing a white box on the table in front of me. It's a brand-new, latest model iPhone.

"What's this?" I frown up at him.

"Lourdes said your phone was broken when you fell." He looks down, and while his tone is stern as ever, I do see a flash of something almost like an apology in his eyes.

Whatever.

"So you're paying for my phone now?"

"Mateo is the reason you broke your old one. He was following my orders."

Orders. I love how he tosses that word around like he's *el presidente.*

Opening the box, I lift the shiny new device. "It's yellow."

He shrugs. "It's as close as I could get to your favorite colors."

Anger mixes with frustration mixes with annoyance. Deacon says my brother loves me. I want to believe it, but after the way he's acted since he returned...

He's nice then he's controlling. He's thoughtful then he's infuriating.

"Thank you." I'm not smiling as I stand and go to the door.

"Where are you going, Carmie?" Valeria looks at me with concern.

I look from her to my brother, with his arms crossed. "I'm going to church."

"By the waters of Babylon, we hung our harps on the willows and wept." Father Molina gazes at the stained-glass windows of our cathedral.

At fifteen, when most kids were defying parental traditions and rules, Father Molina kept me in mass with his subversive sermons. He talked about pushing back against oppression, peaceful resistance, keeping the faith. He appears solemn and reverential, but he's a fighter.

"How could they sing songs of joy with invaders in their land?" His eyes return to us, seated in the pews looking up at him. "Because God was their ally. God brings justice to all."

My eyebrows rise, and I watch as he goes on about God's ability to save us from all our troubles. My mind wanders to my own troubles, and I think about what Mamá would say about worry and fear.

Worry is a story we create in our minds about a future we don't know. The future is always uncertain, she would say. All we have is the present. She had a little quote about the present being a present… It was a play on words. I wish I could remember it exactly, but it was something about how being in the present is peace.

Focusing on the now is enlightenment.

We file forward to receive communion. It's an older church, not too large, but still it has arched, stained-glass windows the original congregation raised money to install. The pews are polished wood with deep red velvet cushions. It's dark and solemn with a good Catholic vibe.

Once we've all returned to our seats, Father Mo holds his arms wide over the congregation, speaking in a strong voice. "May the Lord bless you and keep you. May the Lord make his face to shine upon you and give you rest."

It happens. Calm filters through my chest, and I close my eyes to receive his blessing.

A strong clutch on my forearm snaps me out of my moment of zen. The organ plays a joyful exit hymn, and Valeria's friend Rosalía smiles at me. "I need to talk to you."

"Okay…"

Parishioners file around us heading to the double doors where the priest stands, telling everyone goodbye.

Rosalía is the same age as Valeria, but she's much slimmer with a white stripe running down the middle of her black hair. Her dark eyes are excited. "What are you doing this afternoon?"

I have to think. "Lunch, maybe some painting. I don't have any plans... Why?"

She does a little bounce, grinning wider. "Can you come with me? I got you a job... I think."

"A job?" *What in the world?*

"An art job," she whispers.

Father Molina shakes my hand and says something, but I'm too distracted by... what the heck is an art job?

We're out on the lawn, and Rosalía turns to me. "The rich old lady I work for wants to have her picture done... A portrait? Anyway, she's been having all these artists come to the house and show her their vision or whatever. She hates all of them... So I told her about you!"

She claps, and I'm trying to catch up. "You told a rich old lady I would paint her portrait? I don't really do portraits, Rose."

"Nonsense! You do sketches of people all the time."

"It's not really the same thing..."

She leans closer, gripping my forearm. "This woman has more money than God, Carm. I heard her say she would pay fifteen thousand dollars for it."

My mouth falls open. She has my attention now. "Tell me exactly what happened."

"Well, I was dusting the chandelier in the drawing room, and I heard her complaining they were all kitsch, and she wouldn't hire them if they worked at the Whitney." She's not making sense, but I'm doing my best to be patient. "So I very nicely went over and said my best friend knew a very good artist, and I would be happy to recommend her."

She pauses, and now I grip her arm. "What did she say?"

"She said if she wanted her portrait on black velvet, she'd go to the corner gas station and pay somebody five dollars."

My mouth falls open again. "She said that?"

"Oh, that's not half of what she says. You just wait." Rosalía shakes her head. "Anyways, I showed her your sketch of Sofia. Valeria sent it to me. It's so good. You really captured her personality in the eyes, and—"

"And?"

"And she said if you came by this afternoon, she'd give you a minute of her time. Very dismissive."

"This afternoon?" I feel faint. A fifteen-thousand-dollar job combined with the Arthaus award... I wouldn't need anybody's help.

"I said noon, but she said two." Rosalía shrugs like it's no big deal, something I do every day. "She goes to the First Presbyterian church and then she has lunch."

"I can be there at two." I'm mentally flying through my portfolio. "What can I show her? All my pieces are abstracts..."

"Just show her what you've done. It'll be great." Rosalía squeezes my arm. "And I told her your name was Angela Carmen. It sounds less Mexican."

"It's not going to change my face, Rose."

"Nonsense!" She does a little wave. "You could easily pass for whatever you want."

"An American?" Which happens to be what I am.

"Whatever it takes."

Shaking my head, I give her a squeeze. "Thank you. I'll just show up and be myself."

"That's the best any of us can do."

FROM THE BACK OF THE LYFT, I LOOK UP AT THE MANSION. IS IT POSSIBLE I'm wrong? Double-checking the text Rosalía sent, I verify it's the correct address.

"This is it?" I ask, wishing for some mistake. It can't be...

The driver points to the dashboard map, and I know it's

right. Reaching for the door handle, I carefully step out onto the sidewalk.

"Thank you." I say as the car pulls away.

What's going to happen now? I didn't know Rosalía worked for Deacon's aunt. I've never been to this house. I've never even dared step foot through the doors—as much as Deacon wanted me to.

How small is the world exactly? Sofia would know—because of Disney. Beto would be furious. Straightening my shoulders, I clutch the handles of my portfolio and walk with purpose to the front door. It doesn't matter. It's a job.

How I wish I had that burner phone on me. For all I know, my brother's tracking my calls.

"Welcome, Angela." A statuesque older woman opens the door. "My name is Winona Clarke. You may call me Mrs. Clarke."

"How do you do, Mrs. Clarke."

"If you'll come this way." She leads me through a house that reminds me of an old hunting lodge.

It's paneled in dark wood, and the floors are covered in Persian rugs and animal hides. The furniture is either leather and brass or wood and tapestry, and everything smells like old money and furniture polish. I imagine that's Rosalía's contribution to the home.

Looking down over the foyer is a life-sized portrait of a man with thick white hair and a conquering expression. A white beard covers his jaws, and he holds a tan cowboy hat. He's very Texas in his bolo tie and slacks with oil derricks rising in the background. It's a stately painting, formal and ancient, but looking closer, I see a resemblance.

It's Deacon's grandfather.

The one who supposedly shot mine down.

How strange is life?

"Father always had a flair for the dramatic." Deacon's aunt

Winnie walks ahead of me, and I watch her, wondering what his life was like as a boy here in this stately mansion.

We've never talked about it.

Winnie is tall and slim with really good hair for an older woman, straight and thick, even though it's white. She's elegantly dressed in navy slacks and a filmy, long-sleeved ivory blouse. She has this air about her, a calm confidence like she owns everything. She reminds me of Emmylou Harris.

"What did you have in mind... For your portrait?" I'm not really sure how this works.

"Obviously, it should match what's been done before." Winnie leads me down the oversized hall to a sitting room. "Father was in the oil business. Brandt was into horses. I've only ever taken care of our family affairs, which was more work than both of theirs combined."

She sits in an elegant chair with wooden arms and deep blue fabric. I sit across from her on a leather sofa that sinks deep, putting me lower than her. A white cat with black front legs pops out from under it and rubs against me.

"A backdrop isn't necessary." I scoot forward, giving the cat a quick scrub with my fingers as I do my best to sit taller. "Many old portraits are simply figures in a room or standing beside a chair in *contrapposto*. Think of Michelangelo's David, Mona Lisa, or even Whistler's Mother—"

"I'd prefer not Whistler's Mother." She scowls at me. "I'm not that old."

"Of course not." I swallow a laugh at my unintentional gaff.

"Boots, shoo." She waves the cat away and stands. "We do have many options here at the house. It would make sense, considering it has always been my purview."

"I would suggest a seated pose... Or you could hold an object. Although, you'd want to be comfortable."

"You'd want me to sit the entire time?"

"Or I could work from a photo." Hell, I think I'd prefer that.

"I'd expect you to work on it here, so I could oversee your progress."

"I can work here." Any reason to be out of Beto's house.

She studies me with blue eyes so similar to Deacon's, minus the love. "Tell me about your background. What is your training?"

"I'm a senior at the Roshay studio—"

"Farrell Roshay?" Her eyebrows rise.

"Yes. I've been there two years now."

"How can you afford that?"

"I'm sorry?" *Is that her business?*

"The Roshay Academy is the most elite art school in Texas. How can you afford it? Are you on a scholarship?"

"No." I bite back the answer I'd like to give her. I do want this job. "My uncle pays for it."

"And what is his profession?"

"He owns a car dealership."

"Used cars, I imagine." I don't answer that, and she shifts in her chair. "Did you bring samples of your work? Let me see them."

"Of course." I lift the black portfolio case from the floor beside me.

It's a cheap black pleather case I bought at Michaels. I wish it were nicer, but I suppose it's more about what's inside that counts. Isn't that what everybody says? Somehow I think Winona Clarke missed the memo.

"I see." She turns the plastic pages, quickly bypassing my landscapes. "Who is this?"

She pauses on a sketch I did last year. My throat tightens as I look down on the drawing I hastily slid into one of the back transparent sleeves.

It's my mother behind her camera. She's sitting in a position I remember so well, looking at me as if I'm her subject. Her hand is on her leg, and her arm is slung over the tripod. She's wearing jeans that have holes and are frayed at the knees, and her shirt is a loose navy button-down over a tan tank top.

Her eyes gaze forward with such intensity, and her ubiquitous black glasses frame her hazel eyes. Long, dark hair streaked with gray covers her shoulders like a cape. She looks like a woman who has done great things. It's how I see her in my mind.

Her knowing smile makes me wonder what she's thinking. Probably something about living in the moment. The small lines around her eyes remind me of how she looked at me when I'd say something amusing or wise for my years, as she'd say.

It starts me wondering… Maybe Rosalía's right. I'm not the greatest portrait artist, but something about the eyes captures the spirit. When I look at this sketch, it's like my mother is right here with me.

We're silent, admiring the formidable woman who raised me, who decided I wasn't going to grow up in this place of bitterness and inherited hate.

Yet here I am.

"Who is this, Angela?" Deacon's aunt asks again.

"It's my mother."

Her lips purse, and she looks from me to the sketch. "It's an excellent piece. Can you do something like this for me?"

Blinking up, I try to understand what she's asking. "You want me to find what makes you special?"

It's possible that came out wrong.

Her eyes narrow. "I'll give you a trial period. No promises. If I don't like what you're doing, you're out."

It's my turn to narrow my eyes and study her. "Ten percent up front."

"Five." Our eyes meet, and I hold my tongue. "Impress me, Angela. I want a portrait that causes people to stop and think. Can you do that?"

I don't know…

That is not my answer. I imagine fifteen thousand dollars and moving out of my brother's house, being independent at last. Being free to do what I want.

"Of course. You're stunning." That much is true.

Her blue eyes flinch as if she's trying to decide if I'm being sarcastic. "We'll start tomorrow."

She walks toward the door as if she's finished speaking to me.

"Before I go." I wait for her to stop and give me her attention. "I'd like to have a contract, something in writing that states the terms. We can work out a time frame, signatures—"

One hand on the door, she straightens her shoulders. It's a dramatic pose—maybe how I'll have her stand for the portrait. "I'll pay you fifteen thousand dollars to paint my portrait the way I like it. Is that something you can agree to, Angela? Or do I need to find someone else?"

My jaw tightens, and I think about how painting 'the way she likes it' might go.

Then I think of getting my own place. "I'll agree to it."

"Send me the list of supplies you need, and I'll have everything waiting for you first thing in the morning."

She leaves me alone in the room, wondering if I've made a huge mistake.

"It's like my mother was there, helping me get the job." I'm at Lourdes's small apartment, pacing, trying to get my head around what just happened, what it means.

"So Deacon's racist old aunt is going to pay you fifteen grand to paint her portrait as she sees fit?" My bestie is on her couch with a bowl of popcorn in her lap. "It's like that old song."

"Which one?"

"The one about making a deal with the devil for a boatload of money." She shoves a handful of popcorn in her mouth.

"You made that up."

"What does Deacon think?"

"I haven't told him yet." I'm wondering if I will tell him at all. Hell, I'm not even sure we'll make it past the first week. "It's not a deal with the devil. It's a really neat opportunity. And who knows, maybe she'll get to know me, and we'll get to be friends… It'll be like that other song."

"Which one?"

"The one about love building a bridge."

"More like somewhere over the rainbow." She shovels another handful into her mouth. "That's what happens when you go to church."

"I went to church to get away from Beto." I cross my arms, looking around her one-bedroom apartment. "I've got to get out of his house, Lor."

She crosses her legs under her. "Well, you've got a big job dropped right in your lap. Time to start searching Zillow."

"Yes." I step forward, pointing my finger. "I'll do the portrait, and then if I get the Arthaus award, I'll have another twenty grand—"

"What a life. You go from one high paying gig to another. Next you'll be jet setting to Barcelona, painting portraits of the queen…" Her voice is dreamy, but I'm right there with the bucket of ice water.

"Most fine artists are starving."

She leans back frowning. "So why do it? With your talents, see if you can find a job with a little more stability."

"I could work in design or marketing." *If the very idea didn't give me a full-body shudder.*

She squints her eye at me. "I saw that. You'd hate a job like that."

"Hate is a strong word." My smile is a little sad. "I should try to be interested in something more stable. It would make my life easier."

Sitting forward, she puts the bowl on her coffee table. "Many people work jobs they don't care about during the day to support doing the job they love after hours. Do that!"

Dropping onto the couch beside her, I rest my head on her shoulder. "It's basically what I'm doing now, isn't it?" My head pops up. "Oh, I stopped by to ask if Juliana can take over my shifts at La Frida Java. Indefinitely."

"You did not let him railroad you out of your job. Fuck that 'my sister is not a waitress' bullshit." She imitates Beto in a low, nasal-ey voice like the Godfather.

"No." I exhale a laugh. "If I'm going to work on this portrait at Aunt Winnie's house, I'll have to work during the day, starting in the morning."

"If it makes you feel better, Juliana will be really grateful for the work."

"Silver lining?" I stand, picking up my portfolio. "I guess I should go home now."

"Listen to me." Lourdes puts both hands on my shoulders. "Beto's house is nice, but my couch is open if you ever need it."

"You're the best friend ever." I lean forward and kiss her cheek. "I'm okay for now, but if he's serious about keeping me and Deacon apart…"

Lourdes nods. "I'm here for you."

I give her a squeeze before heading out the door. "Love you, bitch."

"Show that racist bitch who's the *real* bad bitch."

Shaking my head, I groan. "I've never been that bitch. I'll just keep my head down and paint."

"That's my girl. Paint a bridge."

"Over the rainbow."

WITH A CHARCOAL PENCIL, I MAKE A LONG BLACK LINE DOWN THE OVERSIZED sheet of paper. Stepping back, I close my eyes, considering how I can make Winona Clarke unforgettable.

This day was unforgettable, starting with Deacon in my bed and ending with me here, in Beto's garden cottage planning out a portrait of Aunt Winnie.

Deacon and I have texted a few times. He's in Harristown, two and a half hours away. He's well, safe drive... I'm well, I miss him like crazy... He'll be home soon...

I didn't say a word about my new job with his aunt. I don't want him feeling like he needs to do anything. If I'm going to be an artist, I have to be able to work with difficult people. I can't have the men in my life swooping in and smoothing the way for me.

Anyway, at this point, there's nothing to smooth. I'm going in tomorrow for a trial period, and we'll take it from there.

Natural light streams through the open windows of the cottage, and the scent of gardenia floats in on the breeze. I close my eyes and inhale my mother's spirit, focusing on the moment, letting the creativity flow through me.

Winnie's eyes are the same color as Deacon's, which I can see in my sleep, but the emotion flowing from them is very different. Deacon is open and generous. Winnie is not. She's proud... and suspicious. I have an idea of what I'd like to do with her, but it's a little unorthodox. Still, she might go for it.

"I've never watched you work." My brother's voice breaks my concentration.

He stands in the doorway, holding the frame above his head. "Is that how you do it? Sketches first?"

"Depends on what I'm doing." I step back, glad I haven't gone any farther.

"What are you doing?" He lowers his arms and enters the small house.

"Brainstorming." I pick up a damp towel and wipe my fingers.

He nods, going to my portfolio lying open on the table. "I

wasn't sure what I'd do with this place when the realtor showed it to me. I thought it might be a playhouse for Sofia."

"It's a great place for art." I motion to the windows. "Natural light. The breeze keeps the air fresh."

He thumbs through the plastic sleeves, studying my landscapes. "How long have you been doing this?"

"Since I lived in Mexico. Mamá taught me the basics. I took classes at school."

"Some of these are really good. We could frame them, hang them in the house."

I don't know what to say to that. I guess he's trying to be friendly. Too bad he shot all that to hell when he tried to hurt the man I love.

"What's this?" He takes out my sketch of our mother from its plastic sleeve.

Holding it up, he looks at it in a way that makes my chest tighten. The muscle in his jaw moves, and his eyes tense.

"It's our mother." Obviously, he knows who it is.

Clearing his throat, he lowers the piece to the stack. "You have a lot of talent."

His voice is different, and I remember our conversation over breakfast Saturday. I remember what he said about her leaving, why he never came to visit us in Mexico.

I've always kept Mamá on this dreamy pedestal. Our life in Mexico was focused on the present, what we were doing every day. She made her art and she would talk to me like our life there was an adventure. I was a little girl. I never thought about what she left behind.

"I don't want to fight with you, Beto." My voice is quiet, my heart warm, and he pauses in the doorway, looking back.

"Then don't."

CHAPTER
Eleven

Deacon

"IT'S CRAZY TO THINK HOW BUSY THIS PLACE WILL BE IN JUST A few weeks." Noel LaGrange grabs a big box from the stack outside her door.

We're meeting at the store she converted from a feed shed on her family's 100-acre peach orchard in Harristown.

I grab one as well, following her inside. "You got that?"

"Oh sure." She shakes her head, laughing. "I'll be doing a lot more than carrying boxes once harvest starts next week."

She flicks on a window unit, and I place the box beside her cash register. "You guys work hard."

Thinking back to the first year I was here, I couldn't believe how much her family accomplished in one month. Peaches are too fragile to be picked and sorted by machines. They're able to use some tools, but most of it is hand-picking, hand-sorting—backbreaking work in the hottest part of the year.

"Every May I wonder how we're going get everything

done." She laughs, whipping her dark hair into a ponytail on top of her head. "Then we do."

"Jesus loves the little chillll-dren..." Noel's little daughter Dove marches up, carrying a box and singing at the top of her lungs. "All the children of the world!"

"Pipe down, Dolly." Noel takes the box from her and puts it on the counter.

"Miss Tina said we're going to learn it in sign language!" She joins her little hands like a bird flying.

Dove's a character with bright blue eyes and curly blonde hair. I think of Sofia and how the little girls might be friends if Angel and I lived here and she visited us.

"Would you bring the rest of the boxes in from the porch?"

"Okay!" She takes off for the door, and Noel takes jars of face cream and body lotion from the smaller one.

"I've got a lot of stock ready ahead of time this year." She puts the jars on the counter before returning to the register. "I worked all through the spring."

"How's it going?"

"Good." She nods. "I'm dead."

"You could hire someone to cover shifts during harvest."

"I guess, but I don't like sitting around."

"I help with the sorting now!" Dove marches up, carrying an enormous cardboard box, almost bigger than she is. "Uncle Sawyer says I'm as good as the teenagers!"

"Whoa, hang on there." I take the giant box from her, but it's surprisingly light. Opening the flap, I see what looks like a bunch of papers. "What is this?"

"Oh, that." Noel walks over, and we both move the contents around. "It was here when Miss Jessica gave me the place. I wanted her to go through it and make sure it's nothing important."

Miss Jessica is the octogenarian nursing home resident who gave the feed shed to Noel to renovate. Noel cleaned it, painted and wired it, and now it rivals anything you'd see on Main Street, with flowers and a front porch.

I pull out an old ledger and what appear to be receipts. The dates on some are older than I am. "I'm not sure any of this is worth keeping."

"Yeah, she told me to throw it all away, but look here." Noel digs deeper, pulling out a few envelopes and handing them to me. "There are letters…"

Turning the envelopes in my hand, I open the flap and stop. "I guess this might be personal?"

She exhales, shaking her head. "You're right. I should just sort through it all and make a bundle of things I think she really wants to keep."

"I didn't say that—" Dove pats on my leg, and I lift her onto a nearby chair. "It would be nice if you had time, but you're pretty busy."

"Look at this one, Mamma!" Dove holds up a letter with an ornate stamp attached. "Can I have it?"

Noel takes the letter from her daughter and studies it. "I don't know, baby. This one might be worth something. Is that French?"

She hands it to me, and I examine the stamp. "I can't tell. Maybe Vietnamese?"

"Well, that does it." She shakes her head. "I'll go through it tonight and make a stack to take to Miss Jessica."

"You know, I'm just sitting in a hotel room. I could help you."

"Oh, no. It's my old box of junk." She reaches into her purse and pulls out an iPad pro. "Let's stop wasting your time."

She taps over to Quickbooks, and we spend the next half-hour reviewing her business plan, which is on track for thirty percent growth this year.

Noel's a smart businesswoman, so it's a quick, quarterly check-up. She slides the iPad back in its sleeve as Dove holds up another old letter. "Look at this one, Mamma!"

"Ooo, that's a fun one." Noel glances at the envelope, but I look a little closer.

A bright yellow and orange "Greetings from Texas" stamp is in the corner, and the handwriting seems vaguely familiar. A faded return address is in the top left corner, and I remember my dad saying his mother loved to come here in the summer.

"Can I see that one?"

Dove hands it to me. "Isn't it pretty?"

"Yes, it is…" My voice trails off as I read the addresses. It was sent to someone named Winona, and it's a Plano return address. "Do you think Miss Jessica might have known my grandmother?"

"Miss Jessica knew everybody." Noel pops up and looks closer at the letter I'm holding. "Is that from your grandmother?"

"I don't know. I'd like to ask her."

"Okay, fine. We can sort through this now." She's teasing, but I'm motivated.

We only find two more letters in the box, neither from Plano. The rest are receipts and decades-old bookkeeping.

"In my professional opinion, you're safe to toss the rest." I slip all four letters into my messenger bag. "I'll take these to the nursing home tomorrow."

"You sure you don't want to stay for supper?" Noel locks the door to her shop, and we stroll down the hill.

"I would, but I've… got to take care of some business tonight." I want to check in with Angel and pack my things so I can head home early.

"I've got to start paying you for all this somehow."

"Send me some peaches."

"I'll do it." She grins, holding my arm. "One peach care package headed your way!"

Dove takes off running down the hill towards the large, white farmhouse. It's a beautiful place with a sloped, tin roof, white wrap-around porches, and crepe myrtle trees blooming at the corners. The screen door slams as the little girl enters the kitchen, and it's a comforting, homey sound. It makes me think of Angel.

We pause at my car, and I look around the place, thinking about a peaceful life with no angry brothers threatening to shoot me. "Call me if you need anything or if anything changes."

"Nothing changes around here." She steps forward into a hug. "You know that."

I like that.

Back at my hotel, I type a quick text to the number of the phone I got for Angel. *A horse walks into a bar…*

Tossing my device on the bed, I loosen my tie and slide out of my blazer. It was a steamy day, but the window unit in Noel's shop kept us from getting sweaty. I'm pretty sure I can get one more day out of my suit before I head home.

My phone buzzes, and I step out of my slacks before lying on the bed to read her reply. *Bartender says why the long face?*

These corny old jokes were the only game I had as a teenager. Now it's our thing. I text a quick reply, *Because the most beautiful girl in the world isn't riding him right now.*

My thoughts drift to her straddling my lap last night, and my cock starts to harden in my shorts. I slide my hand over it.

A few moments pass, and her reply pops up. *I dreamed I rode a unicorn last night. It had the most satisfying horn…*

Shit. A groan rumbles in my throat, and my fingers curl over my cock. I wish that piece of crap phone had Facetime. *I want to see you naked.*

At a very crowded dinner with my family.

Go to the bathroom.

Insatiable. How was your day?

Good. Noel's going to be the next Burt's Bees. Really wish you were here.

I think about introducing Angel to the Harristown group. She and Noel would be great friends, and I know she'd have a lot in common with Mindy. They're both artists, although Mindy is more interested in commercial arts.

We could get a house out by the lake. I'd be sure it had a room with lots of windows where she could paint. I could take care of her…

I'm ready to do everything with you. Her text stirs a longing so deep in my soul.

I want to do everything with her. *See you tomorrow, beautiful.*

She signs off with a big red heart, and I walk to the shower, flicking on the hot water.

My mind is consumed with thoughts of Angel and me together as I step into the steaming glass enclosure. I love her art. I love her mind. I love the way she teases me, the way she laughs at my corny jokes, the way she cares for the people she loves.

Closing my eyes, I remember her touch, her fingers wrapping around me. I remember her hot little mouth sucking on my lips, my neck, my cock.

Her amber eyes are so round when she looks up at me from her knees. She flickers her tongue along my shaft, pulling me deep into her throat, tracing her fingernails up the insides of my thighs.

It only takes a few tugs to relieve the ache of missing my girl. My ass tightens, and I come long and hard, groaning her name as the water rushes over my back and shoulders. Bracing my hand against the wall, I breathe slowly, coming down, missing the warmth of her body next to mine.

I pull on the hotel robe and order room service. I'll have a cocktail then dinner. In the morning I'll stop by the nursing home on my way out of town, and I'll be in Texas by the end of the day, ready to find some answers and be with my girl.

"DEACON, MY GOODNESS!" MISS JESSICA PATS MY CHEEK WHEN I LEAN down to give her a hug.

She's sitting on a green couch in the activity room of the Pine Hills nursing home where she lives. It's a small place, matching the small town, and the residents range from needing light assistance to hospice care.

"I haven't seen you in ages. Where have you been?"

"How does he look?" Ms. Irene, her blind best friend who also lives in the home is beside her on the couch.

Ms. Irene's straight white hair is styled in a long braid down her back, and her blue eyes gaze in the vicinity of my face. Both old ladies are dressed in flowered smocks, soft pants, and slippers. They appear harmless, but I've learned not to underestimate them.

Miss Jessica leans to her. "He looks like a young Gary Cooper. Tan suit with a white shirt and navy striped tie that makes his blue eyes glow."

She nods up at me, and they ladies shake their heads.

"Stop it, you'll make him blush." Mindy Ray, Noel's best friend and my former college buddy walks up, pulling me into a hug.

Mindy's in jeans and a red sweater, and her long brown hair is in a low ponytail over one shoulder. She started her own marketing business and only works part-time here now, but she still pretty much runs the place.

Stepping back, she inspects me with her arms crossed and her eyebrow raised. "Gary Cooper... hmm... I can see it. You're a little too cocky for Mr. Cooper."

"I'm not cocky."

She makes a *pfft* sound. "You most certainly are."

"I miss all the good stuff now," Ms. Irene sighs.

"Did you come to see Mindy?" Miss Jessica waggles her eyebrows at the two of us, and I take a seat beside her.

"I came to see you."

"Oh, my land, I've waited for this." She puts a hand on her chest. "Cowboy, take me away!"

Shaking my head, I take the letters out of my bag. "Noel found these in an old box at the feed shed. I asked her if I could bring them to you… I think one of them might be from my grandmother."

Her thin brow wrinkles. "Who is your grandmother?"

"Well, she was Kimberly Allen."

The old lady's eyebrows shoot up, and she leans back. "Oh."

Ms. Irene scoots closer. "Kim was your grandmother?"

I'm not sure what to make of this response. "Did you know her? This letter is addressed to Winona… something." I hold out the missive. "The rest is worn away."

Miss Jessica takes the envelopes, sliding her fingers over them as if they're precious relics. "I didn't know Kim very well. She was friends with my sister Winnie. She died… oh, about twenty years ago."

"Winnie?" I had been leaning forward, resting my forearms on my knees, but that name draws me up straight. *Winona… Winnie… Was my aunt named for this lady?*

"It was just a nickname. Winona Fieldstone was her married name."

I slowly lean forward once more, nodding at the letter. "We found that, and I thought you might want it."

She turns it over in her hands. "I don't know why I'd want an old letter. If it's important to you, you can have it." She gives it to me, and I pause, thinking.

"Miss Jessica, did something happen to my grandmother? Something I might not know about?"

Her weathered hand flutters to the neck of her smock. "I have no idea what you know. Anyway, I didn't know her very well. Like I said."

Mindy sits on the arm of my chair. "Sounds like you're sitting on a good story. Spill it, Miss J."

"Melinda Ray! I am not sitting on anything. Mind your business."

Reaching out, I put my hand over hers gently. "It's okay. After my father died, it seems like a lot of my family's history was lost."

"Swept under the rug is more like it." Ms. Irene nods her head.

That gets my attention. It's the exact thing I'm thinking. "Do you know about her?"

Her clouded eyes drift to the ceiling. "Your grandmother was a beautiful woman. Probably the prettiest girl in these parts until Penelope Harris."

"That was Noel's mom." Mindy whispers into my shoulder. "She won every beauty pageant in the tri-county area."

"What happened to her?"

"She was in love with two men, from what I remember. Isn't that right, Jessica?" Ms. Irene looks in the direction of her friend, who's still clutching her collar and looking worried. "Weren't they best friends?"

"Good night, Irene, I was a child. I didn't understand half of what everyone was talking about."

That sounds familiar.

"Well, I did." Ms. Irene nods at me. "Your grandmother married the rich one—who was your grandfather, I guess, since you have all the money."

"Oh, yeah, Deacon's loaded." Mindy gives my shoulder a playful shove.

"But from what I understand, she never got over the other guy. What was his name?"

"Pablo." Miss Jessica holds up a finger. "No... That wasn't it. Marco... No... Juan."

"Oh, sweet lord. I'd say she was getting dementia, but she's always been that way with names." Ms. Irene shakes her head. She leans forward and lowers her voice. "I never knew what his name was, but he was of the Mexican persuasion."

Her lips press together and she nods.

The hairs on the back of my neck prickle. *Holy shit.* "Are you saying my grandmother left my grandfather for another man? A Mexican man?"

"I don't think she ever left him." Ms. Irene's blind eyes drift around my face. "I think she came here after things... went too far."

"Went too far?" I look at Mindy, who's looking at me with raised eyebrows. "Does that mean..."

"You know what it means!" Mindy stage-whispers. "Your grandmother was a ho."

"Melinda Claire Ray!" Miss Jessica swats her with the remaining three envelopes. "Kimberly was a wonderful girl. She just got a little mixed up. It happens."

Miss Jessica is an old maid, if I remember what Mindy told me. Still, I'm not interested in what she knows about love triangles. I'm wondering if this crazy story might be what has Angel's brother so pissed at the Drings.

I take Miss Jessica's hand again. "Do you have any idea where I could find out the other man's name?"

"You have the letter." She nods towards it. "I'm sorry that's all I know."

Looking down at the faded ink on paper, I wonder if I can wait the two-and-a-half-hour drive home to read it... *Nope.*

I'm not even sure I can wait to get to the parking lot.

"Thank you for telling me this." I stand, sliding the envelope into my pocket.

Ms. Irene reaches for Mindy and slowly rises to her feet. She grasps my forearm. "I'm sorry if I upset you with that story."

"You didn't." I lean down to hug her carefully. "You actually might have helped me."

"Well, I hope so. I would never want to hurt anyone."

"I'd better get on back, but I'll be here for the festival."

"Oh, that's wonderful. Come see us, will you?"

Miss Jessica stands, holding my arm. "Don't be too hard on your ancestors. They were human just like us."

"As in everybody makes mistakes?" I give her a wink.

"Exactly." Her tone reminds me of a school teacher, and we walk slowly to the exit. "Jesus said he who is without sin cast the first stone."

"Don't worry." I give her a final hug. "I'm not planning to stone anybody."

I'm trying to get certain people to put down their rocks.

"See you in a few weeks." Mindy gives me a quick hug before guiding the ladies in the direction of the cafeteria.

I dash out to my car, hopping inside and whipping out the envelope. The paper is yellowed and fragile, and the words are faded and written in an ancient, swirling script. Still, they're legible.

Dear Winona,

I miss you so much, my dearest friend. Rogers is gone again. Each time his trips seem to last longer and longer. Brandt started kindergarten, and I find myself alone so much. I used to cry every day.

It's not like spending summers with you in Harristown. How I long for homemade peach ice cream and swimming in the lake, picking peaches off the trees and walking through the meadows...

I scan over her descriptions down to a name that causes my breath to still.

Manuel gave me chocolate with chili pepper yesterday. Isn't that exotic? He brought me lilacs and yellow roses. You should see how beautiful they are together, and the scent...

Manuel. Shit. Here it is. I skim through her descriptions of flowers and dresses and air conditioning until I get to the critical part.

You have to help me, my dear, dear friend. I'm sorry to put you in this position, but I have to stay with you at least until the child is born and we know. What would I do if I were alone here, and everyone saw what I'd done. Rogers would be humiliated.

I can make the journey in a month, and you can help me if the worst happens…

My chest is tight as I finish the letter. It sounds like she came here to have her baby. Doing quick math in my head, if my father was in kindergarten, he was only five or six. Aunt Winnie is seven years younger than he is.

Was this baby Manuel Treviño's? I feel strongly the answer is yes, since I don't know of any other aunts or uncles. If that's the case, what happened to the baby? Where is it?

Looking at the clock, it's after one, and I need to rebook my hotel room. I can't go back to Plano today. I have to find out what happened.

CHAPTER
Twelve

Angel

"**T**HAT'S NOT MY BEST ANGLE." WINNIE IS BESIDE ME LOOKING AT the pictures I've taken using her digital camera.

She's wearing a fitted, dark green V-neck dress, and her hair is gathered in a loose bun at the nape of her neck. Her makeup is subtle, emphasizing her blue eyes, and she has a light stain of plum on her lips.

I think she's stunning, and I flick the buttons on the back, changing the filters and dropping subtle yellows and pinks over the image. "My mother would have loved this camera."

"Your mother was a photographer?" Her voice is sharp. "You drew her with a camera."

"She was an artist. We lived in Mexico, at the foot of the Sierra Madre, and she would take pictures and blow them up and add paint to them. It was a unique style, similar to Georgia O'Keefe."

Winnie's eyes narrow. "Why did you leave Mexico?"

I shrug, looking around. "When she died, I came to live with my family."

"I see." She straightens, walking away from me and going to the fireplace. "How about this?"

Placing a hand on the mantle, she looks towards the windows. I raise the camera and take her photo from several different angles.

"Not bad… I have one last idea. See what you think." I lead her to the chair she was sitting in yesterday and have her turn in the same direction, facing the windows. "Shoulders back. Now let's have this guy in your lap."

Reaching down, I pick up the white cat I noticed yesterday with the black legs and ring-striped tail.

"What?" She laughs. "Boots?"

"I think it adds a whimsical element that shows personality."

Her blue eyes narrow, but she cooperates. Again, I take several shots from different angles. When we're done, I take them all to the laptop computer she provided and plug in the camera.

"You're very professional." She says it like she expected me to be unprofessional, but I let it pass.

"These are my favorites." I bring up four images and she sits in the chair in front of the computer.

"The deal was I would choose my favorite."

"I'm just helping find ones with good highlights. See in this one, your expression is more dramatic, the contrast of shadow and light—"

"I'll look at all of the images and tell you the one I like. You can wait in the hall for me to call you."

Hesitating a moment, I bite back all the things I really want to say to her right now. Clearing my throat, I nod. "I'll take a look at those art supplies."

"Oh, yes. They're just in the sitting room. Through that door." She gestures to a door beside a bookcase.

It leads to a smaller room filled with natural light shining through a wall of windows. "This would be the perfect place for me to paint."

She doesn't answer, and I see a plastic bag sitting on a desk. Going to it, I notice a fifty-dollar bill is also on the table beside it. Ignoring it, I pull out the tubes of oil paint. Turning them over, I study the labels. I'm more familiar with acrylics, but I've been studying tips and techniques for working with oil.

Looking around this small but elegant room, I scan the titles of the leather-bound books on the shelf, *Giant, True Grit, Texas Ranger…*

Everything in this house is massive and old. In addition to the two life-sized portraits in the grand hall, enormous paintings of cowboys and cattle drives hang in prominent locations throughout. I kind of love them for their color and energy and wild spirit.

Winnie calls from the other room. "I've chosen one, Angela."

"Coming!" Grabbing the bag, I start for the door when a ping in my chest stops me.

I remember Rosalía told me Deacon's aunt likes to leave cash lying around to see if they will steal it. My jaw tightens, and I snatch up the fifty, carrying it straight to where she's sitting at the laptop.

"Let me see what you chose. Oh, I think you dropped some money." I place the bill on the desk beside her computer, and she narrows her eyes at it.

Taking the bill, she stands. "I'll have Peter set up the easel in that room if you prefer it."

"Thank you. I'll get started as soon as we sign the contract."

"It was a verbal agreement."

"I prefer to have it in writing."

Again her eyes narrow, and she goes to the door. I turn to the computer and see the photo on the screen. It's the pose I arranged with her cat—my favorite pose, and it feels like a little victory.

THE CANVAS IS BIGGER THAN I AM, BUT I'M NOT INTIMIDATED. I CLOSE MY eyes, take a deep breath, and think of *Spirit*. The energy of that piece allows me to shake off the negativity of my subject and let the images to flow through me.

Lifting the charcoal pencil, I begin. Some artists like to use a grid to work out life sized portraits, but I'm more comfortable using a sketch. Winnie wants it to match the more classical style of the original two works, but I saw her reaction to the portrait of my mother.

That piece is anchored by the eyes and the face, and the rest is more spiritual, emotional. I start with Winnie's eyes, glancing at the photo but also allowing my memory to guide me. As the face takes shape, they seem to take on life. My stomach warms, and I feel as if I'm looking into the eyes of my love.

Perhaps there was a time when this woman wasn't such a bitter old pill. It's hard to imagine. Still, this shared feature makes me wonder if it could ever have been possible. Moving on, I start on her cheeks, the sweep of her hair.

Time passes so quickly when I'm working, I barely even notice it's after lunch until my stomach growls. I'm plotting out the room around her using blocks instead of details. We can decide on that later.

"It's after three." Winnie's voice causes me to inhale sharply. "I'm sorry. I didn't mean to startle you. I assumed you'd be stopping for the day."

"It's later than I thought." Stepping back, I wipe the black off my fingers.

"People always said I have my mother's eyes." She observes my sketch. "She was a very beautiful woman."

"I'm sure." Lifting my pencil, I finish sketching out the surroundings.

"You've captured the resemblance here." She holds her hand towards the canvas. "I like it. You may continue."

Is that a compliment? I do my best not to act surprised. "I'll start laying paint tomorrow."

"You work fast."

"Once I start painting, it'll slow down."

Her eyes narrow, and she surveys me. "How much time will it take?"

"Depends on the weather, but I expect a few weeks."

Her lips tighten, and she seems annoyed. "The article I read said a portrait should take fifty hours to complete. Why would you need longer than a week?"

Why would you ask me how long it takes if you already know?

I don't say that.

"I can't work on it nonstop. When working with oils, you work in layers." I really hate that she has me on the defense. I hate feeling like she's accusing me of being lazy. "I'll start with the darkest colors then add highlights on top. Each layer has to dry or it gets muddy—"

"If you'd like to come over in the evenings to work, I will allow it." She nods as if she's the Queen of England passing down a decree.

"I don't know if that'll make a difference." Rubbing my forehead, I try to think. "I could start earlier in the day then take a break at lunch and return later. A fan would help."

"I'll have a fan delivered in the morning. You can begin your revised schedule then." She marches to the door as if problem solved, pausing before she leaves. "This is for you." She places a white business-sized envelope on the end table.

With a sigh, I collect my things. It's not like I want to hang out in her mansion longer than I have to, but I would like to add this to my portfolio. On my way out, I pick up the envelope. Inside is the signed contract, with the correct numbers and what we agreed to do.

I suppose it's the yin to her yang. She's a racist, bossy bitch, but at least she's a woman of her word. Shaking my head, I'm on my way out when Rosalía meets me.

"How's it going?" She puts her hand on my arm, and we walk to her car together.

"You weren't kidding when you said she was the worst. I thought people like that only existed in the movies."

"I wish. Need a ride?"

"Sure, thanks." Beto's house isn't too far from the Dring estate, and Rosalía chats about her day polishing the silver and Winnie's habit of counting everything afterwards.

She pulls into the driveway, and I pause before getting out. "How can you do it every day?"

"She pays me in cash, and at least she's fair."

Pressing my lips together, I think about this. "Why does she pay you in cash?"

"I think she thinks I'm illegal. She never asked for my social or anything."

Dropping my head against the headrest, I groan. "This woman!"

Rosalía laughs, and we say goodnight. I climb out, walking to my brother's home wondering how Deacon and I will ever merge these two worlds. It feels impossible.

The burner phone vibrates and I pull it out to see a text from my guy. *Staying over an extra day or two. Can I call you?*

Touching the number, I call instead of texting a reply.

"Hey, beautiful. How was your Monday?" His rich voice warms my insides, and I want to thread my fingers in his hair, see the blue eyes that love me.

"The Mondayest." Instead of going into my brother's house, I walk along the sidewalk that loops the lake.

"Busy day at La Frida?"

"Actually... I'm not working at the coffee shop anymore. Juliana took over my shift. I got a job... an art job." God, I sound like Rosalía. "I've been commissioned to paint a portrait. It was kind of out of the blue, but—"

"What?" I hear him smile, and in spite of it all, I smile. "That's fucking amazing. Who are you painting? Tell me all about it."

He can't see me wince. "Let's talk about it when you get home. It's a really neat opportunity, though. If it works out."

"It'll work out. You're the best."

This guy. "I miss you."

"I miss you." I love hearing him say it.

Maybe Lourdes is right, and I did make a deal with the devil... But I see little flickers of a bridge, and I want what Deacon wants. I want our families to like us. Or maybe I'm dreaming of somewhere over the rainbow. My mother did raise me to believe in dreams.

"Why are you staying in Harristown? Is something wrong?"

Now I hear him hesitate. "Maybe I should wait and tell you when I know more. At this point... I'm not really sure."

"Sounds like we're both keeping secrets."

"Fuck that. I hate secrets." He's growly, and I laugh. "Noel had this old letter... it was from my grandmother to her best friend who lived here a long time ago."

"What's wrong with that?"

"I need to find out more." His voice grows quietly serious. "It might be the reason your brother is so angry at my family."

"Oh, Deacon..." My stomach tightens. "Is that good or bad?"

"Too soon to tell." He exhales heavily. "Either way, we've got to know what happened. I feel like I'm getting close to answers."

Nodding, I look up at my brother's house, rising tall in the twilight. "I wish you were here."

"I'll be there soon, Angel. Trust me."

"I do."

CHAPTER
Thirteen

Deacon

"**I**S THERE ANYONE ALIVE WHO MIGHT'VE WORKED AT THE hospital back then?" I'm back at Pine Hills in the activity room with Miss Jessica and Ms. Irene.

They were both surprised to see me again, and when I explained the situation, they apparently already knew most of the story. My grandmother came here pregnant, and she left without a baby. The second part is the mystery. Neither woman knows, but neither one acts surprised either.

Mindy is at the front desk, and we've been ordered not to say anything interesting until she gets back. I'm not waiting.

"Is there a nurse or administrator who might have helped her?" I'm hoping against hope.

Miss Jessica presses her lips into a straight line before shaking her head. "I'm sorry. I wish I could be more help."

"Martha Landry." Ms. Irene nods knowingly. "She was a candy striper, and she had the biggest mouth in our senior class."

"Martha Landry? I don't remember her ever working at the hospital." Miss Jessica looks at her friend confused.

"She got kicked out after a year." Ms. Irene flares her eyes. "She thought she was so cute in that uniform. From what I heard, the boys did, too."

"No!" Miss Jessica hisses.

"Yes." Ms. Irene raises her eyebrows and does a little sniff. "Now *she* was a ho."

Looking back and forth between them, I can't help it. "Why did I think ladies were more… ladylike back then?"

"Because you're an idiot." Miss Jessica snips.

"Please don't spare my feelings."

Ms. Irene starts laughing, and Mindy jogs into the room. "What'd I miss?"

I look up at her. "Any idea where I might find Martha Landry?" *The ho.*

"Well, yeah. She's over in the east wing."

"Are you serious?" Standing fast, I catch her arm. "Can I see her now?"

"Probably."

We take off in the opposite direction. Ms. Irene calls something after us, but I assume it's another little dig, either about us dating or me knowing nothing about old ladies.

She'd be right about the latter.

Mindy checks her phone. "I guess we can see her now. I know she sleeps a lot these days."

It takes less than a minute to get to her room, and Mindy taps on the door. "Miss Landry?" Her voice is hushed. "Are you awake?"

"I'm awake!" A high, wobbly voice answers, and my insides tighten.

Could it possibly be this easy?

We enter the room, and I look around at the papers with childish drawings taped to the walls, framed photos of teens in caps and gowns, couples in wedding attire. A thick old lady sits in a glider across from us. She's wearing heavy, tortoise-shell glasses, and her hair is cut close to her head. She smiles broadly when we enter.

"Hi, Miss Landry." Mindy speaks softly in sort of a sing-song tone as we enter. I linger at the door. "How are you feeling today?"

"Is that you, Gabriella?" She reaches out a hand, which Mindy takes. "I was just thinking about you. How is little Trixie? I bet she started walking."

"She's doing good." Mindy nods, still speaking in that quiet voice. "She took her first steps last week."

Straightening, I frown, trying to understand what's happening right now. Mindy doesn't have a child...

"You're so sweet to come and see me. Is that Roy with you?" She leans to the side, peering at me over her glasses. "My word, if I'd known the mayor was coming, I'd have had my hair done."

"Come say hello, Roy." Mindy makes eyes at me, and I walk over to shake the old lady's hand.

"Hi." I smile, not sure what to say. "How's it going?"

"How are things down at the courthouse?" I look at Mindy for help. She just tilts her head to the side like *play along.*

"Oh... Ah, you know..." I'm trying to think. "Same old same old... Files and fingerprints."

Mindy snorts, and I squint at her. She did not prepare me to role-play.

"Did you get my note about that pothole over on Pine Street? I nearly broke an axle on Tuesday."

"Um... Yes. I did." Mindy's eyebrows rise in approval. "I put my best man on it."

"It better not be that Jimmy Hebert." The old lady scowls, shifting in her seat. "All he does is stand around and flirt. He doesn't do a bit of work."

"I've heard about him." I do my best to sound mayoral, wondering how to get out of this. "I'll have a talk with him this afternoon in my office."

"You do that." She sniffs and moves on to her next complaint. "That Salinas boy was picking his nose again. Tossing newspapers and picking his nose. I have to wash my hands every time I touch my paper."

She goes on longer than I'd like, until finally Mindy finds an exit strategy. "I'd better get the mayor back to work. Important town business."

"Well, thanks for visiting." Miss Landry huffs, shifting in her chair. "You've got my vote next year."

Mindy promises to bring the baby next time. We're out in the hall when she snorts a laugh. "Files and fingerprints?"

"You could've told me she has Alzheimer's before we barged in there."

"You didn't ask!" Mindy does her best to stifle more laughter. "You sounded like a pretty good mayor. I'd vote for you!"

"At least I'm familiar with the town." We stop at the reception desk, and I put my hands on my hips. "What now?"

"You're trying to find a baby born seventy years ago? Why not just go to the courthouse, Mayor?"

"I have a feeling it wasn't recorded. I don't know of any uncle or aunt on my father's side besides Winnie, and it's not her."

Mindy reaches behind the desk and grabs her purse. "Come on. One of the benefits of working here is I know just about all the doctors and nurses at the hospital. Maybe one of them can help us find this baby."

"WE JUST DON'T KEEP RECORDS THAT OLD HERE AT THE HOSPITAL." THE young woman behind the desk makes a disappointed face that kind of annoys me. "A birth certificate or death certificate would've been filed at the courthouse."

"Assuming one was filed." It's possible my annoyance is showing.

Her smile tightens. "Are you implying the hospital did something illegal?"

"Of course not. Thanks for your help." Mindy grabs my arm and pulls me out of the small office. "Don't piss off the clerks. I need them."

"Sorry." I shove a hand in my hair exhaling a low growl. "It's like the answer is right here, and I just can't find it."

"Come on." We head out to her waiting Prius. "Let's go to the courthouse. We should've started there first."

Ten minutes later, it's the same story. No records. Only apologies.

"Told you." We're walking to Mindy's car, and I'm ready to accept defeat.

"It might help if we knew the year this mystery baby was born. You're sure your aunt doesn't know anything?"

"I'm sure she won't talk about it if she does." The air is steamy, and I shrug off my blazer. "The last time I asked her about my grandfather, she said she was too young, no one told her anything."

"You don't believe her?"

Frustration tightens my chest. "I don't know."

"Well, I'm sorry this was a wild goose chase."

"I don't know why I expected anything different." I think about my family's mansion. That big old ancient place. I wonder if something might be hidden there... "Maybe I should just go home."

It's a short drive to Pine Hills. Mindy parks in the administrative lot, and I'm about to head to my car when a high-pitched voice warbles my name. "Deacon! Oh, Deacon! You, there!"

We look up to see Miss Jessica scuffling through the electric double doors with Ms. Irene on her arm. I glance at Mindy, and we jog to where the pair are creeping closer.

"Hey, what are you doing? Trying to escape?" I catch Ms. Irene's arm.

"Deacon, thank heavens." She holds onto me, and I do a slow U-turn, escorting her back inside. "I thought you left."

Mindy is behind us scolding Miss Jessica. "You can't leave the premises without a nurse. You know that."

"I know that, Melinda Claire!" Miss Jessica fusses right back. "Irene was beside herself trying to catch up to you kids. I was keeping her safe."

"What's wrong?" I look at the blind lady holding my arm.

"You ran off so fast, I never got to finish." Inside, I help her sit on a small sofa. "Martha won't remember anything, but her daughter Vandella works with the ladies' auxiliary." She places a hand on her chest, catching her breath. "They keep the unofficial town history. If anybody would know, it would be her."

I look at Mindy, who's watching her carefully. "Are you sure, Ms. Irene? It was a long time ago."

"I'm sure if there's any record, she'd have it. The auxiliary has old diaries and letters." She gives her friend a scolding look. "You should have given them that old box instead of telling Noel to throw it away."

"Why didn't you tell us this before?"

I put my hand on Mindy's arm. "No, it's okay. Where do we find Vandella?"

"I tried to tell you, but you ran off so fast." She turns to me. "She works at the library, of course. It might be too late to see her today, but you could call."

Glancing at the clock, it's almost five. I can't believe we've spent the entire day running all over this tiny town when the answer was at the library.

"I'll call her in the morning."

"Shew, well, that's settled, I'm starving." Ms. Irene stands, holding out her hand. "Let's go eat, Jessica."

"Thanks, Ms. Irene." Mindy looks at me, shaking her head. "Let me know if you need my help tomorrow. And tell us what happens."

"You bet."

Looks like I'm spending another night in Harristown. Reaching in my coat, I pull out my phone to message Angel.

CHAPTER
Fourteen

Angel

I'T'S BEEN THREE DAYS SINCE I STARTED WORKING ON WINNIE'S PORTRAIT. I've finished her hair, face, and torso, and I've started blocking in the background. I confess, I'm pushing as fast as the oil paint and oscillating fan will allow.

I arrive with Rosalía at seven in the mornings and work until lunch, then I take a break and return in the evenings around supper time. Sometimes Winnie sits in the room and reads while I work. I'm tempted to ask her why she doesn't just check the surveillance cameras Rose told me she has, but I don't.

Deacon is still in Harristown on his mysterious quest, which actually is okay. I'm not sure if he'll approve of me working with Winnie. He always acts embarrassed the few times she comes up—not that I blame him. She's the type of relative you want to hide.

It's seven at night, and I'm testing the paint, frowning that it's still damp. *Dammit*. I'm ready to be finished here, out of this house, and away from how hopeless it makes me feel about uniting our families.

"Have you had dinner?" Winnie's voice is behind me.

My hands tighten on the brushes. "Are you speaking to me?"

"Do you see anyone else in the room?" Her voice is sharp, but when my eyes cut to her, she looks away, around the room, almost as if she's embarrassed. "Anyway, if you're hungry, you could join me for a little something... nothing fancy."

WE'RE SEATED AROUND ONE END OF A MAHOGANY TABLE LONG ENOUGH FOR twenty, waiting for the servers to bring out our food. Winnie is at the head, and I'm to her right. The room is enormous, with the same wood-paneled walls and a massive fireplace with an actual fire burning. I realize the air-conditioner must be turned to full blast because I'm not hot at all. Global warming much?

Glasses of white wine are beside each of our chargers, but I won't touch mine. I don't want to give her more ammunition to use against me.

"My nephew usually has dinner with me once a week. When he's in town." Her voice is wistful. "Deacon is like a son to me."

My lips press together, and I do my best to keep my expression neutral. "That's nice."

"He's a wonderful boy... *Man.* He's a wonderful man." Leaning back, she lifts the heavy crystal goblet of wine and takes a sip. "It's so hard to let them grow up."

She doesn't seem to be talking to me, so I look down at my hands in my lap. The door in the back-left corner opens, and a woman enters carrying two shallow bowls. She places each one in front of us, and another woman is behind her carrying smaller plates of chopped grapefruit, and what looks like two different types of oranges.

Leaning closer, I study my plate. *Is this...*

"I have a chef, but this is actually my own special recipe." She lifts a fork of the pale beige and yellow dish, and I don't even need her to tell me. "It's baked macaroni and cheese... and I put an *egg* in the sauce before baking."

She grins like it's so amazing to eat baby food.

"Is that so?" I manage to smile. "Would you mind if I just grab my bag? I left it in the room where I paint."

Her brow wrinkles, and I can tell she's preparing to find some reason to say no. Too late, I'm out of my chair fast, hustling to the room where I left my purse beside my art supplies. I swipe it off the floor and quickly dash to the enormous dining room before she has a chance to finish that sentence.

"Are you taking medication?" She's still frowning as I feel around for the small bottle of Tabasco sauce I keep for emergencies.

"No, thank goodness." Giving the dish a few hits, I toss a few dashes on the citrus as well for good measure. "Would you like some Tabasco?"

"You put hot sauce on your fruit?"

"Try it sometime." Smiling, I give the two dishes a stir and take a bite of her signature baby food. "Delicious!"

She makes a dismissive noise, lifting her wine glass for another sip. "You people and your hot sauce."

"Tabasco is from Louisiana. Avery Island, to be exact." If the Lord is testing me, I intend to pass the test. "Mr. McIlhenny, the Scots-Irishman who invented Tabasco sauce also brought the nutria rat to the United States. They escaped in the 1930s during a hurricane, and now you can find them as far away as Oregon."

"I'd rather not discuss rats during dinner, if you don't mind." She takes a bite of her bland signature dish.

"They're actually more like beavers with big, orange teeth." I take a bite of the citrus, and exhale a happy noise. "Speaking of orange, this is delicious."

"I'm glad you like it." She is not smiling. She's sitting erect with one hand at her neck as if she's protecting herself.

I decide not to inform her people in Louisiana eat nutria. I've had enough fun, and I'm pretty sure she won't make the mistake of inviting me to dinner again.

The sound of forks lightly clinking china is the only noise as an awkward silence falls over the table. I press my lips together as I chew, studying the life-sized painting of a cattle drive hanging on the opposite wall. It's gorgeous, with red-browns, oranges, and yellow highlights.

My dinner is almost done, and I start to make an excuse to get back to work when Winnie breaks in. "You said your uncle is a used car salesman?"

"He owns a car dealership." I manage to keep the irritation out of my voice.

"What does your father do?"

Blinking down, I hold my expression neutral. "He died when I was a little girl."

"Oh." She glances at her plate. "I suppose that's more common in your community."

Our eyes meet, and I'm this close... Instead, I smile. "What do you and your nephew talk about when he visits?"

"Deacon?" A smile breaks across her face. "This and that. Finance mostly. That's his line of work. He's a financial adviser. Some would call him a *wealth* adviser."

I tell myself I can tolerate this woman because she's so obviously proud of the man I love.

She continues wistfully. "I hope one day he settles down with a nice, Texas girl."

"Is that so?" So many snappy replies are on the tip of my tongue, but I want this job—and I *am* a nice Texas girl. So I stand and place my napkin beside my plate. "Thank you so much for dinner. I really should get back to work now."

"Of course. I wouldn't want to block the muse."

Or cause me to take longer than fifty hours... I leave the room quickly. The door closes, and I fall back against it exhaling deeply. Of all the unpleasant dinners... A quick mental reminder of how much she's paying me is all it takes to get me moving, heading to the room where I can get this fucking job done.

It's after eleven when the car drops me in front of Beto's enormous mansion. My brother bought me a Lyft card because his sister "doesn't ride the bus," which I like to imagine him saying in Lourdes's exaggerated Beto-voice.

To be honest, I'm not complaining. I'd be broke paying for my own rides, and I don't like catching the bus late at night. Not to mention, I'm exhausted. My eyes are tired from working on the portrait all day, and my brain is tired from dodging Winona Clarke land mines.

Instead of digging out my keys, I walk around to the back-yard, nearly jumping out of my skin when I see the orange tip of a cigarette in the shadows. My purse falls off my shoulder, and my brother steps into the light.

"Jesus, why are you lurking around back here?" I pull my bag up my arm, annoyed.

"I don't like the smell of cigarettes in the house." My brother walks to the patio, lifting a tumbler of what I assume is his usual Mezcal.

"Then why don't you quit?"

"Why are you coming home so late?"

I exhale heavily, heading to the back door. "I'm working. You know this."

"Hang on." He sits in a metal chair. "Sit with me for a minute."

I stop at the door. "Beto, I'm really tired, and I have to get up at six-thirty to catch a ride with Rosalía."

"Why is this woman making you work so hard?"

"She's not. I just want to finish as soon as possible." It's not entirely true. Winnie still has this idea I shouldn't need more than a week or two, and the last thing I want is her assuming I'm lazy.

"Sit down. I want to talk to you." He leans back in his chair, and my shoulders drop.

Walking slowly to the metal table, I sit on the edge of the chair across from him.

"What?" I don't try to keep the annoyed tone out of my voice.

He frowns. "Don't act like a child."

"Stop treating me like a child."

He takes a drag, causing the orange tip of his cigarette to fire brighter. "I know you think I'm being too hard on you." He exhales before continuing. "You have to trust me, Carmie. I know what's best in this situation."

"Is that so?"

"Yes." His dark eyes level on mine. "Honor is all we have here. These people judge us before they even know who we are… that's why it's called *prejudice*."

"Please don't give me a lesson in English. You pre-judged Deacon without even giving him a chance—"

"I've told you all you need to know about that guy."

"You actually told me very little. According to Valeria, you repeated a story that might not even be true. And it has nothing to do with him. We can't control our grandparents."

He takes another hit off his tumbler, and his white teeth catch the light. I'm not sure if he's smiling or grimacing at me.

"Our father went to his grave a broken man. A poor man." Beto's voice simmers. "His biggest regret was not avenging his father's murder."

I can't answer this.

Mamá talked about the hate here. She talked about shadows drowning out the light—it's why she took me away from this place, away from the anger and bitterness, to her family's estate in Mexico.

She said it was why she made the deep blue and black crosses. She had abandoned the idea of God, but she believed in the symbolism of the cross. She said the vertical was our spiritual relationship and the horizontal was our earthly. She said if our relationship with the vertical was out of balance, our horizontal relationships would not work.

I was so little, I didn't understand. Now I can't help noticing how much my brother's anger sounds like Winnie's bitterness. They're two ends of the same horizontal.

"You don't believe me." He misinterprets my silence.

I don't know Beto well enough to tell him our mother's philosophy, but I'm pretty sure if I mention the cross, he'll get pissed.

My voice is quiet. "I'm very tired. Can we talk about this another time?"

He exhales and stands roughly, shoving his chair back. "You're my sister. It's my job to protect you. That's what I intend to do."

"Even if I don't need protection?"

"Even if you're wrong." He stubs out his cigarette and goes into the house.

I exhale slowly, my eyes warm with tears. I'm tired and I miss Deacon.

Mamá said to love my family more than anything, to be loyal. I wish she were here, because I have so many questions about how to love people who won't give anyone a chance, who won't listen, who are determined to hold onto their wrong assumptions no matter what.

I just really need some wisdom, because I don't believe. And I'm starting not to care.

CHAPTER
Fifteen

Deacon

VANDELLA LANDRY IS A PETITE WOMAN WITH SMALL BLACK GLASSES perched on the end of her nose. Her skin is smooth, and I would think she was in her early forties, if I didn't know how old her mother was and if her black hair wasn't streaked with grey.

"Those were hard times." She shakes her head, looking at the letter I handed her. "People disappeared, people were killed… and the perpetrators walked around in broad daylight."

My stomach tightens, and I'm picking at an old wound. "Do you know what happened to my grandmother?" I need to know this, as much for my family as for Angel's.

"I'm sorry." She shakes her head. "I've never seen her name in my records."

My shoulders fall, and I bite back a swear. These last three days have shown me detective work is not my forte. In fact, it's safe to say I would never want to investigate anything.

Vandella leans in, glancing around. "But I know someone who might know."

That's how I ended up at an old dogtrot shack deep in the woods off Louisiana Highway 528. Vandella gave me directions I almost didn't believe could be real.

Drive out past the old apostolic church, then take a right at the Miller's house the county hauled away last year. Keep going until the pavement ends then go two miles and take a right. When you pass a row of four dumpsters, you're almost there. The dogs will let you know you've arrived.

The only wild card was the house the county hauled away. If it weren't for a mailbox still standing in front of a concrete foundation and a partial brick chimney, I might've missed it.

Now, I'm in my car facing the low house standing in a clearing surrounded by pine trees. It's built of weathered gray wood with a wide opening between the two sides. The tin roof is rusted. It smells like pine needles and wet ground, and at the sound of my vehicle, all five of the dogs hanging around the place start barking. Two are little, a Yorkie and a chihuahua. Another looks like a lab mix, and the other two don't even get up from the porch, a bloodhound and a Rottweiler. I've got my eye on those guys.

Opening the door, I stand out of my car and call across the weedy yard. "Odessa Graves?"

All of the dogs start barking again, but the bigger ones don't move. It almost feels like a joke. After a minute they start to quiet down, and I call again, louder.

The smaller dogs dance around, barking so hard, I'm worried they're going to pop out an eyeball.

I'm trying to decide if I should risk going to the door when a craggily voice breaks through behind me. "Stop that racket!"

Stepping back, I see the hunched figure of an old woman with wild hair. Her pale skin is riddled with lines, and she's wearing a faded dress as gray as her hair. A polished wooden cane is in her hand, and I can't tell if she uses it to walk or as a weapon.

She makes good time to where I'm standing, shading her eyes with a bony hand. "Who are you?"

It's not your usual Southern hospitality greeting. This is old-school, deep woods, *get off my land*.

"Does Odessa Graves still live here?"

"Who wants to know?"

"I'm Deacon Dring... from Texas." She doesn't have a gun as far as I can tell, but I still hold up both hands. "I'm trying to find some information on my grandmother. I hope Ms. Graves might be able to help me."

Her brow pulls together, and she shakes her head. "Don't know any Drings."

"Her name was Kimberly Allen. She would've been here about seventy years ago... pregnant? Vandella Landry thought you might know her."

The old woman starts for the house, and all the dogs flock to her, tails wagging. "I don't know about any pregnant women."

"Please Ms. Graves. It's really important I find out what happened to her. If you know anything—"

She stops and looks over her shoulder at me. "You a lawyer?"

"No, ma'am."

"You work for the TV station?"

"No."

"You makin' a movie?"

"No... None of that." I step away from the car, one careful step towards her. "I'm trying to find a missing uncle or aunt... it's for my family."

Her eyes narrow, and she studies my face for what feels like a very long five seconds. I do my best to show her my sincerity.

"You're too rich to be a policeman."

"I'm just... a businessman." *Close enough.*

She starts walking again. "Come in the house, and I'll see what I can find."

I follow her up the steps to the covered porch. The broad, open passage down the middle serves as a sort of wind tunnel, it attracts a breeze even though the air is pretty still in this part of the country. The right side of the house appears to be her sleeping quarters. She leads me into the left side. The front half is a living room with a few pieces of threadbare furniture, a table, an upright piano, and a door leads to a small kitchen.

It's all weathered wood with dull pine floors, and it all seems to be covered in a film of dust.

"My great grandfather built this house." Odessa walks over to the mantle and takes down a small wooden box. "My mother lived here with her sister after they passed. Then I was born, and my aunt moved to Vidalia."

I'm not sure where she's going with all this, but I don't interrupt her. I watch as she takes a small, polished wood pipe out of the box and stuffs it with tobacco. The stick she was carrying leans against the hearth, and after spending a few minutes lighting her pipe, she walks to a bookcase in the corner.

"My mamma learned to be a nurse in the war." I have no idea which war she's talking about. This woman looks like she could be one hundred years old, judging by the lines in her face. "When she was young, she cared for the wounded soldiers. When she got older, the hospital didn't want her because she had no formal training."

Her voice hasn't changed in tone, so it's hard to know if she's carrying a grudge about this. It's more like she's reciting a history lesson.

"I'm sorry." *Just in case.*

"No need to apologize. You weren't even a twinkle in your daddy's eye when it happened." She takes a long, narrow book from the shelf and walks over to where I'm standing near the door. "Come out here to the kitchen and take a seat."

I follow her through the passage to an even smaller room

with a metal stove against one wall and a large sink across from it. She puts the book on the table and opens it, and I see it's a log with rows and columns. Names and dates are down one side, and some of the columns have entries beside them.

"Folks still managed to find her." Her lips tighten. "I was a teenager when Mamma passed, but I held onto her book. It seemed important somehow, even though most of these people are gone."

Swallowing the knot from my throat, I look closer at the entries. The listings are a mix of male and female names, but the problems all seem to be about the same topic. My eyes flicker to her face.

She studies the entries with a solemn face, and I realize she's the keeper of secrets. Dark secrets. Choices forced upon people by hate or made out of fear or desperation.

I think about my grandmother's desperation, and my chest sinks. "Did she do abortions?"

Odessa shakes her head. "She delivered a lot of babies for people who couldn't go to the hospital for whatever reason. And she helped women who had tried... other ways. She didn't ask questions."

"Would my grandmother have come here to have a baby?"

She shrugs. "It's possible. How much do you know?"

"I have this letter." I hand over the letter Miss Jessica gave me.

The old woman takes it carefully, reading the envelope. "Was this Winona Priddy?"

"I think so?" Hell, I don't know Miss Jessica's last name.

"I remember Miss Winona. I thought her name was *Pretty*, and I wondered what it would be like to have everyone call you that. A real confidence booster." It's the first time she hasn't frowned since I arrived.

"You remember her coming here?"

"She came here alone first, then she came again with a

woman so beautiful… so afraid." Her eyes travel around my face, up to my hair, down to my chin. "It was your grandmother."

"Kimberly Allen."

Odessa's eyes travel out the window into the trees behind the house. Sadness washes over her features.

Reaching out, I clutch her arm a little too hard. "What happened to her?"

"I didn't know that pretty woman's name. I was just a teenager. Still, I could see how sad she was."

"And the baby?"

The old woman turns a page in the ledger, sliding her finger down the rows of names. She turns another and does the same, then another. Her brow is furrowed, and her expression grim. The noise of cicadas is loud in the absence of barking dogs, and it intensifies the isolation of this place.

Finally, she stops, holding her finger on a row, a line in a book. "It's here."

Turning the log to me, she waits until it's in my hands before releasing it and picking up her pipe. She goes to the door and leaves me alone in the kitchen to read the words. My chest is tight, and it takes a moment for my eyes to register the ancient script, faded with the passage of time.

It's here, or at least half of it is. One half of the answer to the question we've been asking. Not the complete story, but an important piece of the puzzle. A sad piece. A piece that makes me want to say this has nothing to do with me, go home, and leave this story hidden deep in the piney woods.

If only I could.

"Do you know what happened next?" I look over to where she stands in the doorway, gazing into the forest, perhaps into the past.

"I know." Ancient eyes, full of compassion, meet mine. "I'll take you there."

CHAPTER
Sixteen

Angel

L YING ON MY BED, I SMILE AT THE CEILING THINKING ABOUT MY GUY. Soft music plays, and I picture threading my fingers in his hair, gazing into his blue eyes flecked with gold, kissing his soft lips. Closing my eyes, I allow the dream of him to sweep away the frustrations of the week.

An hour ago, he texted he was stopping for gas in Marshall, and he wants to see me tonight. I'm ready to meet him anywhere. My body hums with desire. I want his lips on me, his hands. I want to be skin against skin.

Maybe it's my brother's hatred. Maybe it's Deacon's aunt's. Maybe it's simply knowing we're so close to a life together that has me desperate and anxious, missing him more than I ever did in the years we'd been apart.

Today, once again, Winnie decided to sit in a chair and "read" while I worked on her portrait. She criticized everything, and I was starting to think she was laying the groundwork to say she was going in a different direction.

Thanks to my insistence on a contract, she put it in writing that she had the right to refuse payment or fire me if my work didn't meet her satisfaction.

"Is Boots really necessary for the portrait?" She sneered at the cat curled in her lap.

I showed her Renaissance portraits featuring pets, and assured her it was a common practice among the very wealthy to include a family pet, especially a unique one like Boots. Her own brother Brandt had his favorite horse in his portrait.

She seemed to accept this. Then her musing drifted to Deacon, which I felt was a direct test of my ability to keep my mouth shut. When she wondered aloud why he "never dated," I had to excuse myself and go to the restroom.

This evening I finished her portion of the portrait, and after walking around frowning at it from every angle, she finally conceded I'd "captured something"—her words.

A stack of cash totaling $750 was placed in a brown envelope on the small table by the door, five percent of the final payment—confirmation I was hired at least. I took it gladly and left, thanking God it's almost Friday.

Since our chat about honor in the middle of the night, my brother has been MIA. Naturally, I've had a million great comebacks to his "prejudice and protection" speech. Isn't that how it always works? Once I'm out of the situation, I'm a master of snappy comebacks.

Exhaling a slow breath, I lift my phone, wishing it would light up, thinking about my hero... Lourdes called him Prince Eric. That makes me smile. It's been an empty week without Sofia and her little opinions. I miss her. Maybe I'll pick her up after I finish at Ursula's mansion tomorrow... I'm grinning, ready to send a text to Valeria when tapping starts on my window.

My heart leaps to my throat, and I'm off the bed, rushing to the double glass doors to fling them apart. "Deacon?"

Strong arms surround me so fast, and I press my face to his neck, holding him with all my strength, inhaling his intoxicating scent of citrus and soap. My breath hitches, and my stomach is so tight. "I'm so happy to see you."

"I came straight here." His voice is rough, and my body warms with desire.

Large hands smooth down the sides of my hair, cupping my cheeks, and our eyes meet, blue and gold like the sunrise. Stretching higher, I seal my lips to his, hungry for his kiss, his touch. His fingers tighten in my hair as our mouths open and our tongues curl together.

A little noise slips from my throat, and I want him to lift me and carry me to the bed. I want him to fill me, groaning with the same need surging in my veins. Instead he pulls me close, hugging me tightly against his chest. My arms are around his waist, and I'm firm against his body, breathing fast.

"I won't stay." My heart sinks at his words. He kisses the top of my head, my brow. "I just needed to see you, to touch you."

He's pulling back, but I hold him tighter, feeling the tension in his body. "Wait... What's wrong?"

The muscle in his jaw moves, and he looks at our clasped hands, our twined fingers. "So much happened this week."

"Tell me." Tightening my grip, I draw him to the bed, to sit beside me. I know if he stayed so many extra days, it must have been important.

We're sitting, facing each other, and his beautiful eyes focus on our hands, our connection. He hesitates, and his brows pull together. "My father always loved going to Harristown so much... I never knew it was because of his mom... my grandmother."

Now I frown. "What happened?"

He exhales quietly. "She lost a baby there. It was stillborn."

"Oh, Deacon." My heart sinks. "I'm so sorry... Are you okay?"

"I didn't want to come back until I knew everything. I spent the last few days following her trail. It was pretty twisted."

Reaching out, I slide my hand down his arm. "Tell me what happened."

Blue eyes meet mine, and he's not smiling. "My grandmother was a beautiful woman. People who knew her said she was the most beautiful woman they'd ever seen."

"Is that a bad thing?"

"Two men loved her... best friends. She married the rich one, my grandfather." He blinks over my shoulder, and my heart beats faster. "But after seven or so years, she had an affair. She got pregnant and went to her friend in Harristown to give birth."

"Why would she do that?"

"She was afraid my grandfather would see the baby and know what she'd done."

My voice is quiet, my insides trembling. "How would he know?"

"The baby's father was Manuel Treviño."

My grandfather. My throat knots, and I stand, walking slowly around my room, thinking about this, about what he just told me. "You mean... your grandmother had an affair with my grandfather? How is it possible?"

"Apparently, they knew each other. Our grandfathers were friends."

"And your grandmother..."

"It explains the bad blood between our families." He's sitting on the foot of my bed watching me. "My grandfather must have found out."

"So you think Beto is telling the truth?" It feels like a weight is sitting on my chest. "You think your grandfather shot mine?"

Deacon's eyes drop to his hands. "I think I found a motive..."

Honor... Loyalty to your family... Our father died a broken man...

My brother's angry words are in my brain, squeezing my

heart and twisting my insides. Shaking my head, I don't want to think about these events that have nothing to do with us.

"I understand if you want me to go."

"No!" Crossing the room quickly, I climb onto his lap in a straddle, wrapping my arms around his neck and pressing my chest to his. "I want you to stay."

Strong arms are around me, holding me close. We're breathing fast, our hearts beating quickly. We take several long moments, letting the truth of our family's history settle in the spaces around us.

I want to cry. I want to crawl under the blankets with him and hide. I want to go back to the way things used to be. "Remember when it was only us?"

"It was never only us." His voice is quiet.

"We could still pretend." My arms are around him, and I hold on tight. I never want to let go.

He exhales and his arms relax. Sitting up, I find his beautiful face; his sexy lips curl slightly. It's the first hint of a smile he's given me since he returned. It helps my muscles relax. It gives me the smallest bit of hope.

He slides a curl behind my ear with his fingers. "We can't live our lives that way. We have to figure out what to do."

"I don't know…" I kiss his cheek, moving closer to his ear. "I can ignore them for a little while. Pretend this history isn't ours… it's not our problem."

"We do have other things going on in our lives."

Sitting up, I meet his gaze. "Really exciting things."

That gets me a smile, the ghost of a dimple in his cheek, and my stomach warms. "Tell me about your week. I want to know more about this mysterious portrait commission."

My stomach is tight, but I don't want to let anything burst our bubble. "She's a very rich old woman, very difficult. But I'm building a bridge."

"Like Winona Judd?" He leans forward, tracing his lips along mine, tickling my insides with heat.

"It's a popular name."

"If anyone can do it, you can."

We spend the next several minutes lost in a haze of lust and heat and kisses. Deacon slides his mouth into my hair, pulling on the shell of my ear. Whispering hot promises of what he wants to do to me. I'm lost in the sensation of his lips against mine, his hands, his touch.

His dick is hard on my thigh, and he groans roughly. "I left my car out front in plain sight of everyone."

I stand, lowering the sweatpants I'm wearing and climbing him in a straddle. "Then we'd better make this quick."

Rising onto my knees, I cover his mouth with mine, sliding my tongue along his as his long fingers thread in the side of my panties, gripping my ass. My center heats, and I move against him.

His fingers trace a line to the middle of my thighs, and I exhale a moan as he drags them up and down my clit, circling and massaging as I ride his hand.

My voice breaks with desire. "I need you now."

Our hands fumble together, unfastening his pants, lowering them so his cock springs free, so I can line it up and drop, closing my eyes as he fills me, moaning so loud, his large hand fumbles to cover my mouth, thick fingers slipping between my teeth.

My pelvis rocks, and I'm grinding. His face is in my hair, close to my ear, so I can hear his rough breathing, his groans of desire.

"Angel..." It's a hiss of need as his hips lift, driving his cock deeper into me.

His brow furrows, and he lies back on my bed. I lean forward on him, riding fast and hard, feeling the sensations as they whip me higher, tighter, twisting my insides. My breasts bounce, nipples tight, and I can't get enough.

My thighs tighten, my insides tighten, the friction is more than I can bear. My brain is on fire, and I can't slow the movements of my body. It's primal, instinctive. I'm chasing the orgasm that's so close… right there…

"Oh, God…" I gasp as it breaks. My legs shudder, and my back arches as the pleasure shoots through me like a shock. "Oh…" I can't stop the release.

Deacon's hands tighten on my ass, gripping me and moving me up and down on his cock as he breaks.

I feel him pulsing. His lips are at my ear as he comes. "Angel…" It's half-prayer, half-groan, causing my core to squeeze.

We hold each other, not caring about the world around us, not worried about the hate or who might find us. We're like we've always been, in our own place of love and desire and need and satisfaction.

Deacon holds me, rolling us to the side so I'm facing him on the bed. He kisses my nose, my cheek, my lips. "I love you so much."

My heart warms, and I rise up to kiss him back. "I love you."

"Little seductress." He exhales a laugh, shaking his head. "What will I do with you?"

"Stay with me forever."

"If only." He starts to rise, but I hold him.

"Deacon…"

"Angel…" He leans down again, resting his head against my breast. "You make it so hard for me."

"Why should I make it easy?" I grin, holding him, loving how hard it is for him to leave me.

He starts to laugh. "Your brother threatened to shoot me if he caught me with you again."

Everything inside me freezes, and my grip relaxes. "What did you say?"

I remember Beto's gun, his anger, his hatred of everything Dring.

The teasing grin on Deacon's face falters, and he seems to catch himself. "I shouldn't have told you that."

"Yes, you should have." I rise up beside him, straightening my clothes.

"We were all amped up. Everyone was pissed. He was talking out of his ass."

"You should go." I'm off the bed, straightening my panties and going to the window. "We can meet at your apartment next time."

"This is a switch." He's teasing, but I'm freaking out. "Please..."

He's at the window, throwing a leg over the balustrade and sitting. "Come here."

Stepping closer, I put my arms around his neck, my old friend Fear buzzing in my veins.

Dropping his chin, he kisses my lips. "I'm not afraid of your brother. I'll see you tomorrow, and in the meantime, I'm working on this. You trust me?"

He's so beautiful. He's everything to me. If anything happens to him...

"Of course, I trust you." My voice is a broken whisper, and I put my palm against his scruffy cheek.

He leans forward, kissing me longer, pulling my lips with his. I want to hold him, but I need him to go. I can't take a chance on what he just told me.

"I'll call you." One last kiss, and he drops to the pavement, dashing across the back patio and off my brother's property.

I'm breathing fast, terrified. I had no idea when he came here what my brother had threatened, how dangerous our love had become.

My brother is angry and unpredictable. Regardless of what Deacon thinks, I don't know what Beto might do. Would he really shoot Deacon? He's so obsessed with avenging the past...

Either way, I'm not taking a chance.

CHAPTER
Seventeen

Deacon

THE LIFE-SIZED PORTRAIT OF MY AUNT IS UNFINISHED, BUT I'M DRAWN by her eyes and the regal lift of her chin. "You look very elegant. Is that Boots?" Leaning closer, I see the old family cat is in her lap. "That's a fun touch."

"You think so?" Winnie grasps my upper arm, and I've never seen her so excited. "I took a little convincing."

"Is that so?" I can't imagine who my aunt would trust to disagree with her. "Who's doing it?"

"A gifted new artist Angela Carmen, but I don't think that's her real name."

Slanting my eyes, I place my hand over hers. "Why not?"

"She doesn't always respond when I say it." My aunt releases my arm and does a wave. "No matter. I'll pay her in cash."

"That's a lot of cash to hand someone."

"She'll know what to do with it. Those people prefer cash-only payments anyway. Avoids a lot of uncomfortable questions."

"You're assuming she's illegal?"

"What does it matter, darling? She can't help her circumstances."
Winnie motions to the life-sized painting. "Look how beautiful her
work is. I'm thinking of being her patron, commissioning her to do
your portrait."

"That's very big hearted of you." I don't bother hiding my sarcasm.
"Speaking of portraits, why are there no pictures of my grandmother?"

Winnie's spine stiffens. "That's an odd question."

"Is it? She was your mother."

Winnie seems disturbed. "I think they're in the attic with the
rest of her things. Father put them away after she died."

"We never talk about her. Why is that?" I confess, growing up, I
took it for granted. Her death was overshadowed by the loss of my
mother and my father's withdrawal.

"Mother was not very happy." She slips her hand in the crook of
my arm as we stroll to the dining room. "Had she been alive today,
I'm sure she would still be with us, but back then… people didn't
know how to deal with grief."

"Grief?" I'm curious how much my aunt knows of the story,
considering it all happened before she was born.

"She lost a child between your father and me. She was visiting
a friend and went into premature labor. It was very sad. She never
got over it, at least that's what they said."

"I see." I hold her chair as she takes a seat at the table. "How old
were you when she died?"

"I was about the same age you were when you lost your mother."
Empathy is in her eyes. "Let's not talk about it. Our family has not
been lucky in love."

Servers appear with salad plates, and we drift to silence.

I think about her statement and her brief marriage. Winnie married one of my grandfather's business associates, and I'm pretty sure
it was not a love match.

I barely remember my uncle Clarke. My father once said he tried
to tell Winnie what to do, and she walked out.

Angel is on my mind. We exchanged a few texts today, but she had to work, then she had her final art class. My aunt's comment has me needing to see her again, to change my family's luck, regardless of our history.

"Why do you suppose they do it?" She holds a heavy crystal goblet to her lips, sipping her red wine as the servers take away our salad plates, replacing them with steak and new potatoes.

"Do what?" I spear a small red spud and pop it into my mouth.

"This young woman described a beautiful childhood in Mexico. Why would she leave that to come here?"

"I think there are a lot of reasons people like us could never understand." Slicing a bite of steak, I eat the perfectly cooked beef not expecting my aunt to understand the concept of privilege even while sitting in the midst of it. "Why does it matter to you?"

"I'd like to help her. She seems like an intelligent girl. Maybe she wants to go home."

"Maybe you should stay out of it." I take another bite of steak, and she tilts her head to the side.

"I'd say that was rude if I didn't know you better."

I'm not looking to fight with my aunt about the problems of a stranger. I'm more interested in what I've learned. "How much do you know about the way Grandfather acquired his land?"

She exhales, sliding her plate forward and leaning back in her chair. "We've discussed this, Deacon. I was a child, a girl. I was not included in those discussions. It's ignorant and backwards by today's standards, but that's how it was in those days."

"But you married one of his closest business partners. He never discussed it with you?"

"Non-disclosure agreements. Your grandfather was very suspicious." She rises from her chair and goes to the fireplace. "He only got worse as he got older, after Mother died. He didn't trust anyone, least of all women."

Knowing what I've learned, it's like all these dots are just waiting to be connected. My eyes go to the clock, and I see it's after nine. "I think I'll call it a night."

"Won't you stay a little longer?" She puts her hand on my arm, and I cover it with mine.

"I'll check on you in a few days." We're out in the hall when a door opens, the one leading to the side entrance the workers use.

Everything stops when Angel steps into the hallway.

"Oh!" Her voice rushes out on a breath, and my stomach tightens.

She's beautiful in a tight navy tee and jeans that hug her cute little ass. Her curls are in a low ponytail over one shoulder, and when our eyes meet, I can't help smiling. She blinks away fast, and my smile fades.

"Hello, Angela." Winnie's voice is formal. "This is my nephew Deacon. Deacon, this is the young woman I was telling you about."

Angel's family might hate me, but Winnie has no power over my decisions. I'm about to set things straight when Angel reaches forward quickly and shakes my hand.

"How do you do, Mr. Clarke?" She gives me a pointed look, and I stop.

"Deacon's last name is Dring. He's my late brother's son."

"My mistake." Angel blinks away to my aunt. "I won't be late tonight. I'd like to be home by ten-thirty."

"Of course. You've been working very hard." Winnie speaks to her like she's the maid, and I don't like it. "I was just telling Deacon what a wonderful job you're doing. I think he agrees with me... Deacon? What's wrong, darling?"

My eyes are on Angel avoiding my gaze, and I shake my head, returning to my aunt. "I have to go." Leaning forward, I kiss Winnie's cheek then turn to my girl. "Nice meeting you, *Angela*."

Angel does a brief nod before heading into the room where she works.

We're not doing this.

I'm not backing down from being together because things have gotten twisted.

Still, I'll wait.

She'll be home at ten thirty, and I'll be ready for her explanation.

THE BACKYARD LIGHTS STREAM THROUGH THE OPEN WINDOW OF ANGEL'S bedroom. I left my bike in the same place across the street as last week, and I'm sitting in the shadows waiting for her to walk through the door.

Before coming here, I rode through the night out to the tower where we used to meet. I thought about the story of the man who shot his wife and her lover here. As a child, I thought such stories were made up to scare us or to make places seem more interesting.

Now I'm not so sure.

Taking a slight detour, I rode out across my grandfather's land, or the start of it. Our family owns hundreds of miles of forest and grasslands in northeast Texas, leading up to Oklahoma. Was it always ours?

Straddling my bike, I sat at the top of a small hill overlooking the property and shot a quick text to Richland. *Need you to help me research the ownership history of some land.*

He didn't take long to reply. *In El Paso for another week, but I'll see what I can do. What land?*

Mine.

The metallic taste of rain was on my tongue as I sped back towards Lakeside Estates. Now, sitting in Angel's empty room, I listen to the thunder rolling in, making the night even darker. How will she get home? Does she ride the bus at this hour? Anger is rising in my chest when I feel my phone vibrate again.

Sounds like a story. It's Rich.

You have no idea. I hit send just as her door cracks open, and the light from the hall filters into the room.

She doesn't enter, standing in the doorway looking at me sitting in the beige wingback chair across from her.

"You're here." Her voice is soft.

Mine is hard. "Isn't that what you wanted?"

We study each other a moment before she steps into the room and shuts the door behind her. "Are you mad at me?"

"I haven't decided." My foot is crossed over my knee and thunder rolls low in the sky. "Why did you pretend like you didn't know me?"

She closes the distance between us, dropping to her knees. I uncross my legs allowing her to scoot between them.

"I panicked." Her hands slide up my thighs, and she looks up at me. "I didn't want you to get me fired. I really want this job."

"I wouldn't let her fire you."

"Maybe... but she won't like us together."

"I don't care."

"But I do... I've done so much work. It's my art, Deacon." Her voice is soft, eyes round. "Please."

Her thumbs make small circles against my inner thighs, and it's melting my annoyance.

I place my forearms on my knees, threading my fingers in her hair. "You won her over with your talent. That portrait is amazing."

Her cute little nose wrinkles. "She criticizes me nonstop."

"She bragged about you all through dinner... The brilliant young artist she discovered."

That makes her laugh. "Thanks."

"If I'd known it was you, I could've agreed... You're so talented."

Lifting her hands, she places them over mine. "Let me finish before we blow it all up. I want this for my portfolio, for the Arthaus application."

I don't like it, but I can't make her sad. "Okay."

Rising onto her knees, she kisses me. Our lips part, tongues sliding together, and her fingers fumble to my shoulders. My hands slide lower, pulling her waist closer to me, threading my fingers under her shirt to her soft skin.

We move faster, her fingers rise to my neck. She exhales a soft noise, and heat fills my stomach.

"I want to taste you." It's a rough whisper, and she stands slowly, looking down as a curl slips over her shoulder.

My hands are on her waist, fumbling with the button on her jeans. Her fingers are in my hair, and I kiss the skin below her navel. "Deacon..." she sighs in a tone I love.

"What the fuck?" A sharp voice rips through our moment.

Angel is jerked back, and Beto stands in front of me, seething. "What the fuck are you doing in my house?"

"Beto, you're hurting me!" Angel's face contorts with pain, and I'm on my feet.

"Let her go."

"What did I tell you?" He reaches behind him, pulling out a black handgun. "The next time I saw you with her?"

"Beto!" Angel screams, jerking her arm against his grip. "No!"

Her brother doesn't move. His eyes flash, and he's holding the weapon in my stomach.

"Put it down before you hurt someone." My voice is low. I don't want to taunt him. I don't know how far he'll go.

"Get the fuck out of my house." He takes a step closer, still gripping Angel by the arm.

She's no longer struggling. Her eyes are fixed on the gun.

"Beto, please." Her voice trembles. "I'll do whatever you want."

"Get out." He shoves her back hard, and I lunge forward,

putting my hand over the cool metal and turning it away from me.

It goes off with a sharp pop, and warm liquid spills over my hands. Fear seizes my chest, choking my breath.

"Fuck." Beto's lips tighten, and he drops to his knees.

I'm holding the gun as Mateo enters the room.

"Beto!" He's shouting, grabbing cloth to stop the blood, and I'm trying to figure out what just happened.

The gun slips from my hand to the white fluffy rug.

Angel is on the floor, terrified eyes flying between me and her brother. "Beto?"

It's all happening so fast, but it feels like time has slowed down. Mateo rolls him onto his back, pressing a towel into Beto's side. His eyes are closed, and blood is all over his stomach.

"No…" Blood on my hands, my arms, my jeans.

"I'm going to kill you!" Mateo screams at me, fire in his eyes.

"Angel, call 911." My voice sounds strange, and I'm backing to the window. "Hurry!"

Mateo lunges for the gun on the floor, but I beat him to it, snatching it up and holding it loosely in my hand. I'm not a killer. I don't know what the fuck to do right now.

"Go, Deacon!" Angel's voice is hoarse with tears. "Just go… Now!"

"But…" I'm torn between wanting to help and knowing I can't.

Mateo stands, pulling Beto up with him. He hauls him over his shoulder, turning for the door. Angel is right behind them, and I'm left standing in the room with her words echoing in my ears.

I do the only thing I know to do. I pick up my phone and leave through the window, running across the lawn to my waiting motorcycle.

CHAPTER
Eighteen

Angel

"**W**E'RE SORRY, THE NUMBER YOU HAVE REACHED IS NOT available." Pressing the end button, I hang up and try again.

The burner phone Deacon bought me is in my hand, and I've been calling him nonstop for five hours. I don't know if he turned his phone off or if he left it in my bedroom or threw it away. Is he avoiding my calls?

Valeria is with me in the hospital pacing and praying. She's been here since Mateo called her. My insides are raw, and I can't seem to stop shaking. I don't know how this happened.

One minute I was in bliss, wrapped in Deacon's arms, filled with joy and wonder and lust and desire. The next, my brother was twisting my arm and yelling at my love, pulling out a gun and threatening him…

"It's going to be okay, Carmie." Valeria sees the fresh tears sliding down my cheeks and pulls me into a hug. "Everything is going to be okay."

She brought me clean clothes, but my brother's blood has stained my hands. I can't seem to stop crying.

"I said it was an accident." Mateo is beside us speaking low and not making eye contact. "I said he was cleaning the gun and it went off. He didn't know it was loaded."

"Is that not what happened?" Valeria looks up at him with astonishment then to me.

"It's what happened." Mateo looks at me as if to silence me. "I'll take care of the rest."

He turns and leaves us standing there as he exits the hospital, and I know he's going to find Deacon. My stomach shudders, and a fresh wave of tears floods my eyes. I've got to stop him. I've got to find Deacon and warn him.

"I have to go." I have to find my love before Mateo does.

"But your brother!" Valeria grips my arm, and I feel like I'm being torn in two.

"Miss Treviño?" A calm, female voice joins us in the waiting room. "Would you come with me, please?"

Valeria holds my arm as we follow the doctor into a smaller room with a glass door. She closes it, and we take a seat, holding each other's hands.

The doctor looks at Valeria, and I quickly explain. "This is my cousin. She helps take care of things."

"I see." The woman nods, her expression serious as she places X-rays on the black screen on the wall and flips on the lights behind them. My heart beats so hard, I feel faint. "Your brother is a very lucky man, Miss Treviño. The bullet glanced off his rib here..." She circles a white blob on the slide. "Otherwise, it would have been a fatal shot."

"Otherwise..." Valeria repeats her words slowly. "Would have been... So he's okay?"

"He's not out of the woods just yet, but yes. He should make a full recovery."

"Oh, thank you Jesus!" My aunt crosses herself.

My eyes close, and more tears stream down my cheeks.

"It's very important never to clean a loaded weapon..." The doctor goes on about gun safety, a lesson I don't need, and all I can think about is getting to Deacon.

Things have gone from bad to worse, and I need him to hold me. I'm so afraid.

"If you'll just excuse me." My stomach is churning. "I need to go to the restroom."

I barely make it out the smaller room when I have to lean into the garbage can beside the door and throw up.

"Oh, Carmie!" Valeria is with me at once, sliding her fingers through my hair, pulling it away from my face. "Honey, it's going to be okay."

"I'm sorry." I take the tissues the doctor hands me, using them to dry my face and wipe my mouth. "I'm so sorry. I think I'd better go."

"Are you okay, Miss Treviño?" The doctor watches me, and I nod.

"I just need to lie down."

Pulling out my phone, I punch up the Lyft app. As I do so, I notice the slight bruising around my forearm. Valeria notices it as well and steps between me and the doctor, who is explaining what comes next for my brother.

The bullet exited his torso, so he doesn't need surgery. Still, the doctor says he'll have to stay in the hospital a few days.

My phone pings the Lyft is here, and I head for the door. I've got to find Deacon before Mateo does.

A RED BLOODSTAIN MARS THE FLUFFY WHITE RUG COVERING THE DARK wood floors of my bedroom. My brother's gun is in front of the chair where Deacon sat. It brings on a fresh wave of tears, and I stumble to my bathroom to grab one of the thick white towels.

Placing it over the stain, I collapse to my knees, pressing my hand to my lips. Beto's going to be okay, but I don't know where Deacon is. Reaching out, I take the gun and carry it to my bed, pushing it between the mattresses.

I don't know if the police will come here or if Mateo's explanation will cover what happened. I know nothing about this man my brother wanted to set me up with—who he is or why he's here.

My limbs are heavy as I crawl onto the comforter and lift the burner phone to try one more time. I dial Deacon's number, and the robot voice answers. My hands drop, and my eyes close.

Pain twists in my chest, and I feel like I can't breathe properly. "Where are you?" I whisper, turning my face to the pillow. "I need you…"

"Where is he?" The stern voice pulls me from a dreamless sleep, and I blink around my bedroom confused.

Sunlight streams through the window and Mateo stands over me. His eyes are red and lined, and his jaw is set.

"What time is it?" I can't believe I fell asleep.

"It's almost nine."

Almost nine? I sit up too fast, and my head spins. Nausea rises in my throat, and I jump out of the bed and go to the bathroom, turning on the faucet.

Mateo is right with me. "Where is your boyfriend?"

"Would you get out, please? I need to use the toilet." He glares at me a moment before going to the door.

I push it closed behind him and turn the lock. Leaning over the sink, I hold cool water to my neck, too my cheeks. The nausea slowly subsides, but my eyes are swollen. I look pretty rough. Chewing my lip, I realize I left the burner phone in my bed. *Shit.*

Quickly using the restroom, I open the door and find Mateo looking through the papers on my desk. "What are you doing?"

He walks to where I'm standing. "Where is he?"

"I don't know." Pushing past him, I start for my bed.

"You're lying." He catches my arm, hazel eyes flashing. "Stop protecting him. He almost killed your brother."

"Let me go, Mateo." My voice is firm. "Beto came at him with the gun. It was an accident."

"This does not go unanswered. I'm in charge until your brother's back on his feet." His grip relaxes, and I jerk my arm away, going to my dresser and pulling out leggings and a tunic top.

"I have to get to work."

"You tell me if you hear from him."

Yeah, right. I scoop the burner phone off my bed, hiding it with my clothes as I return to the bathroom and close the door. Dressing quickly, I dust some powder on my nose. I can't hide my red eyes. My heart is beating fast, and I'm ready to get out of this house.

I missed my ride with Rosalía, so I take the keys from the rack in the kitchen to the silver MINI Cooper I've never driven. I hate to drive, but this car feels solid, and it goes fast. Two things I want right now.

Parking on the street in front of Winnie's house, I jog to the side entrance and go straight to the room where I paint. As usual, she's there reading, and when I walk in, she narrows her eyes.

"You didn't arrive with Rosalía today. I hope that isn't a sign of things to come."

Looking around the room, I try to figure out a nonchalant way to ask if Deacon is here. "I wasn't sure if I should come early... with your family in town."

"Family?" Her brow furrows.

"Your nephew? Isn't he staying with you?"

"Deacon? Goodness no. Why would you think that?" She shakes her head.

"He was here last night, so I just assumed he was staying with you."

"Deacon has a penthouse apartment downtown. He was on his way out when you arrived last night."

My bottom lip goes between my teeth, and my heart sinks. "So he's not here?"

"No… not that it has anything to do with you." She stands and crosses the room to me, brow arched. "Have you been crying?"

Clearing my throat, I turn my face away. "My older brother had an accident last night. He's in the hospital."

She's quiet, studying me, and I go to the canvas, not really in the mood to paint. I want to collapse in a heap and cry. My stomach is in knots, and all I can think is Mateo out there waiting with a gun. I can't possibly paint.

"If you're not feeling well today, I think you can take a long weekend."

My eyes widen, and I glance over my shoulder. "You're giving me the day off?"

She turns, strolling to the chair and picking up her book. "I understand family obligations. Just don't make it a habit." That last bit is sharp, but I don't give a shit.

"Thank you." I grab my bag and hurry out to my car, taking the iPhone Beto bought me out of my bag.

I suspect he uses it to keep tabs on me, but with him in the hospital, that's out the window. I don't know how to drive downtown, and this phone has a map application on it. I'm typing in the name of Deacon's penthouse tower when the burner starts buzzing in my purse.

Tossing the iPhone aside, I dig in my bag. The face says unknown number, but I don't let it stop me. "Hello?" My voice is breathless.

"Hi, ahh… Is this Angel?" The male voice sounds a little familiar, and only one person calls me Angel.

"Yes! Are you with Deacon?"

"Hey, this is Richland Wells. I'm a friend of Deacon's."

"Rich! Yes, I remember." My heart is beating so fast. If he's been in an accident...

"How's your brother?"

I put my hand over my nose to stop the tears. "He's going to be okay. They're keeping him a few days, but he's going to recover." The guy makes a noise of relief, and I can't take it anymore. "I'm sorry, are you with Deacon? Please, can I speak to him?"

"You want to speak to him?" It sounds like he's talking to me and someone else.

"Yes! Of course, I do. Is he there?"

A bit of shuffling, muffled voices. *He thought I didn't want to speak to him? How could he think that?*

"Angel?" The warm male voice in my ear causes my heart to melt.

"Deacon?" My breath hiccups, and I can't stop the fresh tears. "Oh, Deacon..."

"Don't cry, beautiful." His voice breaks. "Your brother's okay?"

Nodding, I sniff before answering. "The doctor said he's going to make a full recovery."

"Thank God." Deacon exhales heavily. "I'm sorry, Angel. I fucked up everything."

"Where are you? I've been so worried."

"I'm in El Paso with Rich. I asked him to do something for me... I came to help him, then I'll turn myself in."

My voice goes high. "You can't do that. There's no need."

"I shot your brother, Angel." His voice is tight.

Clearing the thickness from my voice, I shake my head. "He's going to be okay. You are not going to the police. It wasn't your fault. He came at you with a gun..."

It's quiet on the line. "You still want to see me?"

"What? I've been calling and calling."

"You told me to go." His voice is quiet. "I thought you hated me."

"Hated you? How could I ever—" My voice breaks again, fresh tears. "Tell me where you are. Send me the address."

"I don't want you coming here. You need to be with your family."

"I need to be with you."

"I don't like you driving by yourself—"

Now I'm getting frustrated. "Text me the address!"

His breathy chuckle fills my ear, and my stomach warms. "Okay, beautiful. But I want you to call me every so often so I know you're safe."

"I'll see you tonight."

Turning the wheel, I go back to my brother's house and grab that rolling suitcase. It doesn't take long to fill it with everything I own. I'm never coming back to this house again. I don't know if that means I'll sleep on Lourdes's couch or I'll move in with Deacon, but I won't be here.

I put the envelope of cash in my purse and my suitcase in the car, and I collect the paintings I brought home from class yesterday. I grab my few paint supplies from the cottage and download the pictures I took of Winnie's portrait onto my laptop, leaving the iPhone on the kitchen counter. I don't want any of his gifts.

Pausing at my car, I press my lips together. This is a problem. Taking this car is maintaining a connection… But I have to get to El Paso.

My brow furrows, and I exhale a growl, looking up at the enormous mansion towering over me. "Fine, you fucking win this round."

I'm going to take this car for now, but it's not mine. I won't give him any power over me. It's not my will that takes this vehicle, it's my need.

And I need to be with my love.

CHAPTER
Nineteen

Deacon

BETO'S ALIVE.

Cloud shadows drift across the Franklin Mountains as I sit and watch from the balcony of Skeeter's El Paso home. The minutes crawl as I wait for her to arrive. She texted me on a gas break that she was making good time, but my insides ache with needing to see her.

After Beto was shot and Mateo carried him out... and Angel screamed at me to go, I struggled with what to do. His blood was on my clothes and hands, and I had to at least get clean.

Stopping at an old-school gas station, I used the dirty restroom to strip out of my shirt, doing my best to wash my hands and arms in the tiny stream of water coming from the sink.

Wearing only my jacket and jeans, I sped along Interstate 20 contemplating my next steps. Shock drove me. For all I knew, I'd just killed a man. I'd lost my love, I'd lost everything.

How could Angel ever forgive me for killing her brother?

My life was over.

Closing my eyes briefly, I leaned harder on the throttle as grief washed over me. When I opened them again, I saw the sign for new developments in Fate, and I knew what I had to do.

Before I went away. I had to be sure the past would be made right, and I didn't trust Winnie to do it. Leaning forward into the rain, over the handlebars of my bike, I set a course for El Paso. Rich was working on this, but I had to find the truth about the past. I owed that much to Angel and her family—especially if Beto were dead because of me.

Now Angel's saying he's alive. He's going to recover... And she doesn't hate me.

Standing, I walk along the balcony willing time to move faster.

The French doors open, and Rich walks out holding two beers. "Drink something before you get heat stroke."

Taking one, I rub the back of my neck. "Not sure this is the right choice for dehydration."

"It's been a rough twenty-four hours. You just got some great news. Beer is the right choice."

"I'm not a killer."

"I never thought you were." He leans back, taking a long sip of Modelo. "If a guy comes at you with a gun, that is not murder. It's self-defense."

"Yes, but I broke into his house."

"You were the guest of his sister, who is an adult and invited you there."

Taking a drink, I nod, wiping my lips with the back of my hand. "Then she screamed at me to get out." Flashbacks of the blood, of Angel crying on her knees... all of it hits me like a sucker punch. "I'm a fucking fool."

"Ease up on my friend Deacon." He's joking, but I'm not.

"I actually thought I'd introduce myself to her family, tell them we were in love and wanted to marry. I thought they'd welcome us with open arms. We'd have a party, a big wedding. Happy ever fucking after."

"You've always been a cocky bastard."

"Asshole." I take a longer sip of beer.

He exhales a laugh, leaning forward. "You know, most couples expect the same thing. It doesn't make you a fool. How were you supposed to know your family had a history to rival the Montagues and Capulets?"

Shaking my head, that reminds me. "How's it going with the title search?"

"No dice." He polishes off his beer. "Deeds that old aren't stored electronically. But, lucky for you, I know how to search the county archives."

"I can help—"

"You'll just get in the way." He rubs a hand through his messy blond hair. "Plus I'm interested now. This is fucking fascinating. You think your grandfather cheated hers out of Fate?"

"It's what they think." I don't mention the baby, my grandmother, or the murder allegation.

"I want to know who's right." He grins at me, blue eyes crinkling in his tanned face.

The sound of tires on gravel below draws our attention. My chest tightens, and I'm pretty sure it's her.

"Nice ride." Rich stands.

She steps out of the driver's side, and the wind pushes thick, golden-brown curls over her shoulders. Her dress swirls around her slim body, and using one hand to shade her eyes, she looks up at me.

She's so fucking gorgeous. My breath stills in my lungs. "Angel…"

"Go." A grin is in his voice.

I barely hear it.

I'm jogging down the massive wood staircase, through the open foyer, and out the front door as the words hang in the air.

I hesitate on the porch.

Our eyes meet, and a tear traces down her cheek. "Deacon…" It's a mixture of longing and exhaustion, and my uncertainty is gone.

Closing the space between us, I pull her into my arms, tucking her sweet head against my chest and inhaling deeply… *jasmine.* Relief hits me like a rush of life in my veins, and the fist in my chest unfurls.

"I thought you'd given up on us."

Lifting her chin, she gives me a teasing smile. "I'm very determined."

Leaning down, I press my lips to hers, ready to push them apart and claim that sassy mouth.

A throat clearing pulls us up short. "Sorry to interrupt this beautiful reunion scene." Rich twirls a set of keys in his hand. "I've got to head on back to Dallas now."

My brow furrows, and I check the time. "You can't drive to Dallas. It's late—"

"Dude. BP has a private jet." A car slowly makes its way up the long driveway, and he tosses the keys to me. "Uncle Skeeter won't be home until Monday. You two stay and do something you've never done."

Lifting my chin, I squint one eye at him. "Like what?"

"Spend the weekend together as a couple. Have fun. Go skinny dipping in the lake. Take selfies." He jogs out to the waiting vehicle. "Lock up before you leave."

Angel drops her forehead against my chest, and I call after my friend. "Thanks, man."

He waves out the window, disappearing down the two-lane road leading away from the secluded compound. I slide my hands down Angel's smooth arms, threading our fingers, palm against palm.

"I'm so glad to see you."

She makes a humming noise, arching her back and rising on her toes to kiss my lips. "I've missed you so much."

Her eyes are the color of sunset, and she feels like heaven in my arms. Our mouths reunite in a slow kiss, lips pulling, tongues touching. Heat fills my stomach, and I pull her body against mine, loving the feel of us chest to stomach to thigh. I'm ready to take her inside. I want us to be completely reunited.

"Did you bring any bags?"

Her whiskey eyes meet mine. "I brought everything."

Stepping back, she goes to the small car and opens the trunk. One rolling suitcase is inside, and I take it from her. "This is everything?"

"It's what's mine. I'm never going to that house again."

"Angel—"

"I'm an adult, I have money, and I'm done with trying to include them in our lives." She puts her purse on her shoulder and takes out what looks like art supplies from the back seat. "Beto tried to kill you."

"And I nearly killed him in return."

Her eyes flash to mine. "None of this would have happened if he hadn't attacked you."

I can't argue with her. "The police will have questions."

"Mateo told them Beto was cleaning the gun and it went off. He didn't know it was loaded. I don't think they're going to pursue it."

Our feet crunch on the gravel as we walk to the porch. "So I don't need to turn myself in?"

"You didn't do anything wrong."

Inside, I put her suitcase on the landing before pulling her into my arms again. "Are you okay with that?"

Her chin lifts, and our eyes meet. "It's what's right. Now where's that lake? I'm ready to go skinny dipping."

ANGEL'S SOFT BREASTS FLATTEN AGAINST MY BARE CHEST. WATER LAPS AT our shoulders, and her body is warm against mine. She eases the pressure in my chest, the relentless stress since that gun went off.

Leaning forward, I capture her lips, parting them so I can stroke her tongue with mine as her legs rise and wrap around my waist.

Her lips trace a line to my ear. "I want you to fill me."

It's a sultry whisper that tingles my erection. I reach down, grasping my cock and sliding it up and down until I'm at her opening, thrusting inside.

"Fuck," I groan as wet, clenching heat surrounds me.

"Deacon…" She whispers hungrily at my ear, and my eyes close, my hips thrust upward.

"Mm… yes…" Hot murmurs as our mouths kiss and pull, devouring lips, cheeks.

I lightly bite the side of her neck, and she moans, tightening around my cock. She rides me, pushing her thighs against my waist. Fingers thread in my hair, and her chin lifts.

Her full breasts are at my mouth, and I catch a hard nipple, pulling it with my teeth. Sweet water is on my tongue, and she pulls me deeper. I'm right on the edge about to come.

"Come for me." My hands grip her soft ass, and I move her, doing my best to hold on as she chants my name, moaning softly.

"So good…" She holds my face, sweeping her tongue in my mouth.

Our mouths seal together, tongues unite, and her pelvis moves like a wave against mine, up and down, blowing my mind.

"Fuck." I'm losing control. My ass tightens, and one more massaging pull from her hot little body is all it takes. I start to come.

"Oh, God…" She gasps, shuddering and scratching my shoulders.

My lips are on her neck, and we rise together, higher and higher, pulsing and swirling, holding and touching… Until we're breathing hard, hearts beating fast, as we come down, hugging each other tightly, returning to this moment.

Opening my eyes, I gaze across the placid lake. The surface shines gold with the setting sun, and it's so peaceful, as if nothing terrible is waiting for us anywhere.

Walking with her in my arms, I lower her so I can see her pretty eyes. They're sunset and dreams and all of my future.

I slide my palms along her cheeks, kissing her cute little nose. "I love you."

Her eyes flutter closed, and when they open slowly, they shine with unshed tears. "Deacon…" She puts her hand against my face, sliding her thumb along the top of my cheek. "You own my heart."

She's in my arms, and our kisses are slow and languid, sated and happy. "Remind me to thank Rich for this."

A pretty smile breaks across her face, and she laughs. "He's on the permanent Christmas card list."

"Are we starting a list now?" Holding her hand as I go to where we left our clothes.

"Absolutely. One for Christmas cards and one for switches."

She's behind me, and I hand her my shirt off the dry grass to wrap around her naked body as I pull my jeans over my hips. "I thought it was lumps of coal."

"Those are for throwing."

I chuckle, hugging her to my side, my arm around her shoulders as we walk back to the house. She's a centerfold with her hair wet in only my shirt and those sexy lace panties. The sun is dipping behind the horizon, creating layers of red, orange, yellow, and blue across the sky.

"I want to paint this." Her voice is quiet, dreamy. She looks up at me, and her eyes blend with the horizon. "I want to paint you."

Lifting her hand, I kiss her fingers. "Sounds hot."

A brown sack is on the back steps with a receipt attached from L&J Cafe. "What's this?"

My phone has a text on the face. "Rich says, 'Enjoy the best Tex-Mex in the city. Tell Angel not to be too critical. I'm sure she's had better.'"

Her lips press in a smile, and she shakes her head. "I'm sure it's delicious."

We're in the kitchen, and I put a Dos Equis in her hand. I take out the contents of the bag—flautas, pollo en mole, with sides of chips, salsa, and guacamole.

We carry the entire spread out the back door to Skeeter's airy patio. Ceiling fans and the breeze make it pleasant, and as the sun goes down, so does the temperature.

I click on the gas fire pit, and yellow twinkle lights are strung around the edge of the roof. An enormous pillow is on the floor beside a low table. I take a seat, and Angel crawls between my legs, dipping a chip in salsa and feeding it to me.

"This salsa is the best I've had." She crams a loaded chip into her mouth, crunching loudly. "Okay, Valeria's is really good... But this is *really* good."

"It's hot." I reach around her for my Modelo. "Give me some of that mole."

"Mm... Try this." She holds a flauta to my lips, and I take a bite of the roll.

Nodding, I lift my chin. "That's good. Mole."

"Okay, okay..." She giggles, cutting a piece of the chicken covered in brown sauce.

I groan in approval at the fruity, spicy, hot sauce with the chocolate undertone. She polishes off another flauta, and when we're good and full, I lift her to her feet, pulling her onto the couch where she curls up at my side facing me.

"I guess we never really got to do this." Her head rests on her hand, and I slide a curl off her cheek with my finger.

"I was always gone. Why did you ever wait for me?"

Leaning forward, she kisses my lips briefly. "Have you seen you?"

"So it's purely physical?"

"Yes."

Reaching down, I grab her ribs, and she squeals a laugh, nearly rolling backwards off the small couch.

"Take it easy, sex kitten." I catch her, pulling her to me again.

Her arm goes around my waist, and she lifts her chin, tracing her lips along my jaw. "We missed some things, but we did what mattered most."

"Which was?"

"We talked about our hopes and dreams. You always supported my art."

"You're fucking talented as shit. Of course I support you. That portrait of Winnie is stunning."

She leans her head against my chest. A minute passes, and she sniffs. I frown, giving her a little shake. "What's wrong, Angel?"

Meeting my eyes again, hers shimmer with light. "I love you so much."

Cupping her cheek, I lean in for a real kiss, lips parting, tongues sliding together. She exhales a noise, and I'm ready for more. Sitting up, I sweep her into my arms and stand, carrying her into the house.

"What are you doing?" Her mouth is at my ear, tugging it with her teeth.

"Taking you to bed."

CHAPTER
Twenty

Angel

"Favorite Green Day song?" Deacon kisses a line along my jaw, and I'm vibrating with freshly fucked happiness and so much love.

He's between my thighs, propped on his elbows, and we're both naked in an enormous California king-sized bed surrounded by soft white sheets and a silky beige duvet.

After our conversation about missing out on the little things, he decided we needed to catch up on all the minutiae of teen life we missed.

Sitting forward, I trace my lips along his brow. "American Idiot." Then I drop back, shaking my head. "No... no, no... Boulevard of Broken Dreams."

We both sing at once, "I walk a lonely road..."

"Good one." He gives me that killer smile, the dimple ghosting his cheek. He is so damn fine. "Your turn."

"Uh..." I try to think. "Favorite Nicholas Cage movie?"

His brow lowers over those devastatingly blue eyes. "Was that a thing?"

"Sure! He's made a buttload of movies." I remember all the guys going on about him in *Into the Spider-Verse*.

"Hm." He looks around. "He was the dark Spider-Man in Spider-Verse, but that was more recent…"

"Oh my lord, you all know that one!"

He blinks at me a crooked grin on his cheeks, and my stomach flips. "Who's we all?" I love his sexy, teasing voice. I love having him between my legs, making love whenever we want. "Spill it, Carmelita."

"Boys. All you boys." I can't resist. "I'm not your aunt."

His forehead drops to my stomach. "How can you work for her?"

He rolls onto his back, and I curl up beside him like a cat, using my foot to pull the sheet a little lower so I can admire the lines of muscle in his stomach, the V leading past his waist. I'm lost in a haze of lust when he gives my shoulder a little nudge.

"Hey…"

"Huh? Oh, your aunt." Stretching higher, I kiss his cheek. "She's paying me very well."

"Good." He stretches his arm out, wrapping it around me. "You're worth every penny."

"You're so sweet to me."

"I'm not sweet. I'm honest. Now, what's yours?"

"What?"

"Favorite Nicholas Cage movie."

"Oh!" My head drops to the side, and I exhale trying to think. "*Raising Arizona*… No! No no… *Moonstruck*."

He chuckles, and rolling forward into his chest, I meet his eyes. "Why are you laughing?"

"You do that every time." He looks at me like he's done since I arrived.

He starts with my eyes, gazing into them with so much feeling, then he goes along my hairline, down my neck to my shoulders, my breasts… It's like a slow, loving touch, memorizing everything about me.

"Look at me." I lift my gaze to his blue eyes burning bright. "You are my family. It's only you and me. Always."

This guy.

Rising onto my knees, I straddle his waist, leaning across his chest to press my lips to his. "Nothing can keep us apart."

I feel his dick stirring at my backside, and I want to slide lower, to put him in my mouth and blow his mind.

Instead, he grips my upper arms. "Ride me."

It's a rough order, and I'm instantly wet. A hot breath escapes my parted lips, and reaching behind me, I grip him, hard and thick in my hand, sliding up and down as his jaw tightens. Guiding my body over his, I line us up and drop. His eyes close with a low groan.

He's watching me, dark and intense, and I want to put on a show. I want him to come so hard. I straighten, arching my back and rocking my hips faster on his dick. I cup my breasts, lifting them and making them full and round. His blue eyes follow my movements, and tingles spread beneath my skin, down my legs.

I move faster, back and forth, and the friction of my clit against his shaft has me losing control. He lifts his hips, driving deeper into me as I lean back, placing my hands on his thighs and sliding faster, faster…

He sits up in the bed, catching a hard nipple in his mouth and giving it a firm suck. It registers straight to my core, and I gasp on the edge of orgasm.

"Oh, yeah…" It's a strangled whisper.

His fingers lightly trace my ass as I move. "So fucking hot…"

He slips a hand between us, rubbing his thumb over my clit, and I electrify at the sensation.

"Deacon…" It's a frantic moan. His finger moves faster, making me jerk with every pass.

His dick slides higher, hitting that spot that makes me see stars. He doesn't stop, and I'm losing focus. My vision blurs.

"Oh, God… Don't stop. Don't…" I'm rising on my knees, bouncing on his dick as instinct takes over.

My stomach twists, feral noises scrape from my throat. Every nerve in my body is on fire, and I ride his cock until I break.

Like touching an electric fence, my body jerks and shudders. He grips my ass in both hands, holding me against him as he groans deep, pulsing and filling me. His fingers cut into my skin, and I hold him, wrapping my arms around his shoulders.

His body trembles, and I feel him moving inside me. His heart beats hard against my breast, and he's breathing in my ear. Kissing my hair, loosening his grip.

My arms are tight around him, and his arms band around my waist, holding me flush to him. Our breathing moves in time. I lower my cheek to his shoulder, and I'm sure I'm on another planet, another world where the only things that exist are this beautiful man and the love we share.

How could that ever be wrong? Why should we pay for the sins of our grandfathers?

I don't like that thought crowding my blissed-out state, but our reality is only a few hours away, and while we can't pretend forever, we can pretend for a few days…

"TURN TO YOUR SIDE." MY EYES SWEEP DEACON'S NUDE TORSO. AS I DRAG the kohl pencil down my large sketch pad.

"At least it's warm." He quips. One leg is bent, and a small towel covers his lap. "I wonder where you're planning to hang this one."

I'm shading the lines of his muscles, the planes of his shoulders, when I realize he's teasing me. "Do you need a break?"

"I'm good." A sly smile curls his lips, and my favorite dimple catches my eyes, distracting me for a moment before I get back to work.

Sliding my hand along the page, I return to the smooth highlight of his pecs... his beautiful body. My eyes narrow as I look at him again, so unaware of himself sitting there naked and amazing.

"I've never had someone sit for me before outside of class."

He looks up from his phone. "Good."

It's so emphatic, I laugh. "Good?"

"I don't want you looking like that at other guys."

"Looking like what?"

His eyebrow arches. "Like you're all flushed."

"You make it hard to concentrate."

That only feeds his ego. His blue eyes darken, and I shift in my seat, clearing my throat. "I need to finish this so I can send it with my Arthaus application."

"When is it due?"

"This week, and it's very important."

Then he grins. "So I'm distracting?"

I don't answer, moving to his stomach. Eventually, I'm going to get down to his pelvis and then all bets are off.

Drawing him is like touching him, but slower. It's examining every line, memorizing every square inch of skin, every shade and nuance. It's the most intimate thing we've ever done.

"Tell me about your mom." He takes a drink of the water bottle I put out for him along with some snacks. "You said she made you want to be an artist? I know she was a Buddhist. How did that happen?"

Pausing a moment, I take a breath. It's a good distraction, and it's something we haven't talked about very much.

"She went to art school in California. It's where she learned different philosophies." Looking up at the mountains rising along the skyline, I try to remember her. "She never told me why she turned to that belief system over our family's tradition. I was raised strict Catholic, but she resisted."

"Do you think that's strange?" Blinking back to him, I see he's watching me with that familiar intensity. So interested in everything I say.

"I didn't then." Lifting my pencil, I return to work on his perfect abs. He is such a Michelangelo. "Maybe I don't now... I mean, knowing what I know. Once or twice she mentioned the life she left behind. She would talk about hearts consumed with revenge and hate and how it was cancer in your soul."

"She left her husband and her son." His voice is gentle, not accusatory. "Didn't she feel bad about that?"

My brow clenches, and I slide my pinkie finger over his abs on the page. "I was so little. I never thought about that. I never asked, and she never said."

Deacon shrugs. "It would explain why he's so angry. My mother died when I was young. It hurt to have her gone, but at least I knew she loved me."

"Mamá loved her family..." My voice is sharper than I intend, and Deacon's eyes blink to mine.

"Hey, I'm sorry—"

"No, I'm sorry." Shaking my head. "You're right. You're absolutely right. It's a fair question. I don't know the answer." I look down at the paper. "Maybe she wanted them to come to her?"

"I would come to you."

I smile and make two strong lines for the outside of his thighs. His powerful legs are lined with muscle all the way to his calves. I'm inching my way higher when his voice breaks the silence.

"Tell me about her art. What made you want to be an artist like her?"

Sitting straighter, I think about this. "She said you become a part of life through art. She said she found her voice in her art. She loved Georgia O'Keefe. Her boldness and wildness... She had this quote by her that said, 'I could say things with color and shapes I couldn't say any other way.'"

I think about the quote now and how true it is.

"She seems like a really interesting lady. Problematic... but hey, aren't we all?"

Our eyes meet again, and I laugh "Apparently so, even when we try not to be." Pushing off the couch, I carry the sketchpad to where my naked love reclines. "Take a look and see what you think."

He catches me by the waist and pulls me down on the cushion between his legs. Taking the drawing, he holds it up as I lean my head back against his shoulder.

"This is amazing." He kisses my temple. "One thing bothers me. Right around here."

He moves his hand around his eyes and brow, and I frown. "What's wrong with it?"

"He doesn't look as happy as he ought to be."

Tilting my head, I feel a grin pulling my cheeks. "How can we fix it?"

The sketchpad is forgotten as he turns me in his arms. "I have an idea."

Heat is in his eyes, and I climb onto my knees as our mouths collide, ripping that small towel away and straddling his lap. He cups my breasts through the top of my thin dress, and I shrug out of the sleeves, allowing it to fall around my waist.

I love when he devours me, and I rise higher on my knees, lifting them closer to his mouth. Only this time when he kisses the soft peaks, making his way to my straining nipples, I jump when he pulls one with his teeth.

"Oh..." It's not a cry of pleasure, and he frowns.

"Too rough?"

I kiss his forehead, working my way down to his cheeks as I slide lower. "Must be tender from last night... or after dinner... or skinny dipping..." I punctuate each time with a kiss.

He grins, moving his hands under my skirt and grazing his

fingers along my slippery core. "We've done it a lot. Do you need a break?"

"No, thank you." I smile, covering his mouth with mine again, pushing his lips apart and sucking his tongue.

He kisses me back with equal desire, and I slide my fist up and down his thickening member. He groans, and I feel it in my core.

"I want you inside me," I whisper hotly.

Gripping my waist, he turns me on his lap, and with one deep thrust, I arch, pressing my back against his chest and rotating my hips as I ride him in reverse. His hand slides to the front of my lap, fingers circling my clit, and I rock faster, sending him deeper, feeling him hit the spot that makes my eyes roll.

"Oh, God," I gasp, squeezing him inside me.

"Fuck, yeah," he groans.

I love it when he groans. I love it when I can hear the struggle in his voice.

Reaching over my shoulder, I hold his face and drag my tongue along his neck, tasting the salt of his skin, the scuff of his beard.

His fingers move faster, and heat rises in my legs. We're frantic with desire, desperate for more of each other, for everything. We chase each other's mouths and skin. He cups my breasts, teasing my hardened nipples as we move.

Desire prickles beneath my skin, tingling every nerve ending. Orgasm races through my blood. His thrusts grow sharper, plunging deep as I break into shudders on his lap. His arm is a band of iron holding me tight, pressing me against him as he comes, as I ride with him higher, lost in a swirl of heat and lust and union.

DEACON'S ARM IS OVER MY WAIST, AND HIS BREATHING IS LOW AND rhythmic. I'm lying on my back, gazing at his beautiful face as the wind moves his thick brown hair across his brow.

A smile curls my lips, and I trace my finger lightly along the sweep of a wave, just above his skin, not touching. I don't want to wake him. My heart beats for him with so much love.

Crawling carefully to the side, I lift the sketchpad and start a new drawing, losing myself in the lines of his forehead, the cut of his cheekbone, the square jaw covered in scruff. My stomach tingles. He's a god in repose, something you would see in a Greek temple or a Roman coliseum.

He's mine.

My eyes heat, and I'm so emotional lately. My love for him has always been strong, but I've never been such a cry baby.

A strange scent floats by on the breeze, an animal, and my throat closes. I'm shocked by my body's sudden revulsion, and jumping to my feet, I barely make it to the half bathroom just inside the patio door before I throw up my small breakfast of toast and coffee.

I flush quickly and step to the sink to put cool water on my face and neck, and I remember being at the hospital, talking to the doctor. Then I remember the next morning with Mateo. I'd chalked it up to stress, but closing my eyes, I filter through the dates...

I've got to know for sure before I say anything, but my chest trembles. My stomach tightens, and my insides squeeze. I'm excited and I'm scared, and I can't breathe. And I'm terrified...

If this is true, I have no idea what happens next.

CHAPTER
Twenty-One

Deacon

THE SKY SPREADS OUT IN FRONT OF US BRILLIANT BLUE AND GOLD. THE sun dips toward the horizon, and it's like fire rolling beneath the clouds. Angel is behind me on the bike, slim arms tight around my waist, and we're flying along the freeway headed up to Mount Cristo Rey.

Placing one hand on top of hers, I give it a squeeze as satisfaction spreads across my stomach. We've spent the last twenty-four hours growing closer than we've ever been, talking about everything, loving each other whenever we want. It's like a little honeymoon...

It's amazing.

And I've decided.

Nothing's stopping us anymore.

Wind pushes against my face, and we rise higher, following the trail up the mountain. As the sun drops lower, we can see the lights of Juarez flickering on to the south. It's crazy how close the two places are.

Reaching the top of the small mountain, I ease off on the gas and we slow. No one else is here, and I park the bike, removing my helmet and reaching for hers. Our eyes meet, and we don't speak. We're in this magical place at this time of day when it feels like anything can happen.

The air is a little cooler at this altitude, and I pull her against my side, wrapping my arm over her shoulders as the breeze swirls around us. Her skirt swirls around her beautiful legs, and I think about those beautiful legs being mine, her beautiful heart belonging to me, her talented mind and caring soul.

We climb the wooden staircase leading up to the enormous cross with the massive statue of Jesus standing in front of it. It's not a crucifixion, as the Christ's hands are facing down, palms spread over the cities as if in blessing or prayer.

I'll take both.

Standing on the crown-shaped platform at the base of the monument, we gaze upwards, absorbing the solemnity of the moment as the sky turns red above us. The air is crisp and dry. Dipping my head, I press my nose to the top of Angel's head and inhale.

Exhaling slowly, it's time.

"I thought it would be easy." My voice is quiet. "I knew people like Winnie would be a problem, but I could handle her. Now we're in a dark place." She tenses, and I tighten my embrace. "I wanted to do this differently, but now I don't want to wait."

Turning to her, I hold her left hand as she looks up at me. "Nothing will change my love for you, Angelica Maria del Carmen." Lowering to one knee, I take the ring I've held since April out of my inside pocket.

"Deacon..." She inhales sharply, pressing her hand to her lips as her eyes heat.

"I want you to be my wife." Looking at her slim hand so delicate in mine, I place the ring on her third finger. "Will you?"

She drops to her knees, her pretty eyes shimmering as she nods quickly. Emotion tightens my stomach. She blinks and two tears fall right before she dives into my embrace, wrapping her arms around my neck.

Clearing the thickness in my throat, I look up at the sky around us, the hands spread over us in blessing. "Don't cry, beautiful. I'm going to make you so happy."

She smiles through tears, her hands on my shoulders. "You already have."

Rocking back on my heels, I pull her to my chest so I can seal our lips together, tongues entwining. She climbs into my lap, pressing her body to mine as our kiss deepens, emotions surge between us.

My mouth moves down to her sternum, and I wrap my arms around her waist, holding her tight against me, listening to her heart beating like wings in her chest. My beautiful angel.

"I saw a movie once…" Her voice is soft, thoughtful at my ear. "This couple couldn't be married by a minister, in front of their families, because of a war… so they said the words three times, and they were married."

"Look at me." I lift my head, and I'm determined, forceful. "I'm going to marry you in front of God and everybody."

A smile creases her face, and she nods, blinking as another tear falls. "I want that too… But I want you to know, I'll marry you right here, even if it's only the two of us promising at Jesus's feet on this mountain in the desert."

Love burns in my chest, and I look up at the monument, at the sky. I like her idea. It's sacred and perfect.

Rising to stand, I help her to her feet. "Three times?"

"Let's say it together."

Holding both her hands in mine, I look directly in her eyes and repeat the words as she says them.

On the third time, I'm sure it's in my mind, but the air seems to still. A final ray of sunlight cuts through the red-orange clouds, and the force of our promise surrounds us, binding us together.

We're changed.

Leaning down, I kiss her again gently. It's a holy kiss, a kiss that defies the hatred and prejudices of our families. A breath apart, our noses touch. We smile and possessive warmth surrounds my heart. We've created something unbreakable.

Returning to the house, her body is pressed against my back like a hot promise of what's to come. Her hands are on my waist, but I feel her fingers fumble with the edge of my shirt, lifting it and tracing the lines across my stomach. Tingles move below my belt, and I lean harder on the throttle.

The wind washes around us, the sky stretches purple and gold as we cover the miles, racing down the mountain road to the city below. Consummation is hot in my blood when we finally arrive at the house.

Pulling up the long driveway, I park at the edge of the porch. We're off the bike, whipping off the helmets and leaving them on the steps as we stumble up them, falling into each other's arms through the doorway.

Our lips fumble for each other's, our hands are everywhere. Hers pull up my shirt. I'm unbuttoning the front of her cotton dress. I lift her, and she holds my neck, fingers threading the back of my hair as we seek out skin, cheeks, mouths.

I want to be gentle, but my jeans catch my ankles, and I stumble, catching us as we fall on the stairs leading to the second floor.

I'm sitting with her on top of me, and I groan. "That's going to leave a mark."

We both laugh, diving into each other again. I'm too hungry to care.

My hands are under her skirt, tearing her thong away. She gasps, clutching my shoulders and pushing me back, dipping her head to pull my dick in her mouth.

"Ohh, fuck." My head drops back with a groan.

She's licking and sucking, and my fingers slide into her hair. My hips rise involuntarily. It feels too good. My eyes squeeze shut as pleasure snakes up my legs. Her head bobs faster, pulling me deeper. My cock hits the back of her throat, and I groan low, shakily. I'm close...

But I don't want to come this way. I want to be inside her, holding her.

Reaching down, I manage to lift her to me. "Come here."

She comes off with a pop and a frown, and I pull her onto my lap. "I want to hold my wife when I fuck her the first time."

"I want to hear my husband groaning my name." Her eyes are hot, and she's so fucking sassy and perfect.

"Don't worry, beautiful. You always blow my mind. Even when we're not having sex."

Her soft breasts are against my chest, and I sink deep into her slippery-hot depths. Our mouths unite, and we move, flowing together, rising higher, finding that place of bliss like we always do.

Exploding through space until we're floating down to Earth again, holding each other close, sharing each other's breath. Sharing everything.

Forever.

"I THINK YOU SHOULD GO BACK TO BETO'S PLACE." IT'S PRE-DAWN, AND Angel's packing for the drive back. She's actually worried about losing time on Winnie's portrait.

"You're joking, right?" She cuts those pretty eyes at me.

"Actually, I'm not. I think it's the best thing—for now."

I passed a restless night, her beautiful body draped over mine, staring into the darkness searching for another way, but the only way forward is not creating a bigger rift than already exists. For now.

"I'm not going back there." Shaking her cute, stubborn head, she places her art supplies in the suitcase, wrapping the pencils and brushes in paper towel and dropping them in a large Ziploc. "Mamá took me away from that life. Now I understand why."

I study the oval diamond ring on her finger. With the rose-gold setting it's beautiful on her elegant hand. "Your brother loves you. His anger is justified. Us living together will only make things worse."

"I'm your wife."

Catching her arm, I pull it to my lips, kissing the soft skin of her wrist. "Not on paper."

"A piece of paper isn't going to change anything."

"At least we'll be legal." Pushing off the bed, I walk around to face her, sliding a curl off her cheek. "I know we're going to wait, but when we do have children, you'll miss your family."

She stiffens, blinking away from my gaze. "Maybe. Maybe not."

Catching her chin, I turn her eyes to mine. "What about Sofia? You love her."

"Don't bring Sofia into this. She's just a little girl."

This plan makes my stomach hurt, but I know it's the right thing to do. If we're ever going to make peace with our families, we have to do this the right way.

"Just try. I'll fix this, and we can plan our wedding."

"Maybe some things can't be fixed."

Leaning closer, I kiss her temple, taking a hit off her sexy scent. "Trust me."

"I want to, but I'm not sure I can anymore." She exhales heavily. "I didn't mention this… Mateo is waiting for you in Plano. With a gun."

"Shit." Stepping back, I rub my forehead. *Waiting for me?* "What does that mean?"

"He said shooting Beto can't go unanswered." She shakes her head. "It's stupid. Beto's going to be okay… I'll make him talk to Mateo. Stop him."

She zips her suitcase closed, and I lift it off the bed, hating the fact she's leaving, hating the idea of her not being with me all the time. Hating the idea a guy's waiting for me with a gun—*what the fuck?*

We walk slowly to her car, and I put the suitcase in the trunk. "Look at me." I catch her arm.

She slams the trunk. "I am looking at you." Her eyes meet mine, and her voice is soft, determined. "I've only ever looked at you. I've only ever trusted you."

Her words hit me straight in the heart. "I said I wouldn't let you down, and I won't. I love you. You're my wife."

Stepping closer, she rests her forehead against my cheek. A moment passes, and her hands go around my waist.

She speaks softly, like we did at the monument, at Jesus's feet. "I love you… I love you… I love you."

Leaning down, I kiss her with all the promises I've made, all the promises I have inside of me waiting to be made. "Now and forever."

Fire burns in my belly to fight for us, to protect what we have. Our world isn't ending, it's only beginning, and I defy anyone who tries to keep us apart. I want to bring this family together, but not at the cost of losing us.

As much as I hate it, maybe some promises can't be kept…

CHAPTER
Twenty-Two

Angel

"I TRUST YOUR FAMILY SITUATION HAS IMPROVED?" WINNIE SITS ON the chaise across from me, a book in her hand, watching me closely.

"Mm…" My brush pauses as I think about her question.

I rushed back to make an appearance at her house today. After Friday, I didn't want her to think I'm lazy or my family life is too sordid for me to continue. Despite what Deacon says, I'm not giving her any reason to doubt or stereotype me.

"The situation has changed."

"And your brother?"

I haven't called Valeria, but Lourdes said Beto would be going home tomorrow. I haven't heard anything about Mateo, which worries me.

"He's better, thank you."

She situates herself on the couch with a grunting noise, and I return to the deep brown and green of the bookcase behind her. I added highlights to her dress, I finished the cat. Now I'm looking at her profile on canvas thinking this woman is my family. *Mi familia.*

My eyes narrow as I consider this new reality.

Before coming here, I stopped at New Hope to transfer my one suitcase to Lourdes's car. We talked on the drive back, and she agreed to let me sleep on her couch for now. She told me everyone has been talking about what happened with Beto, and they've all been speculating over where I was this weekend.

"What the fuuuu...." She almost had a cow when she saw the ring on my finger.

It's beautiful, a peach-oval diamond in a rose gold setting with diamond-baguette daisies on both sides of the band. Smiling, my hand goes to my chest, and I feel it where it hangs on a chain inside my shirt. I was not expecting a ring or a wedding, of promises. I'm engaged... We exchanged vows.

The entire weekend was magical and beautiful.

But as frustrated as I was with him wanting to go back in the closet, I realize looking at the woman sitting across from me, he's right. All the pent-up emotions, the binary thinking—if we moved in together, it would only fuel their hatred.

The base of the bookcase is complete, and I step back. "I'll stop here and let this dry. Tomorrow I can add the spines. If there are any favorite books you'd like me to add, let me know."

Winnie sets her book aside and walks over to inspect my work. I collect my brushes and wipe them down before dipping them in fast-drying saffron oil for the night. I'll give them a more thorough cleaning when I'm finished.

"I like what you've done with this." She circles her finger around the shading on her dress.

"Thank you." I set the brushes aside and pick up my purse, ready to go.

"You're different today." She crosses her arms, studying me.

"Am I?" *She has no idea.*

Her arms drop, and she lets out an irritated huff before going to the door. "I'm glad your family is well. I wouldn't want you to be unable to finish."

"Don't worry. I'll finish."

I'm right behind her at the door, but as soon as I step into the hall, the scent of onion from the kitchen hits my nose, and my throat closes. *Oh, God, no.* Saliva pools in my mouth, and I bite my upper lip until my eyes water. My hand covers my lips, and I pray I make it outside before she stops or decides she needs to tell me one last thing.

Bolting through the door leading from the hallway, I push through the servant's entrance and make it behind the shrub just before I puke the finger sandwich I ate at New Hope before coming here.

"Oh, God." I cough, my eyes flooding with tears.

I don't have cool water or even a cloth to clean my face. Sniffing, I lightly tap the tears from under my eyes and hurry down the driveway towards my waiting car. Lourdes agreed to help me return it to Beto's tonight, but first I have to take care of something on my own.

I'M IN THE WAFFLE HOUSE BATHROOM, SITTING ON THE CLOSED TOILET, staring at a pink plus sign and realizing my life has completely changed.

It's possible I'm in shock, because I don't feel afraid or even anxious. A part of me welcomes this. I'm having Deacon's baby. My stomach fills with butterflies, and my fingers flutter to the ring hanging from my neck. I slip it on, contemplating my next move.

I can't tell Lourdes.

I can't tell anyone until I tell Deacon.

He texted earlier saying he was at the land office with Rich. *I love you. Call me when you're done.*

I'd read his words, but I haven't had a chance to respond. I still have to finish my last errand involving my brother.

Standing, I cap the test and drop it in my purse. Then I throw everything away and wash up quickly before heading to my best friend's house.

"Finally." Lourdes meets me at the door, keys in hand. "I thought I was going to have to drive to the bitch's house and save you."

"You mean the witch's house?"

"How's that bridge over the rainbow going?"

She follows me out to the driveway, and I pause before getting in my ride. "Deacon says she likes me… But I'm not venturing over any rivers any time soon."

"So it's a bridge, but not a very reliable one?"

"Exactly."

It's twilight when we arrive at Beto's mansion. Lourdes's apartment is on the south side of town, near Valeria's house where I spent my teen years. Beto lives in the rich part of town, where nobody knows their neighbors and the yards look like children never play in them.

My stomach tightens as we pull into the driveway, and I want to get out of here as fast as possible.

Leaving the car parked outside the garage, I put the keys in the glove compartment and jog to where Lourdes is waiting. "Let's go."

I'm just about to get in when a strong hand grips me by the arm. "Here you are."

Beto stands behind me, and I twirl away, doing my best to get my arm out of his grasp. "You're home early."

"I don't like hospitals." His hold on my arm loosens, and I can tell he's weak. He seems winded, but he's still angry. "Where have you been?"

"None of your business." My voice is low and cold. "You forfeited that right when you pulled a gun on Deacon."

"I told you never to see him again. I told him never to come here." Dark eyes flash at me. "He was trespassing in my home."

"He was my guest."

"He's not allowed here."

"Which is why I'm moving in with Lourdes."

Beto's jaw clenches, and he leans down to look at my friend through the window. I step between him and the car. "If you have a problem with it, talk to me."

I won't have him menacing my friend.

Straightening, he crosses his arms, looking down at me. "Go to Lourdes. I know where you are."

"Call off Mateo."

His brow lowers. "What does that mean?"

"He's got a gun, and he's hunting Deacon. I want you to make him stop."

My brother huffs a laugh, and his arms drop. He turns and starts up the driveway, but at a slower pace than his usual forceful swagger.

"Beto!" I call after him. "Call off your dog."

"Mateo does what he wants. I have no control over him."

My heart beats faster as I watch him walk away. "If anything happens to Deacon, I'll tell them you were responsible."

Sickness is in my throat. I don't like making such threats against my brother, but I have to keep the father of my baby safe.

He pauses, and without turning, calls to me. "And I'll tell them how I was really shot."

"You came at him with a gun."

"He was a trespasser in my house."

I've been dreaming of my baby, of Deacon's face when I tell him, since I left the Waffle House bathroom, but now I'm afraid. I don't know how to make my brother do what I want.

We're in the car, and Lourdes watches me with wide eyes. "Mateo's after Deacon?"

"Do you know where Mateo lives?"

She shakes her head no. "I met him for the first time after Beto came back. He came with him from Mexico."

My head hurts, and my stomach is churning. I've got to get to a bathroom or I'm going to blow my cover in front of my bestie. Rolling down the window, I let the cool night air caress my forehead, and I wonder where Deacon is right now.

I need to get to him.

CHAPTER
Twenty-Three

Deacon

"T HE OLDEST RECORDS WE HAVE IN THIS BUILDING ONLY GO BACK twenty years." The woman kneels before an open drawer in a long filing cabinet. "My guess is you need something older than that."

She's skinny, and her stringy, light-blonde hair is twisted in a little knot at the back of her head with a pencil stuck in it. She looks up at us through metal-rimmed glasses. I watch with frustration as her fingers crawl along the manila folders, occasionally pausing to open one.

"I'm actually surprised these are still here." She lifts out another folder then drops it back. "The county gets rid of the old records on a yearly basis."

"Gets rid of?" Rich takes a step forward. "What does that mean? Shreds?"

"They're considered historical record, so they're not shredded. They might as well be." She straightens with an exhale. "They store everything in a warehouse off Tenth Street. It's old, deteriorating. Rat-infested."

Rich grimaces at me, but I'm excited.

I give him a nod, and he rubs his hand through his shaggy blond hair. He's dressed in jeans and a polo shirt today, which means he hasn't been in the office. I'm in jeans and a dark tee, and I'm not going anywhere until we get some answers.

"Would it be possible for us to go there and look around?" His tone is far more relaxed than mine would be.

The woman stands with a grunt, pushing the heavy file drawer closed. "You've got to have a license to poke around in there, or permission from court."

We follow her back to the front of the building.

I can't stand it anymore. "Aren't those covered by Freedom of Information?"

"Some are. Some files are not. In the warehouse, they're all together, and nobody's there to make sure you're not poking around in other people's business."

Rich exhales a laugh, leaning on his elbow on the front counter. "Aw, come on, Mary. You've known me long enough to trust me with other people's business."

She cocks her hip to the side and squints an eye first at me, then at him. "I wouldn't go that far, but here's what I'll do."

Pulling the pencil out of the knot at the back of her head, she reaches under the counter and takes out a small pad of forms. I watch her write tomorrow's date, sign it and rip it off.

"This will get you inside for one day." She holds it up towards Rich. "If you get caught with your nose where it's not supposed to be, I'm going to deny ever giving it to you."

"You just cost me three months of favors." We're out in the car, and Rich hands the pass over to me.

"It looks like a hall pass."

"You'd better decide what you're looking for, because you've got one day."

Up to this point, I wasn't sure what I was looking for. "If the timelines add up, the swindle would've occurred sixty-five years ago."

I'm thinking about the secret baby, the murder allegation... I'm sure it all happened around the same time.

"But you're going to need proof the land ever belonged to Manuel Treviño, which means—"

"I'm going to have to go further back than that." How far is the question.

"Needle in a haystack."

"Maybe not." If I calculate how old my grandfather would've been when he was able to start buying land, I can guess his then-best friend would've been doing the same.

"I'm sorry, I can't join you tomorrow. I'm meeting with the guys about the El Paso work all day."

I admit, I'm disappointed. I could use some help if this warehouse is as massive as it sounds, but I'm not giving up. "No way, man. You've helped me a lot. I appreciate it."

He parallel parks outside the entrance to the Foster Building, and I give him a firm shake before getting out. "Thanks for this weekend."

"No problem." He winks. "I hope you made the most of it."

I lean back before closing the door. "She said yes."

"Yeah, she did!" He slaps my palm before shaking my hand. "Congrats. Now we're getting somewhere. Now I understand why this is all so urgent."

"It's her family." I rub a hand over my jaw. "She says she doesn't care, but she will. If this is what it takes to make peace, I'm going to find it, and I'm going to fix it."

"Captain America."

"Ah." I push him away. I don't have time for his sarcasm.

"I'm serious. What's that saying about fortune helping the pure in heart?"

"I think you made that up."

He laughs. "Well, it sounds good. I believe in you."

"Thanks."

"Let me know if I can help."

We say goodnight, and I'm across the sidewalk, pushing through the front doors as he pulls away. Waiting in the empty, glass-walled lobby for the elevator to descend, I fish my phone out of my pocket and shoot a quick text to Angel.

How's the couch? Not too late if you want to come over…

My chest tightens. I can't think of anything I'd love more than to curl up with my girl and sleep tonight. Among other things…

The hairs on the back of my neck rise as a shadow moves in the small sitting area across from the elevator. Angel's warning about Mateo is on my mind, and I fall back, looking around quickly for anything I might use as a weapon.

My adrenaline kicks up, and I'm raising my fists when the streetlight falls across her face. "I made up an excuse to slip out."

"Angel." We rush together.

I wrap her in my arms, and warmth surrounds my heart as the stress of this day melts away. The elevator dings, and we step inside, rising quickly to the penthouse suite. We're across the foyer and into my room as we're finishing our first sentences.

"I missed you so much." I kiss the top of her head.

"I thought about you all day. How was your drive back?"

"Long. I wondered why I didn't just follow you this morning."

"You had to lock up the house, make sure we didn't leave anything on."

Inside my apartment, I lead her to the kitchen. "Wine?"

She climbs onto a barstool, hesitating before shaking her head no. "I'll pass tonight."

For a minute, it feels like she wants to tell me something, but she doesn't. "How was my aunt? Bitter as ever?"

"Actually, she was nicer than usual."

"Good." I go to the refrigerator and pull open the door, taking out cheese and milk and eggs. "She'd better treat you like a queen."

"I'm not royalty." She says the words softly, like she's remembering something.

"Feel like dinner? Signature mac and cheese a'la Angelica?"

A smile breaks across her pretty face. "Sounds perfect. Although… I think I'll have it your way tonight."

"You're kidding?" Holding the door open, I motion to the plastic bags of peppers and onions. "I stocked up."

"Oh, no!" She laughs, putting her hands over her face. "I've kind of been having… heartburn lately."

Frowning, I fill the quart saucepan with water and put it on a high flame. "I'm sorry. I might have Tums in the hall closet. No promises."

"It's okay, I have some."

Her voice is so soft, and she seems so distracted. While I wait for the water to boil, I walk around the bar to where she's sitting and wrap her in my arms. "What's going on? Did something happen today?"

Nestling her cheek against my chest, she exhales softly. "I brought the car back to Beto. He's home. He came outside and confronted me."

"I wish I'd have been there."

"No." She shakes her head, and I step back, meeting her eyes. "He wouldn't call off Mateo. He wouldn't back down from any of it. I'm so mad at him."

It's a sad, soft lament, and I lift her hand, kissing her fingers before stopping cold. "You're not wearing your ring?"

"I am." She reaches around her neck, tugging on a silver chain and pulling the diamond out of her shirt. "I thought it was better if I kept it hidden until we're ready."

She slips it on her finger, and I give it a kiss before going to where the water is boiling. I drop the noodles in and start the cheese sauce.

"Tomorrow I'm going to this warehouse where they store a bunch of old records."

Her eyes are round as she watches me. "You think you've found something?"

"I think it's going to be like the end of *Raiders of the Lost Ark*." Stirring the cheese mixture, I take the boiling pasta off the stove and transfer it to a pan, pouring the creamy sauce on it and covering it all with shredded mozzarella and parmesan.

"I wish I could help you." She sits on the stool watching, her pretty face on her hand, her diamond gleaming in the lights.

"You keep doing what you're doing with Winnie. I'm working on this."

Once dinner is in the oven, I set a timer and circle the bar to where she's sitting. Her hands are on my waist, and she looks up at me. "I was thinking today how Winnie is my family now, too."

"I like hearing you say that." Using my thumb, I slide a curl away from her eyes. "I know we've got a little ways to go, but we're going to win this."

"Is it a race? Or a war."

Thinking about the question, I don't like either of those options. "It's a test."

CHAPTER
Twenty-Four

Angel

DEACON'S BLAND SIGNATURE DISH IS ACTUALLY THE PERFECT COMFORT food for my sensitive stomach. We curl up on the couch, bowls in hand and while he has a glass of dry white wine, I stick to carbonated water.

He's holding a linen envelope from the stack of mail he sorted before we sat down. "The Cattleman's Masque is this weekend."

"What's that?" Taking another bite, I snuggle deeper into his overstuffed leather couch.

While he finished cooking, I changed into one of his sweatshirts and a pair of boxer shorts and thick socks. I'm surrounded by fresh linen, citrus, and yummy Deacon scent.

"It's this big, annual fundraiser every year at the Palace Casino." He takes out an elegantly engraved invitation with script writing, tissue, and double envelopes.

"The Palace?" I scoot up higher on the couch, taking it from him and reading the formal invitation. "I don't know how to gamble."

"It doesn't matter. It's just a bunch of people with too much money standing around gossiping." He takes a bite of dinner. "They'll gamble and raise all the money."

"What for?"

He shrugs, setting his bowl aside and takes a sip of wine. "One year it was Keeping Texas Wild... I think they stole that from Austin's stay weird campaign. Another year it was to protect the Mustangs or their habitat—"

"Oh! I love that one!" Sitting higher, I think about *Spirit*. "What's this year's?"

"Does it say on the invitation?"

Turning the paper in my hand, "I don't see anything."

"Winnie would know." He reaches for me, pulling me onto his lap. "I told her I was bringing a date this year."

He smiles up at me, and I put my hands on his neck, leaning down to kiss his soft lips. "Who were you planning to ask?"

"I had this one girl in mind." He kisses my neck, and I close my eyes, loving the feel of him strong in my arms. Loving the heat he stirs in me with his mouth. "She's really pretty. She's actually my wife... In a way."

Leaning back, my stomach squeezes when I catch his mischievous blue eyes. "I thought you were a single guy."

"No way." He kisses me again. "I'm married to the most beautiful girl you've ever seen."

"You don't say."

Scooping his hands under my butt, he stands in one fluid movement, carrying me to his bedroom. "I do say." He tosses me on the bed, and I laugh as I barely bounce on the firm mattress. "What's the word, beautiful? Go with me as my date to this snooty function where all of my aunt's friends will be there showing off?"

"Wait... All of Winnie's friends will be there?" My stomach twists, and I feel scared and a little anxious. "Are you sure—"

"I'm positive." He leans across the bed, resting his fists on the mattress on either side of me. "I'm going to show you off—and who knows, I might have solved your family's problem by then, too."

"What will I wear?"

With a quick kiss, he straightens. "I'll give you my card and you can get whatever you want from Nieman's. Ask one of the clerks to help you. It's formal, so go all out."

"I… don't know…" My voice trails off as he pulls off his tee, revealing his bare, lined torso. I fall back against the pillows, admiring the sight of my gorgeous future husband… current husband?

"Don't know what? Don't know if you'll go? You're going."

Clearing my throat, I collect my thoughts. "I've never had a clerk help me. It sounds expensive. I don't know about spending your money—"

"You're my wife." His dark brow lowers, and he leans down to pull off his jeans. "I want you to have a beautiful dress and go with me to this damn party. It'll be the first year I enjoy it."

He straightens, facing me in nothing but boxer briefs, and my breath disappears. "Okay…"

"You know, when you look at me that way, I can only think of one thing I want to do to you."

Little wings flutter inside my stomach, and I slide lower in the bed. "What's that?"

"Here." He climbs over me, strong arms on either side of my head as he lowers his body over mine. "Let me show you."

STANDING IN FRONT OF WINNIE'S PORTRAIT, SO MANY THOUGHTS SWIRL IN my head. I had planned to tell Deacon about the baby after dinner last night. It's why I went to his apartment building… Also, because I was worried about Mateo.

Then he started talking about the masquerade this weekend

and dresses and formalwear. It's a celebration, and I imagined getting home after, everything quiet as I tell him the happy news, and us celebrating. Maybe with sparkling grape juice and a card, something memorable.

Then he started undressing, and I kind of forgot everything else. My lips curl with a smile as I think about his sexy body. I did some more work on his portrait while we were in El Paso, surrounding his torso in bright blue and shading it with orange... It's different from my usual work, but it's an appropriate evolution. My life is changing.

I remember his proposal, my tears. *I'm going to make you so happy...*

"Looks like you'll be done this week." Winnie's voice pulls me out of my daydreams.

"I think I will." Stepping back, I inspect her likeness, surrounded by all these rich things she loves, with the indifferent cat in her lap.

"I brought you this as a partial payment." She holds out a thick brown envelope, and I realize it's more cash.

"You don't owe me any payment—"

"I am well aware of that. However, you're clearly on track to finish, and I obviously like what you've done." Her tone is clipped, and she glances briefly at my waist. "I thought you might need the money now."

"I don't know why I would need an early payment... But if you're offering, I'll accept it." *Don't look a gift horse in the mouth.*

Her lips press and she nods sharply. "Not that it's any of my business, but if you need a doctor... I know one who can help you."

For a split second, I'm confused. *Does she mean for my brother?* "I'm sorry, I don't understand—"

"Enrique found vomit in the flower bed this morning. You ran out so suddenly last night... I simply put two and two together."

She lifts her chin in a self-righteous manner, and my jaw clenches. *Of all the stereotypical…*

"You assumed I was pregnant."

Her eyebrow arches. "Are you not?"

My cheeks burn hot, and while I'm excited and happy about the baby, I'm pissed I can't rub it in her face—that it's Deacon's, that we're engaged, or that we're kind of even married… in a way.

"That's what I thought. You might think me unkind, but I've seen many promising careers cut short by unexpected… arrivals. I'd hate for that to happen to someone as talented as you."

"Nothing is being cut short." Snatching the envelope out of her hand, I stuff it in my purse. "You can keep your doctor's referral."

"I wasn't trying to offend you. I simply wanted to help."

"I don't need your help. With all due respect, mind your own business."

Turning to the canvas, I pick up my brush and hold it a minute while I calm my breathing. I imagine telling her the father is her dear, precious nephew… Who I happen to be madly in love with. Instead, I swallow my annoyance and focus on finishing this job.

"Well, I'm sorry if I offended you."

I don't answer, and she quietly leaves the room.

CHAPTER
Twenty-Five

Deacon

S TANDING IN THE CENTER OF THE COUNTY WAREHOUSE BUILDING, I'M surrounded by boxes stretching to the back wall and stacked to the ceiling. It's not as big as Hangar 51, but it's just as daunting.

The guard left me at the door to figure out the order, if there is any.

Stopping at the closest box, I open the lid and look inside. Manila folders are mixed with brown envelopes in stacks that look like someone emptied file drawers into boxes and taped them shut.

If that's the case, these boxes have to hold years. Scanning the documents, I find the year 1968 on this one. Too early.

Shoving it back in the pile, I dig a little deeper and pull out another folder, opening it. *Yes...* The date is also 1968. I pull out a black marker I shoved in my jeans just in case and mark this box 68.

Going down a few rows, I pull up at what I hope gets me back ten years. Lifting the box off the stack, I open it and repeat the process. My stomach is tight, and I realize I'm holding my breath when I read the date 1975.

"Shit." I swear out loud.

"Ready to give up?" The female voice calls to me from the front of the room.

Using the marker, I write *75* on this one and go back to where I started. "Not yet." Once I'm back at the original box, I walk forward what I hope is ten years.

"There's supposed to be an order to this madness, but I think everyone stopped caring in the 80s." Mary lifts the lid on the box closest to her and waves a hand in front of her face, coughing. "So much dust. Think you need a mask?"

"I'm not allergic." And I'm in a hurry. The longer this needle hides in the haystack, the longer it takes to mend our bridges.

"This one's 1971. What year are you after?" She drops the lid and looks around the large room.

"I'm guessing the second half of the 1940s."

Mary's brown eyes widen. "You don't know the year?"

Exhaling deeply, I look down. "My grandfather would've been buying property up to 1950. If he went in with someone it could be as early as 1945."

She passes me, heading toward the back of the room. "Those are going to be some of the first records put here. Older stuff is usually claimed by the historical society."

My stomach tightens, and I feel a little encouraged as I follow her to the back of the room. "You think you can find it?"

"No, but maybe we can isolate the location." She pulls the lid off a box and lifts out an envelope.

It's paper-thin and yellowed. "Now we're getting somewhere."

"Let me see."

She turns it to me and smiles. "Fifty-two."

"Here." I take the marker and put a 52 on the outside of the box.

"These numbers are supposed to do what you just did." She runs her finger along a barcode printed on a sticker on the side of the box.

It has a mixture of letters and numbers I can't decipher. "Do you know what they mean?"

Her lips press into a frown, and she shakes her head. "I wouldn't even know where to start looking for a scanner for it."

"At least I'm getting warmer." I go to the next box and lift the lid, digging deep into the contents.

I make a note 50 and go five rows down. Mary continues searching row by row, closing boxes and helping me note them.

"I've got it!" Holding the folder up, I open it to show the year is 1945. "Now let's see what this is."

She hustles up to me, and we try to read the narrow, ancient script. "It's almost like a straight line," she whispers.

At the top is a triangular drawing with measurements marked out.

"Find the name." We scan the page reading closer until we hit it.

"Hathaway." Mary shakes her head and returns the documents to the folder. "You're going to have to go through every one of these."

We both assess the size of the box, and I look at my watch. "I've got six hours."

"You've got serious determination."

"I've got reasons." Putting the box on the floor, I take a seat, ready to spend as much time as I have searching.

"What's the name we're after?" She opens the next box and pulls out a folder.

"Treviño. Dring is good, but I'm really looking for either a combination of Dring and Treviño or just Treviño."

Her brow furrows. "Mexican?"

"American."

Her chin lifts and she opens the top folder, running her finger down the page. "Partnerships complicate things. They didn't always keep the most complete records for such situations. Any chance you know the DBA?"

"As far as I know, they were 'doing business as' themselves."

We search in silence, moving boxes aside as we finish going through them. We move on to 1946, page after page, until I'm better at recognizing birth records from death records from marriage licenses from land ownership.

My eyes are starting to cross. It's way past lunch, and my stomach is growling. I'm up to 1948 when Mary freezes, scrambling to her feet with a yellowed document in her hand.

"What was that name again? Treviño?"

I'm on my feet just as fast, meeting her where she left the box. "Manuel Treviño."

She stops, and I lean down to look closer. A map is drawn at the top of the page, and I feel my heart beating faster as I recognize what I know is my family's land leading up to Oklahoma.

"This is it." I take the fragile sheet of paper from her, holding it carefully, reading the dates, the agreement to purchase, the smaller section drawn out as his—although in reality, it's not that small.

"I don't want to be a wet blanket, but this only shows they owned it at one time a long time ago." Our eyes meet, and she's frowning slightly. "Anything could have happened after this. He could have sold it, lost it in some financial downturn…"

"He didn't." I feel more certain of it than anything.

"Still, you can't prove he didn't."

I'm less worried about that aspect of the story. What I needed most is right here, proof the family's claim is real. I have a good idea where I can find the rest of the story, and it's in that ancient old house where Winnie lives.

"Can I have this?"

Mary winces and slowly shakes her head no. "I'm sorry, Deacon. As far as we know, that's the only copy left."

"Moldering here with the rats in an old warehouse where no one even knows it's located?"

"Pretty much." She's apologetic, and I consider what might happen if I bolt. "Is there a copy machine here?"

Two hours later, I'm back at Winnie's with the original land deed and a copy in my breast pocket, hoping to catch Angel before she leaves.

No luck.

"Deacon! What a pleasant surprise." My aunt meets me in the foyer with her arms wide, pulling me in for a hug. "The masque is this weekend, so we can't do our usual dinner date. Would you like to have dinner tonight?"

Glancing at my watch, I see it's after six. "Wow, no."

She huffs a laugh. "Don't give it a second thought."

"Sorry, I didn't realize how late it is. I was just hoping I could poke around in the attic a minute."

"The attic?" She pulls her head back frowning. "It's so hot... and really, what on Earth—"

"I'll just be a minute." Sprinting up the massive wooden staircase, I climb one more and go to the back hall away from the bedrooms where the rectangular door is overhead.

Stepping back, I open it and lower the wooden ladder before charging into the stifling heat. A naked bulb is perched on a beam in the open space. It's a framework of two by fours and insulation, and it's hot as hell. It smells like old paper and dried goods.

Carefully, I step on a thin plank covering the wood frame of the ceiling.

"Deacon?" My aunt calls from below. "What are you looking for?"

Straightening, I look across the massive space with boxes arranged in every nook and cranny. *Wasn't I just here?* Fatigue hits me like a hammer. I don't need a permit to search this house. I can come back tomorrow, after I've rested.

Returning to the ladder, I slowly climb down, wiping the sweat off my brow with my sleeve and folding the wooden ladder into the door before lifting it shut.

"My goodness what a mess." Winnie waves a hand in front of her face. "What's come over you?"

"I was thinking about Grandma Kim... your mom."

"I know who Grandma Kim was. Why are you so fixated on her all of a sudden?"

"You said her things were in the attic—"

"Perhaps not all of them, thankfully. Do you have any idea how hot it gets up there in the summertime?"

"I can imagine." Rubbing my hand over my mouth, I realize how much of her stuff is probably lost. "Did she keep a diary or anything that you know of?"

"I don't know, Deacon." Winnie starts up the hall, waving a hand over her head. "If you're not staying for dinner, you'll have to excuse me. I'm hungry."

"Okay." I jog to catch up with her, giving her a sweaty hug, which makes her holler. "If you think of anything let me know. See you Friday."

"Brute." She follows me down to the door, and I catch a warm smile on her cheeks. "You're still bringing this mystery date?"

"Yep." *My beautiful wife.*

"I can't wait."

CHAPTER
Twenty-Six

Angel

"**D**ESCRIBE YOUR PHILOSOPHY OF ART." I'M SITTING ON DEACON'S lap in front of his giant desktop computer filling out the Arthaus application.

It's been a week and no sign of Mateo. Every night we've slept in Deacon's penthouse apartment, with the doorman guarding us below and layers of security between us and the street.

My main worry tonight is making this deadline. "Oh, man... I don't know."

"Yes, you do." He nudges me in the side. "You told me all about it in El Paso."

"I did?"

"You did, and it was passionate and moving."

"You're thinking of something else." I look over my shoulder and give him a sly wink.

"No distractions. You have to get this in tonight."

"Okay... ugh... I hate when they make me write." Scrubbing

my fingers on my forehead, I try to put the words together, but it feels like a jumble. "Why can't I just paint my philosophy?"

Again, I'm dressed in his boxer shorts and sweatshirt, belly full of mac and cheese. I was finally able to show him *Spirit* in real life, which he insisted on hanging on his living room wall.

The portrait I painted of him is in the bedroom.

"Here." He puts his hands around me on the keyboard. "Tell me your philosophy, and I'll type it."

Turning my face, I kiss his cheek. "Let me stand up and walk."

For the next several minutes I talk through my feelings about art. "It gives me a voice… I find ways of expressing myself in color and shape that I'm not able to do with my mouth and hands… It's a way of touching people, making them think, making them change their way of thinking… Art can take the mundane and make it magical."

Deacon's fingers fly over the keys, and I wrinkle my nose. "Does that sound dumb?"

"Not at all." His eyes are fixed on the screen, and he's typing quickly, finishing with a sharp little tap. "You sound like someone I'd give a twenty-thousand-dollar scholarship."

Leaning down, I kiss his lips. "It's a residency."

"I'd give it to you."

"You're biased." Sitting on his lap again, I cross my legs and read the words he's written, and my chest tightens. "You made me sound really good."

He kisses my cheek, right beside my ear. "I just wrote what you said."

I spend the next several minutes uploading my photos of *Spirit*, of Winnie's portrait, of Deacon's portrait, and a few sunsets and figure drawings. My final is the sketch I did of him while he slept.

"Hey, I've never seen that one."

"I did it while you were sleeping." I hold my finger over the mouse, hesitating as my stomach trembles before clicking submit.

Exhaling heavily, I turn in Deacon's lap and put my arms around his neck, burying my face in his shoulder. "I did it."

"You did it." He scoops me under the butt, carrying me to the bedroom. "Now it's time to get some rest. I have to be in the office all day tomorrow, then I've got to follow up with Winnie about my grandmother."

"I can't believe you found that old deed." He showed me the yellowed paper with my grandfather's signature on it over dinner.

Carefully touching the signature, I tried to imagine the man who held onto his land, who made an agreement with his best friend to carve out a section for his family, and who according to my brother had it stolen away.

"You think it's all connected?" Lying on my side in the bed, I wait as Deacon climbs in beside me in only his boxer briefs.

"I think it's very possible my grandfather found out what happened and set out to destroy the man who stole his wife." He reaches for me, and I turn, spooning my back against his firm chest. "I think I can understand his motivation."

Deacon's nose is in the back of my hair, and I thread our fingers. "Didn't you say your grandfather was gone all the time, leaving her alone with a five-year-old?"

"That's what her letter said." His voice grows sleepy.

"I think you know better than to do something like that." Threading our fingers, I place our hands over my stomach, thinking about the little life growing there.

Closing my eyes, I drift to sleep on a dream of us in the desert, in the shadow of the Sierra Madre mountains, our baby in my arms.

"Don't look at the price tag." Lourdes sits across from me in the plush dressing room at Nieman's.

"I can't help it," I whisper, dropping the small white square hanging from the sleeve. "And that's on *sale!*"

I'm standing in front of a gold-framed, full-length mirror in a deep red gown with a plunging V in the front and a high slit up the leg. It's tight over my waist and stomach, and I can't help thinking it might be my last time for a dress like this for a while.

"This dressing room is the size of my bedroom." Lourdes leans forward. "I can't believe they just let us back here."

"Deacon called first." I turn to the side, looking down my back. "I think I like the black one better."

"Which one? You tried on three."

"The one with the silver belt."

"Ohh... yes. Super elegant."

"Have you made your choice, Mrs. Dring?" My heart stops at her words, and Lourdes inhales a quiet hiss.

Pride, embarrassment, a little smug happiness warms my chest. I feel my cheeks warm, and I can't help a smile. "Yes, I like this one."

I motion to the floor-length black dress with the high slit on the leg.

"Ah, yes. The Carolina Herrera. Would you be needing shoes to complete the look?"

Lourdes and I exchange a glance, and she raises her brows like she does this all the time. "She'll need some black heels, yes."

"I'll have our recommendations sent over from the shoe department. Do you know your size?"

Clearing my throat, I manage to answer. "Seven and a half narrow."

"Very good."

The elegant older woman leaves the dressing room, and as soon as the door closes, we explode into whispers.

"Mrs. Dring?" Lourdes leans forward.

"I am wearing my engagement ring..." Holding out my

hand, I admire how the peach stone sparkles like a drop of fire on my hand in this light.

"Yeah, but no wedding band."

"Maybe I left it at home?"

"I would never know. You haven't slept on my couch once since you supposedly moved in with me."

We straighten up in time for my fitting and finishing up my purchases for the party. The clerk helps me select a feathered mask to compliment the dress with sequins and silver accents. Then she offers to have it all shipped to Deacon's penthouse, so I don't have to carry heavy bags. I had no idea stores even did stuff like that.

"Longest shopping trip ever!" I cry as the wind pushes my hair around my head through the open windows.

I've got my feet on the dash and the music is blasting J'Lo's "On the Floor." Lourdes and I sing the Na-Na part at the top of our lungs. I'm trying to remember the last time I felt so happy and free.

"Oh, no." My bestie turns the music down as we pull into her driveway, and I recognize Valeria's Honda.

My happy-free feeling dims. "Why are you saying that?"

"She's been calling for you."

"Why didn't you tell me?" Sitting up quickly, I trace my fingers through my wild hair, pulling it into a scrunchie.

"I kept forgetting."

I'm not sure why we're whispering. We're both grown women. Lourdes puts the car in park, and we go into the house together.

"Carmie!" Sofia's little voice echoes through the house. "I've missed you!"

She runs straight to me, and I swing her up on my hip, hugging her as she squeezes my neck with all her four-year-old strength.

"Oh!" I grunt playfully. "I missed you, too!"

She sits back on my arm. "I started camp on Monday and we went to the museum, and I saw some arts, and I told Mamma none of them were as good as yours. And Mamma said we needed to come see you to see your art, and I said I wanted to see you because I didn't want you to go to Ursula after Uncle Beto broke all your stuff—"

"My goodness, Soph!" Lourdes cries. "Take a breath."

I'm smiling so much my cheeks hurt, listening to all her words with big eyes. "You've been a busy little lady!"

"Come here." Valeria pulls me and her littlest daughter into a hug. "I haven't seen you in so long. Not since the accident. Where have you been?"

"Working… here…" I'm stalling.

"Lourdes said Juliana took over at the coffee shop for you."

"You know I've been working on that portrait." My hand rubs circles on Sofia's little back as she puts her head on my shoulder.

I notice Lourdes's eyes widen, but it's too late. Valeria catches my hand, pulling it to her face. "What is this?"

"Ahh… Haha…" I force a fake laugh. There's no getting out of this one. "It's ahh—"

"It's an engagement ring." My cousin's eyes narrow, and her lips press together. "You're engaged, and you didn't bother to tell your family? See what this boy is doing to you?"

Sofia's head pops up. "I want to see your ring."

I move my hand around to show her while keeping my eyes on my cousin. "It just happened a few days ago."

I'm hesitant to say it was over the weekend. I know exactly where that will lead—to her pointing out I was getting engaged while my brother was in the hospital. Instead, I state the obvious.

"If my family acted a little more civilized, I'd be more excited to tell you these things."

"You're really going to marry that boy?"

"Deacon is a man, and yes. I'm really going to marry him." Sofia slides down my waist and trots to the small living room and turns on the television.

Valeria catches my arm and pulls me towards the door. "Come with me."

We go outside, and my arms cross automatically. Valeria looks at me and shakes her head. "Don't be like that."

"I've said all I have to say about this."

"You're acting like Lola."

"I'm not acting like Lola. I didn't come to your house looking for a reason to criticize you, yet here you are."

She exhales heavily and rubs her forehead. "You need to go back to Beto's. He needs you."

"That's not going to happen."

"Why?" She extends her hand, then slaps it down against her thigh. "Why are you doing this to your brother? He's weak. He's been shot—"

"For his own actions." I can't listen to her defend my brother anymore. "Where's Mateo?"

"Mateo?" Her brow furrows. "Why do you care where he is?"

"He has a gun, and he told me he's looking for Deacon."

"A gun?" Valeria shakes her head dismissively. "Boys get heated up during fights. I'm sure he's cooled off by now."

"How well do you know him?"

She shrugs, walking towards the house. "He came here with Beto. I don't know him very well."

"Then you can't say he's cooled off." I step forward pointing my finger. "You say my behavior causes problems. He's the problem."

Her lips part like she's about to say more, but I'm not interested in more. I've got my phone out, and I'm calling a Lyft to take me downtown to Deacon. I can't stand here and listen to any more of this ignorance.

The app is ticking, and I'm not looking at her. Still, she speaks quietly. "You're a beautiful artist, Carmelita. You're like your mother. Your family misses you. We want you with us. We love you, Carm."

Her words hurt, but I'm not letting her pull me into her web. My phone dings, and the black Ford Escort is here. I don't say goodbye as I step inside.

CHAPTER
Twenty-Seven

Deacon

S TEPPING INTO THE TWINKLE-LIT FOYER OF THE PALACE CASINO, I CAN'T help tugging at the neck of my tuxedo. I hate shit like this.

Angel wanted us to meet here. She wanted to surprise me. I huff a laugh and shake my head, going to the bar and ordering a scotch neat.

"Deacon!" Aunt Winnie comes up to me and puts her arm on my shoulder. "What are you doing here alone? Haven and I are just dying to meet this mystery date of yours."

"Hi, Ms. Wells." I step forward to kiss Rich's mother's cheek. "Where's Rich?"

"Oh, you know Rich." She shakes her white-blonde hair. "He does whatever the hell he wants."

"It's true." As entrenched as she is in Plano society, Rich's mother was changed by their brief foray into white poverty.

It made her a more decent human being than most of my aunt's friends. Most of them are bored old biddies with too much money waiting for the next scandal.

"I'll be sure to find you when my date arrives." I can't wait to see her face when she realizes her gifted artist is my fiancée.

"You do that." Winnie kisses my cheek. "Cecilia and I have been taking bets."

My eyebrow arches. "On what?"

"Blonde or brunette, darling." She waves her hand as if I'm being ridiculous. "What else?"

I'm not even going to answer that one. I take a hit of my scotch and watch as couples file through the double glass doors at the bottom of the stairs. I'm just slipping on my felt mask when I see her. My mouth goes dry, and the blood races below my belt.

Her eyes are downcast, watching her feet as she climbs the marble staircase in a floor-length, long-sleeved black dress that flows in silky waves around her slender, hourglass figure. She's surrounded by couples—men in tuxedos and women in evening gowns—but they all fade to black and white as she rises higher.

A smooth, tanned leg appears through the thigh-high slit in the front of her dress, and the neckline dips daringly low, showing off the soft peaks of her breasts. Her hair is parted in the middle and sleek in a bun at the base of her neck, and a silver belt accentuates her small waist.

Even with a black feathered mask covering her beautiful face, I'd know her anywhere. I'm off my seat closing the space between us as she reaches the top step.

"You are so beautiful." I take her hand, pulling her close to my chest. "Remind me to send a thank you to the sales clerks at Nieman's."

Amber eyes behind the elegant mask blink up at me, and a hint of a grin teases her full, berry-stained lips. "Do I know you?"

"Probably not." I lift her fingers to my lips and kiss them, gratified to see my engagement ring perched on her finger. "I'm a party crasher, here to steal your heart."

"You'll have to excuse me." She lifts her chin to speak near my ear. "I'm meeting my husband."

The warmth of her breath, the tickle of her lips causes the muscles around my cock to tighten.

"Husband?" I pretend to disapprove. "You're much too young and beautiful to be married."

"Oh, no. I'm very happily married."

"Well, he's a very lucky man."

She blinks up at me. "You're wrong. I'm the lucky one."

Leaning closer, I study her full lips. "I really want to kiss you right now."

"Maybe we can step out on the balcony where no one will see."

"I suppose we ought to make an appearance before I smear your lipstick." Pulling her hand into the crook of my arm, we enter the main casino.

For the fundraiser, the roulette wheels and blackjack tables have been moved to the perimeter, leaving a large, open dance floor. A gold-embroidered banner encouraging us to "Feed Texas" spans the top of a stage where a brass band plays standards.

Walking to the floor, I pull her into my arms and slow dance to "Irreplaceable You." She feels so good. She's the only thing that matters to me. I kiss her lightly on the forehead. Her eyes close, and the pull between us is so intense. I close my eyes, and it's just us…

Until the song ends.

The band cranks up a fast-paced ska-type song I don't recognize, and my hand slides down to Angel's. Our fingers thread, and I lead her off the floor—straight to Winnie. She's holding a white mask on a stick in front of her eyes. It has yellow feathers to match her yellow silk evening gown. Cecilia Westbrook is in a cornflower blue dress with an elaborate feathered mask attached to her face.

They're cats ready to pounce.

"Deacon, my dear." She smiles, holding out a hand to Angel. "And who might this be."

My hand is on Angel's waist, and I feel her body stiffen. I slide my arm around her, pulling her closer. "Winnie, let me present Angelica Maria del Carmen Treviño. Angel, this is my aunt Winona Clarke."

The mask moves from in front of my aunt's face midway through my introduction, and I watch her gleeful smile morph into something between shock and horror.

"Did you say…" Her voice is drowned out by Cecilia's loud voice.

"Why, he's dating a little brown girl!" My aunt's bestie gives me a smug look. "How open-minded of you, dear."

My reply is sharp. "She's not a girl, she's a woman, and—"

"Deacon." Winnie grasps my arm. "May I see you outside for a second?"

She gestures with her mask in the direction of the French doors spaced along the outer walls. They lead to a large patio area overlooking a man-made lake.

"Of course. Angel and I would love to speak to you outside."

"No…" She shakes her head. "I meant *alone.*"

"You can say whatever you need to say to the both of us." My tone is final.

"Yes, Winnie." Cecilia is enjoying this in a way that's pissing me off. "What do you need to say?"

"If you don't mind, this is a family matter." My aunt clutches my arm, attempting to pull me away from the group.

My grip tightens on Angel's hand. "Angel will be family soon. I asked her to marry me."

Winnie's face pales, and she blinks from Angel to me. "She's a Treviño."

It's not what I expected her to say. I thought she recognized

Angel from painting her portrait day after day, but clearly spending two weeks with her didn't warrant a memory.

Angel hasn't spoken since this entire confrontation began, and I check her expression. It's hard to read behind the mask.

"Yes. Angelica Treviño. You know her as Angela Carmen." Angel's hand tightens in mine, but I know she finished the portrait today. I know my aunt paid her, and if she hadn't, I was fully prepared to ensure she honored her commitment.

I'm so proud of my girl.

Winnie drops her mask altogether. I make a move to catch it, but I see it's attached to her wrist by a loop. "You're Angela…" She points at Angel before turning fiery eyes on me. "You knew this whole time?"

I catch her pointed finger in my fist. "Whatever you're about to say, I'd advise you to stop right now and rethink it."

Her chest rises and falls fast, but she presses her lips together in a tight line.

Angel's cheeks flush, and she leans into my shoulder. "Would you get me a drink, please?"

I hesitate, looking from her to my aunt. "Of course. White wine?"

She shakes her head. "Ginger ale would be fine."

I'm puzzled by her choice, but I'm sure it has more to do with my prejudiced aunt's stereotypes than anything. "Winnie, would you like a drink?"

My aunt is not smiling. "Vodka rocks."

"You got it." Lifting her hand, I kiss Angel's knuckles. It feels like she's trying to get rid of me, but before I head for the nearest drink station, I look at my aunt. "Don't ruin this."

"I can't even begin to guess what you mean."

"You know what I mean." I lower my brow. "Angel is important to me."

"Deacon, I have no intention of ruining anything."

"Good." I linger with my hand on Angel's back, but her eyes are downcast. Exhaling a breath, I give her a little pat. "I'll be right back."

I want to trust Angel knows what she's doing, but I'd be lying if I said I wasn't concerned. Avoiding any familiar faces, I make my way quickly to the beverage station, keeping my eyes on the women.

CHAPTER
Twenty-Eight

Angel

D EACON MOVES SWIFTLY THROUGH THE CROWD, GLANCING BACK every few moments. He's stunning in a tuxedo with his dark hair swept back, his blue eyes glowing with love, lined with concern.

Rather than dancing around the elephant in the room, I decide to get this over with fast. Rip off the band-aid.

"I know you're angry." I remove the mask from my face, meeting Winnie's narrowed gaze.

"You lied to me."

"I did no such thing."

"You were at my house, day after day, and you never said a word." Her voice is cold, and I can't tell if she's angry or hurt.

"You never asked." I'm doing my best to be non-confrontational.

I want her to say whatever she has to say, and I want Deacon to be right—I want us to be friends. We're going to be family.

"That's so like your kind. So smug." Her arms cross. "You

took my money today and never said a word about seeing my nephew or me tonight."

"My kind…" I exhale shaking my head. "I accepted payment for my artistic service. My personal life is not your business."

She sniffs, lifting her chin. "And is that his?"

Her eyes drop to my waist, and my chest tightens. "Yes."

"Now it makes sense. Deacon is the most eligible bachelor in the city. He could be with any woman here tonight. Of course, he's doing the right thing."

"He doesn't know about it yet." I resent the implication I'm using my pregnancy to trap him.

"Why not?"

I glance to where he's standing at the bar waiting, tall and slim in his tuxedo. He rises above the other men standing around, handsome as a model, glancing in our direction every so often. *So protective.* Our eyes catch, and he smiles, warming my stomach. I love him so much.

"It's really early… I wanted to wait for a special moment." Returning to her, I do a little shrug. "I thought tonight might be a good time. After the ball."

"You've been living with him?"

"I've spent a few nights at his apartment."

Her hands go up, and she does a little wave. "I've had enough of this. Tell Deacon we'll talk about this later. I'm going home."

With that she turns and walks away, leaving me standing in front of the cluster of tables all alone. Deacon is settling up with the bartender, and I recognize a familiar voice.

"Carmen?" Looking around, I see a guy I recognize from Valeria's old neighborhood.

"Chris?"

He's wearing a white coat, and I realize he's one of the waiters. "What are you doing here?"

"I—"

"Hey, sorry that took so long." Deacon appears at my side.

I smile up at him, taking my soft drink out of his full hands. "Your aunt had to go."

"She did?" He looks at the vodka he's holding and then towards the door. "You want this?"

"No thanks. This is an old friend Chris…" Turning back to the guy, I'm confused when I see he's scowling. "What's wrong?"

"You're here with him?" Chris nods, motioning with his tray at Deacon.

My mouth drops, and I'm about to answer when Deacon steps forward to shake his hand.

"Hey, how's it going? Chris you said?" He's friendly, open. "I'm Deacon."

"I know who you are." Chris's black eyes flash at mine. "He shot your brother."

"No, that's not what happened—" I step forward to stop him, but he backs away, moving farther into the crowd.

Deacon watches him go before turning to me. "Not sure what to do with that."

Anger tightens my throat. If my brother is spreading lies, putting Deacon in jeopardy… "I know what to do about it," I say under my breath. I'm going to visit him tomorrow.

"Where did my aunt go?" Deacon's scanning the crowded room.

"She left. Said she'd talk to you later."

Our eyes meet, and we both seem a bit deflated.

"Hey." He puts his drink on the high table and his hands on my waist, pulling me closer. "We're supposed to be having fun tonight. Let's dance."

Nodding, I follow him back to the floor, where we get cozy and sway to the instrumental version of "Beyond the Sea," and my mind drifts to Sofia. It feels like a year has passed since Beto destroyed everything, and Lourdes called Deacon my prince. He is my prince, but unlike that fictional princess, I'm not giving up anything to be with him. My brother is not a king, he's not my father, and he's not going to threaten our love.

We dance. We sample the barbecue skewers on platters. I sip ginger ale, while Deacon sticks to scotch. The only members of the old guard who approach us are the men. They shake Deacon's hand, ask how his business is going, welcome him back to town.

I feel the eyes of all the old women in the room on us the entire night, and I'm sure we're the subject of much gossip, the same gossip that sent Winnie running for the hills. I can't decide if I think she's a coward or if she did it to avoid engaging.

Haven Wells is the one older woman who asks to meet me. "I adore your dress."

"Thank you." I do a brief nod. "Deacon bought it for me."

Her white-blonde hair is styled in a chin-length bob, and I know immediately she's the mother of Deacon's friend Rich, who has yet to make an appearance.

"I heard you two are engaged?" She smiles, looking up at my date. "Is this true?"

"It is." Deacon catches my hand, threading our fingers and showing her my ring.

"It's gorgeous. Did you pick it out together?"

"No—he completely surprised me with it." The diamond flashes in the light, and I imagine him picking it out, keeping it a secret...

"Brave boy." Haven nudges him in the side, and he shrugs.

"I figured if she didn't like it, I'd get her another one."

"Another one!" I cry, and he laughs.

Haven leans into me, clinking her champagne glass against my tumbler. "Mental note." She does a little wave, circling into the crowd. "Have a fun night, kids."

"I like her."

"She's one of the better ones." He puts the glass down and catches my arms. "How are you feeling?"

Tilting my head to the side, I look up at him, a smile curling my lips. "I'm ready to go if you are. I have something special in mind."

"Is that so?' His eyes light, and he steps closer, cupping my cheeks and lifting my chin as he leans down, speaking at my ear. "We're not too far from our tower if you'd like to make a little detour."

My eyes flutter shut as his warm breath skates over my neck, making me shiver. His thumb touches my chin, and my body heats. "I could be persuaded to take a little detour."

It's not like the baby's going anywhere.

Without another word, he clasps my hand, leading me to the large, glass foyer where we entered.

He's walking fast, and I catch the side of my dress, laughing as I do my best to keep up. "You're going to make me trip."

My heels click on the marble floors, and as soon as we're outside, he turns my back to the wall, covering my mouth with his. Our lips seal, and I'm flooded with heat as our tongues curl and the scent of citrus and soap flood my senses.

Hands slide up my sides, cupping my breasts over my gown. I moan, tasting him, smelling him… His hands slide down my back to cup my ass, and I'm on fire.

"As gorgeous as this dress is, I've wanted to put my hands all over your naked body all night."

"I want your hands all over my naked body." It's an urgent request.

"Wait here while I get the car."

He leaves me hot and bothered as I watch him jog to the VIP lot. On wobbly legs, I stroll to the end of the walkway to wait for him. It doesn't take long for him to pull up in his sleek black Audi two-seater.

I'm about to open the door when he's out in a flash, circling the front and holding it for me. "I got this."

We're inside and speeding down the highway in no time. His large hand rests on my thigh, rising higher, following the high slit of my dress. Shifting in the buttery leather seat, I uncross my legs, loving the heat rising with his touch. His lips curl as his eyes watch the road, and I sigh at the first slide of his finger against my crotch, sheathed in silk.

"Why don't you slip those off?" Heat is in his voice, and I'm so wet.

"I'm not sure if I can in this skirt." Wiggling side to side, I reach under, trying to maneuver my hands beneath the floor-length gown. "I don't want to rip it."

"I'll rip it." He's hungry, aggressive, and I'm vibrating with need.

"I need to stand. How much farther?" My voice is breathless.

"Not much." His hand returns to the smooth skin of my thigh when his phone buzzes on the console. "Probably Rich making excuses for why he never showed."

I'm ready to say it doesn't matter, when I see it's Winnie. "It's your aunt."

"I don't care." His hand slides higher up my thigh, and as much as I want him to touch me, I can't help wondering what she'll say to him.

Will she tell him about the baby?

Will she say I'm trying to trap him?

It's like cold water on my heated body. "Should I see what she wrote?"

His hand leaves me, and he makes an annoyed sound as he picks up the black phone and swipes his finger across the face before handing it to me. "Old cock blocker. We might as well read it together."

"Are you sure?" I feel bad for breaking the mood.

"Positive."

My tongue wets my bottom lip, and I lift the phone to read the words aloud. "Come to the house after you've taken her home. I have the diary you asked for. You need to see it."

"Mother fucker." Deacon's voice is a hiss. "I knew she had it."

Cold fear trickles through my chest as I watch the muscle move in his jaw. "What does that mean?"

The mood in the car completely shifts. "It's about our grandparents."

"We have to go."

CHAPTER
Twenty-Nine

Deacon

"**Y**OU WERE GOING TO LET ME SEARCH THE WHOLE ATTIC?" I'M SO fucking angry, I'm doing a good job keeping my tone civil. "When you had it the whole time?"

Winnie's dressed in her floor-length navy velvet robe, and her hair is wrapped in that white turban. "The things in my mother's personal diary are private. I didn't know your reason for wanting to see it. I was protecting her memory."

I'm breathing fast, and while I understand this, I'm still pissed. "You could have told me that. We could've talked it out."

"Does she have to be here." Winnie eyes Angel.

Angel stands at once, starting for the door, but I catch her hand.

"Yes." My voice is firm. "This involves all of us."

Winnie looks directly at Angel. "Did you come here straight from the masque?"

Angel nods.

"So you didn't—"

"We were on the way home when you texted." Angel's voice is quiet.

I hold out my hand. "May I see the diary, please? This is pretty important to us."

Winnie's lips tighten, and she slips her hand in the folds of her robe, taking out a brown-leather clad book. It's slimmer than I expected, but clearly old.

"I guessed the part you wanted to see. The bookmark is there."

For a moment, I hold the small book, allowing the significance of it to seep through my fingers. This book could be the key to everything. *If only it could fix things…*

Carefully, I open the cover. The room is so quiet, you could hear a pin drop. I'm pretty sure I hear everyone's breath swirling in and out. I'm at the section Winnie marked. My fingers turn the pages carefully, delicately, like it's as important as the constitution. Hell, it could be.

I've just found the place when a loud banging on the stained-glass front door snaps us all to attention.

"Open the door!" A male voice roars. "Deacon Dring? I know you're in there. I know you have my sister."

I know who it is, but Angel says the word. "Beto…"

Winnie leaves the room, catching the side of her robe and dashing down the hall. At first I think she's going to answer him, but she strides with purpose in the opposite direction. I don't have time to wonder. Beto is beating on the door like he's a fucking storm trooper.

Angel catches my arm, speaking softly. "Let me talk to him."

"I don't like the sound of this." Protective anger is hot in my chest.

"I can handle my brother. Give me a second to talk to him."

"You're not going out there alone."

"Deacon." Her slim hand touches my stomach. "He's my brother."

Reaching out, she turns the brass deadbolt, walking out onto the front steps. "Beto?" Her voice is strong, firm. "Why are you here?"

"The question is why are you here?" He's dressed in only dark jeans and a white tank, but he's wearing a belt, which I'm pretty sure has a holster on it. "Chris said he saw you at that big party tonight."

"I went to the Cattleman's Masque with Deacon."

"So you think you belong in this world? You think they won't chew you up and spit you out like they do with all our kind?"

"I think you need to go home. You have no business being here."

"I'm not leaving without my sister." His voice is a quiet roll of thunder, approaching danger. "Papá would expect me to protect you from these people."

"These people." Angel exhales a laugh. "You sound just like them. You all use the same words. You all share the same hate. It's senseless, and it's not Deacon and me."

"Let's go." He steps forward and catches her arm, and I'm out the door.

"Let her go." I remove his hand and stand beside her. "Angel is my fiancée. If you have something to say, say it to me."

Beto's dark eyes gleam. "Are we doing this again?"

"I'm not doing anything. You're going home."

The loud *click-click* of a gun echoes at my shoulder, and I step aside to see my aunt holding a massive, double-barrel shotgun at her shoulder.

"Oh, shit." I pull Angel behind me.

Winnie's cheek is lowered as she looks through the sites, which are leveled point blank at Angel's brother. "Get off my place."

Beto's hands go up, but his smile holds steady. "What is this? Hiding behind some old lady now?"

"This old lady is going to put a hole in your head the size of Texas if you don't get off my land." Winnie's voice is fierce, and her blue eyes flash cold fire.

"Your land." Fury kindles Beto's eyes. "Give me my family, and I'll get off *your land*."

"Looks like you have a problem with English. *Habla Inglés?*" Winnie still hasn't lowered the gun.

He looks from me to my aunt, and the muscle in his square jaw moves.

I've never seen my aunt this way. "Winnie, maybe you should put the gun down before someone gets hurt."

"I don't need your protection, asshole."

"Beto?" A scuff of shoes on the driveway draws my attention, and a shadowy figure jogs up. "Chris told me he saw them—"

"Stay back, Mateo." Beto's eyes haven't left my aunt's, and he's holding one hand out, stepping slowly down the stairs.

"He tried to kill you." Mateo's eyes land on mine, and he whips out a pistol.

"No!" Angel screams, throwing her body against mine, chest to chest.

A sharp pop cuts the night, and the scene shifts into fast motion as my whole world falls apart. Angel drops, sending us both to the ground.

My arms tighten around her, and we land on the hard stone. For a split second, I'm disoriented.

"Angel?" Her body is heavy, and fear seizes my heart.

She's not moving. Warm wetness is on my hands. I remember this… I know what it is.

Blood.

"Call 911!" My voice breaks.

"Oh my God," Winnie lowers the shotgun and pulls a phone from her robe. "911? We need an ambulance, immediately. A young lady's been shot. Please hurry."

"Angel?" I'm holding her, rocking her.

"Deacon?" Angel's eyes squeeze, and she lets out a soft cry. "It hurts…"

A clatter of metal on stone, and Mateo watches us dumbfounded.

"Mateo!" I shout. "Look at me…" My voice crackles with controlled rage. "I will find you. I will finish you."

Now I have hate.

He takes a step back then turns and runs, disappearing into the night.

Beto drops to his knees. "Carmie?" He lifts his sister's limp hand. *"Mija…"*

My gaze is fixed on Angel. "You did this."

"No…" He shakes his head, moving aside as Winnie appears, holding a thick towel.

"Press this into the wound." Her face is white as a sheet. "EMS is on the way."

I take the towel, holding it against Angel's back, securing it with my arms. "I'm here, baby. It's going to be okay. I've got you."

Her body shudders, and my arms tighten around her, applying pressure, trying to stop the bleeding. "I can't feel my arm…"

"Don't try to talk."

"I wanted to take you to Mexico." She trembles, and I rock her, hugging her.

Lowering my head, I put my lips against her cheek. "What?"

"I wanted you to see the mountains…" Her voice trails off.

"We're going to see the mountains." My voice breaks. "I'll take you there."

In the distance, I hear the wail of sirens. My heart is sick, and I can't think of anything but making them hurry, making them get here before it's too late.

There's so much blood.

"I can't breathe…" Her eyes are closed, and her pretty face is so pale.

The sirens grow louder, and I see the lights flashing at the end of the street. Beto limps to the edge of the driveway, moving into the shadows. I'm not interested in him. My entire focus is on my love, fading in my arms.

"Stay with me, Angel." A hot tear hits my cheek. "Don't fly away. Don't leave me."

The ambulance screeches to a stop, and the scene grows chaotic. A gurney appears, and people are running back and forth. I can't take my eyes off Angel's pale face, so relaxed and beautiful.

Two large men surround me. "We have to take her now, sir."

"Let her go, Deacon." Winnie's hands are on my shoulders, but I can't fathom her words. They're the worst thing I've ever heard.

"She's so warm." I hold her closer to my chest, lowering my face to hers, unwilling to let her go.

"Deacon, you have to let them take her."

"Sir, you have to let her go."

My brain is reeling.

I can't let her go.

They force my arms apart, and I think I'm losing my mind. My world is imploding, then my aunt destroys my soul.

"Please do everything you can… She's pregnant."

CHAPTER
Thirty

Deacon

MY EYES ACHE, AND I CAN'T STOP MY THOUGHTS.

"What's happening?" I growl, pacing like a caged tiger. Winnie arranged for Angel to be taken to the private wing of the Methodist hospital, where our family is treated by private physicians. She brought me clean clothes, and we've been waiting ever since. It's like being in a plush prison.

We rushed here from the mansion. I rode in the back of the ambulance with Angel, but I couldn't get close for the paramedics doing everything they could to stabilize her, stop the bleeding, monitor her vitals.

Even though I was shoved aside, I was relived to be in the same space, to know she was alive, even if she was fighting.

"The bullet entered her shoulder." One of the big male attendants was on the phone with the doctor the entire drive. "No exit wound."

As soon as we arrived, she was taken from us, rushed to emergency surgery to remove the bullet and hopefully repair the damage to her arm and shoulder.

I think about her not being able to paint. I think about how she turned, putting her body between Mateo and me, and I realize I would be dead right now if she hadn't. My face drops to my hands, and I fight the tears.

Clearing my throat, I look up at my aunt. "How did you know she was pregnant?"

Winnie shifts on the leather couch, adjusting the throw over her legs "She was sick at the house one evening. I took a guess."

"You guessed she was pregnant?"

"Sit down, Deacon." Winnie reaches out her hand. "You'll make yourself ill."

I let it go she avoided my question. "Why didn't she tell me?"

"I think she was planning to tell you tonight."

I rub my fingers over my eyes. It all makes sense now. That's why she wasn't drinking—I try to remember the last time I saw her drink alcohol. It was last weekend. She must've just found out. "I had no idea."

"Fathers are often the last to know." Winnie stands and walks to the window, looking out at the black night.

My chest is tight, and even though I've only known a few hours, I desperately don't want to lose our baby. "Where's the fucking nurse?"

A cheery young man has been popping in every hour or so to let us know the surgery is progressing and everything is fine. His updates are all the same, but his perky face is wearing on my nerves.

"Language, Deacon, please." She turns, not seeming that offended. "Surgery takes time. You want it to take time."

Noise outside the door draws our attention, and I look up to see Lourdes rushing in, her red-rimmed eyes round with worry. "How is she? Oh, God, I can't believe this..."

"I can't believe we're back at the hospital." Valeria reaches out her hand, and I take it.

Sofia is on her hip, and when she sees me, her little chin quivers. "I want Carmie."

I reach for her, and she leans into my arms, putting her head on my shoulder. I close my eyes a moment, thinking about our baby, how it could look like this little girl.

My voice is thick. "I want her, too."

My aunt stands and straightens her blouse. "Who are these people?" Her tone is decidedly unfriendly, and I hate her choice of words.

"Sorry…" I gesture between the women. "This is my aunt Winona Clarke. Valeria and Sofia are Angel's cousins. Lourdes is her best friend."

"Nice to meet you, Mrs. Clarke." Lourdes is apologetic. "I texted and asked if we could come."

"I see." Winnie lifts her chin with a sniff. "I'll leave you with your friends, Deacon."

"You don't have to go." Valeria's hands are clasped, and I can tell she's been crying. "We don't mean to intrude."

"It's late. Deacon will call me or text if anything changes."

She leaves, and Lourdes frowns up at me. "Did we scare her away?"

The image of my aunt on the front porch holding a double-barrel shotgun in Beto's face floats through my mind. "I don't think she's scared."

I don't know what's going on in Winnie's head—other than her prejudice is strong. At this point, I almost wish she'd pulled the trigger. The thought is bitter in my mind as the door opens and that asshole steps into the waiting room.

"I wanted to check on my sister."

"You've got a lot of nerve coming here."

"I'm sorry, Deacon." Valeria's voice is quiet. "Beto asked to come with us."

I pass Sofia to her mother, not taking my eyes off Angel's brother. "Get out."

"You can't keep me out." He limps closer. "I'm her brother."

"You're the reason she's in surgery."

"It's not true." He holds out a hand like he's so innocent. "I never wanted Angel to be hurt."

"You only wanted me to be killed." I'm slowly closing the space between us.

"Beto…" Valeria's voice trembles. "Maybe you should wait at home."

"I have a right to be here."

"Don't talk to me about rights. You refused to call off Mateo, even when she asked you to."

He doesn't deny it because he can't. I'm on him now, and he steps back. Sofia whimpers from behind me, and Lourdes interjects.

"Can't we put this behind us for now? Focus on Carmie?"

"I want you out of here." My breath is a rasp. "My days of making peace are over."

Beto's back hits the wall, but he doesn't back down.

His white teeth clench behind his tight snarl. "I didn't come for peace. I came for my family."

"She's not your family anymore. She's mine." I grab his shirt in both fists, slamming him against the wall. "If I see you touch her again, I'll put a bullet between your eyes."

Sofia cries more, but I don't care. All I see is my beautiful love lying in my arms, struggling for breath. All I see is a tiny baby I never knew slipping away from me.

All I see is red.

He sniffs, trying to twist out of my grasp. "I'd expect nothing less of a Dring."

"You should have expected more. I wanted more." I give him another slam against the wall, and a glass falls from the shelf. Lourdes makes a frightened noise. "But you tried to take everything from me." I breathe down his nose.

"All right, then, who could use some news?" A cheery male voice bounces in from behind us, but it changes quickly. "Oh… Oh, no! What's happening here? Security!"

Surprisingly fast, we're surrounded by two guards who pull us apart.

"Get him out of here." I snarl. "He doesn't belong in this room."

The guard grips Beto's arm tighter. "Let's go, pal."

Beto doesn't even try to struggle. He only glares at me as the guard escorts him out, leaving me bitter and broken, sitting on the couch with my hands in my hair.

The pleasure of telling him off, of almost hitting him is overshadowed by my pain. This is never how I wanted our story to end.

The melee is cleared, and the perky male nurse returns to where we're sitting.

"Well, that was exciting." He puts his hand on his chest, tilting his head to the side. "Now who's ready for an update? I've got a little good news, and a little bad news.

CHAPTER
Thirty-One

Deacon

WINNIE SITS ACROSS FROM ME BEHIND THE MASSIVE MAHOGANY desk. "So you see, the property wasn't exactly stolen—"

"But it was taken by force."

My grandmother's diary contains the full account. After my grandfather found out about the affair and the lost baby, he went on a warpath with one goal in mind: Destroying Manuel Treviño—and he had the connections to do it. He had Manuel convicted of embezzlement, he had him thrown in jail, and he had all his lands confiscated and redistributed to the county.

"They were immediately plunged into poverty."

"That's the oil business, Deacon." Winnie is dismissive. "It's always ups and downs. One day you're on top of the world, the next you have nothing. Remember what happened to the Wells?"

"What happened to them was political, flooding the market, things they couldn't control. What happened to Angel's grandfather was straight up revenge."

"Potato, potahto. He should have been saving for a rainy day."

As much as I want to rail at her, her behavior since the shooting has quelled my impatience. For all her misguided beliefs, she's making steps in the right direction, and it's progress I'd like to continue.

"I'm going to make it right." Leaning back in the leather chair, I straighten the cuff of my shirt beneath my blazer.

"How do you propose to do that?" She leans back in her desk chair, steepling her fingers at her chin.

Pushing off my thighs, I stand. "I'll get Rich to help me determine the market value of the land, and I'll gift it to the family."

"No." Winnie stands, holding up her hands. "I don't want any part of this. What Manuel did was wrong. He seduced your grandmother, and my father was entitled to his revenge."

"I confess I'm surprised to hear you take this position. You saw your mother's letters, her complaints of neglect…"

"It doesn't excuse what happened."

"No, but it puts it in perspective." Pausing at the door, I squint back at her. "I'm not doing it for my grandfather. I'm doing it for Angel."

"It's water under the bridge." My aunt walks around the desk. "From what I gather they don't need the money anyway."

"It doesn't matter. I promised Angel I'd fix things, and I intend to keep that promise."

Winnie shakes her head, a hint of sadness in her eyes. "Some things can't be fixed."

"This can."

BETO'S HOUSE LOOMS LARGE AND EMPTY OVER THE TREE-LINED ROAD. I remember the first time I came here, and it was filled with music and dancing and family.

It's a shadowy husk of that night—a night that ended in violence.

Looking up at the stone structure, I can't help thinking he

put himself here. His stubbornness, his vendetta, his refusal find common ground.

"You have to be able to see things from all sides if you're going to change." Valeria had said that night two weeks ago in the hospital waiting room.

It was the night she lowered her walls and we became friends.

Now I'm hoping I can do the same with this angry lone wolf. I press the button for the doorbell and wait. Minutes pass, and no one comes.

I follow the walk around to the back patio, where I smell cigarette smoke and music playing softly.

"Beto?" I open the metal gate carefully. "You back here?"

He's at the iron table, a tumbler of clear liquid in front of him and a cigarette smoldering in the ash tray. He's in a white tee this time with his black hair back in a small ponytail.

When I step through the gate, his dark eyes flicker up to mine, and he looks like he hasn't slept in a while. "What do you want?"

"Something we've never done." Squaring my shoulders, I enter the patio.

"What's that?"

"I want to have a civilized talk with you."

He huffs a laugh, lifting the cigarette from the tray. "Is that so?"

I'm wearing a gray suit, and I don't plan to stay long. I've got a plane to catch in an hour, and I'm looking forward to spending this evening miles away.

Reaching into my breast pocket, I take out one of two long envelopes. "For the past month, I've been searching for answers. I went to Harristown, I went to the county seat, then I went home. You know what I learned?"

"I'm not playing games. Tell me or get out."

Asshole. "That story you told me was real."

"No shit. What difference does it make now?"

Stepping forward, I place the envelope on the table beside his hand. "In this envelope is the fair market value of your grandfather's land—provided you sold it today." He starts to speak, and I hold up my hands to stop him. "I know, it's not the same. We don't know if your grandfather would have sold Fate. We do know there's no oil there."

"It's developed, commercial real estate."

"Yes, it is. If we had been alive, perhaps we would have done something different. We weren't."

He lifts the envelope, and opens the flap, glancing at me once more before sliding the check out slightly. His brow furrows. "What's this?"

"That's your half." Another step forward. "I'm extending this as a peace offering. I want us to be friends."

He doesn't move.

He stares at the envelope, still as a stone, then stands. "I never wanted to hurt my sister."

Acid is in my throat, but I force myself to hold steady, to focus on making peace. I promised Angel. "Okay."

"If I had known—"

"We don't have to relive it." My jaw clenches, and I can't stop myself from asking. It haunts me, an echo of pain in my stomach. "Have you heard from Mateo?"

"No. For all I know he's returned to Mexico."

"He'd better stay there." Then I do something I never thought I'd be able to do—I extend my hand to shake his.

He hesitates a moment before reaching out and clasping my hand. "This doesn't change how my grandfather died."

Our hands are clasped, and I hold his gaze. "No one knows what happened in that room that night. You and I faced off in this house, and you were shot. You could have been killed. Was that my fault?"

His jaw tightens, and he thinks about my question. Our hands are still clasped, and he nods. "We were both at fault."

"I wouldn't say that—"

"I told you to stay away from her."

"You knew I wasn't going to do that."

His lips press into a line, and he releases my hand. "We'll release that story to the past."

"When I get back, we'll go for a drink."

"I'll have the family here. We'll have a party."

"Put it on the calendar for March."

He nods, and a ghost of a smile curls his lips. "Our family will reunite."

"What's left of it."

I'm pulling into the private parking lot for chartered planes. My bags are checked through, our flight plan has been filed, and I'm aching to be in my seat and in the sky.

Even a few days feels like too long now, and I can't wait to see how much progress the workers have made.

Inside the Gulfstream G3, a lone flight attendant helps me with my carry on. "Welcome, Mr. Dring. I've got whiskey or beer—"

"I'll have a scotch if you have it."

"Of course." She nods, moving to the front of the small plane. "The captain said as soon as you're in your seat, we're clear for takeoff."

Easing out of my blazer, I put it on the chair across from me and take a seat. "Let's go."

Four hours later, I'm in a car headed out of Cuidad Victoria, northwest towards the rising peaks of the Sierra Madre mountains.

My phone buzzes on the seat, and I glance at the face. The words sit on the screen, and I start to smile.

He orders a beer and a mop.

While I was waiting for the car to come around, I'd sent a text. *A skeleton walks into a bar…*

The road grows narrower and turns to cobblestones as I enter the Villa de Santa María de Aguayo. Colorful houses rise in layers along the foothills of the mountains.

It's exactly as she described it, exactly as it was when I left two days ago to settle matters with our families. I approach the ranch house, which is in the in the process of restoration, and warmth spreads across my stomach when I see her.

Angel stands on the front porch beneath a strand of yellow twinkle lights. She's in a thin cotton sundress, and her feet are bare when she walks to the top of the porch steps.

Stepping out of the car, I pause a moment to take in the beauty of her waiting for me. Her stomach is just starting to show the smallest baby bump.

I grin, and she blinks quickly, her cheeks flushing. "Did you miss me?"

"I always miss you when you're gone."

Closing the door, I leave my bags for later. It's a beautiful night, and my lady is looking at me like I'm the best thing she's ever seen.

She's the best thing I've ever seen, and I want her in my arms.

CHAPTER
Thirty-Two

Angel

"**T**ELL ME ABOUT MY BROTHER. WHAT DID HE SAY?"

The white sheets on our king-sized bed are rumpled from our love-making, and we're surrounded by sheer mosquito netting. Workers have finished this half of the house, and it's like a luxurious resort. Through arched windows, we can see the purple peaks rising in the distance during the day. At night, the moon shines overhead, bathing us in silvery light.

Deacon's head rests against my chest, and he smooths his palm over my growing belly. "She's getting bigger."

The warmth in his voice makes my chest squeeze. I reach down and trace my fingers through his hair. "We don't know if it's a girl yet."

"She's a girl, and she's going to be as beautiful as her mamma, with a cute little dimple at the top of her cheek."

"Is that so?" I rise up on my elbows to look at him, but a sharp pain makes me drop quickly onto the mattress again. "Ouch."

His head pops up. "What happened?"

"Just forgot I'm still healing."

After the surgery to remove the bullet from my shoulder-blade, I spent a month wearing a tight bandage from my neck to my elbow, while the bullet wound in my shoulder blade healed. Since graduating from that, I've been doing physical therapy, but I still have to work on the muscles of my right side.

Deacon frowns, shifting his position so he's behind me, cradling my upper body in his arms with his palms never leaving my stomach.

It's like since almost losing us, he never wants to be far away. He even complained about returning to Plano for two days while he discussed his plans with Winnie then completed the transaction with my brother.

I give him another nudge with my elbow. "Tell me what happened."

"Winnie thought it was overkill. She actually surprised me—she took her father's side, like he was the victim and what he did was justifiable."

"That is unexpected." We're quiet while I consider this angle. "I'd think the woman who charged out of her house brandishing a double-barrel shotgun and ordering my brother off her property would be a bit more understanding of her mother's predicament."

"Tell me about it." He kisses the top of my shoulder, and I melt into his firm chest. "I guess she knew her father better. We had that in common—her mother died when she was young."

"I never knew that." Tracing my finger along Deacon's forearm, I can't help thinking if what happened to me could possibly fuel his over-possessiveness now. "We all lost our mothers young."

His arms tighten around me, and his voice has an edge. "We're breaking that chain."

Turning my head, I kiss him slow. I don't want him worrying about me. "I'm not going anywhere."

"No, you're not."

Our eyes meet, and our love burns so strong.

"Tell me about my brother."

"He's alone in that big house." Deacon exhales heavily. "I felt kind of bad for him."

"You're kidding." I twist around to look at him again, and his eyebrows quirk.

"I did."

"I hope you told him it's his own damn fault."

He pulls me into his embrace again, positioning me so his hands can slide over the baby. "I told him we should get together sometime for a drink. He suggested a party for the whole family at his place in March."

My brow furrows. "March?"

"I suggested March—nine months from now."

"Oh…" I shake my head. "I'll probably need an extra month to be on my feet again."

"We'll change it to April."

We're quiet, looking out the arched windows, listening to the hum of insects in the night, the croak of frogs. I'm thinking about being here, in my favorite place with him. It's what I've always wanted.

"You fixed it."

"Hm?" Sleepiness has entered his tone. "What's that?"

"You said you'd fix it. I said some things couldn't be fixed. But you said they could, and you did."

His face moves into my hair, and he inhales deeply. "We fixed it. We all gave a little."

"But you gave the most."

"And I got the most in return."

Reaching over my shoulder, I cup his cheek, holding our faces together as I close my eyes.

Once I thought being in Deacon's arms was like diving off

a cliff into a pool of wonder and happiness. Now I realize those were little girl fantasies, and while they're still true, it's so much more than that.

Being in Deacon's arms means being supported by a partner who will fight for me, who will hold my hand when I have to fight, who will wait for me when I need some space, and who won't give up until I've slain my monsters.

Together, our love is healing. Our love is creative and pure. Our kisses are reckless, but they're not irresponsible. We're wild and free, like the horse in my painting. Our spirit is groundbreaking and revolutionary, brave enough to heal the wounds of the past and forge a future of unity.

My hand is over his on my belly as I drift to sleep with these visions in my mind, as I plan my next painting, as I take my next step into a new world.

THE PEAKS OF THE SIERRA MADRE ARE TIPPED IN GOLDEN LIGHT, AND A mist surrounds the mountain tops. I slipped out of bed at the break of dawn with my camera to capture the light streaking the ripples of mountains, the gleaming off the sunrise on the colorful houses dotting the foothills.

It's a warm morning, and I'm in a thin cotton dress, barefoot as I walk along the stone pavement leading up the hill from our house into the scrub bushes and banana trees.

A month has passed since Deacon returned. The workers have finished updating and basically transforming my mother's house into a modern villa. Deacon took the lead in making sure we could divide our time here and not lose contact with our family and business back home, but he allowed me to maintain the elements I loved so much growing up—the rustic décor and open-air patio, the large porch where we can sit and listen to the children playing or the birds singing. The vivid colors, open windows, stone floors, and twinkle lights tracing the arches of the high ceilings.

My mother's spirit is alive in this place, and I've hung her pictures alongside my paintings throughout. Satisfaction warms my chest when I see their complimentary nature. She was one end of the spectrum, and I am the other.

A flutter in my stomach draws my attention, and I slide my palm along my stomach. "I hear you, little one." I whisper. "You're a part of this. You're going to make your mark in this world."

"Talking to yourself already?" The deep voice draws my attention, and I look up to see my brother standing at the top of the path.

His arms are crossed. He's dressed in dark jeans and a short-sleeved shirt, but he does something wholly new. He smiles as he walks to where I'm standing, and when he reaches me, he pulls me in for a hug.

"You're early. Are you by yourself?" I hug him sideways.

"I don't like those little planes." He puts his arm across my shoulder, and we walk slowly towards the house. "How are you feeling, *mija?*"

Exhaling softly, I look over the garden, where an arch has been assembled on a rise with the mountains in the distance. "Ready to be a bride."

"It's a good day for a wedding." His voice is warm, calm, and I think my brother is on a journey to peace.

I think it started the night I was shot, and we decided the violence had to end.

"Your cousin's worrying herself sick." He shakes his head, reaching for the door to let me in the kitchen. Valeria and the rest of them are flying in this afternoon. "Not enough time to decorate the house, the dress won't fit, the cake won't be right…"

"She might be right about the dress." I laugh, holding my stomach. "Every time I try it on, it gets a little tighter."

"La Sierra Madre." My brother muses, looking out the open window.

Holding out my hand, I clasp his. "I'm glad you're here. She would have wanted you to be here."

He gives me a tight smile. "I want to believe that."

"Then do."

HOURS LATER, I'M SURROUNDED BY FAMILY. "WAIT! I MISSED A SPOT." Lourdes is behind me with a large curling iron attempting to coax my hair into a smooth cascade of curls.

We're in a large suite preparing for the ceremony—on the opposite end of the U-shaped house from the men. When it's time to emerge, we'll meet in the middle and file down the walk together to the top of the little hill where the priest will be waiting.

"My head's too tight." Sofia tugs on the garland arranged around a braid on her head.

"Stop it, Soph!" Lourdes catches her little hand, moving it away. "I'll fix it in just a minute. Let me finish with Carmie."

Valeria charges in the room dressed in a flowing, pale green dress. She has an envelope in her hand, and she's squinting as she reads the address.

"Deacon said I had to give this to you right now." Looking up, she freezes, clutching her hand to her chest, her eyes filling with tears. "Oh, Carmie! You are so beautiful!"

My eyes heat at the sight of her unshed tears, and Lourdes shoves a tissue in my hand.

"Stop!" she cries. "No tears until the ceremony."

"I'm not crying." Sofia tugs on her garland. "My head hurts."

"Come here." Lourdes lifts her onto a chair and starts rebraiding her hair.

"What's in the envelope, Ma?" Lola sits on the purple chaise at the foot of the guest bed.

"Oh!" Valeria, takes the business-sized envelope from her

chest and holds it to me. "I don't know. Deacon saw it and said it couldn't wait. He wanted to give it to you himself, but—"

"It's from the Palladium gallery!" My hand goes to my chest as my breath disappears.

"What's that?" Valeria watches me worried as I sink to the bed in my strapless ivory gown. "Careful with your skirt."

She arranges the full chiffon skirt around me, but my entire focus is on the thin envelope in my trembling hand. "They award the Arthaus residency…"

"Oh shit!" Lourdes cries, and Valeria pinches her arm.

"Language!"

"Sorry! Sorry, Sofia." My bestie dashes to my side, watching me with huge eyes. "Do you need me to open it?"

"What's the Arthaus residency?" Lola tugs the skirt of her pink chiffon gown higher so she can scoot to where I'm sitting— where I'm having a mini panic attack.

The baby moves in my stomach, and I slide my hand over her in a soothing way. "It doesn't matter…" I say softly, doing my best to calm my racing heart. "Whether I got it or not, it doesn't matter."

"Give it to me." Lourdes holds out her hand, and I pass it to her.

She rips the flap open and takes out the ivory sheet. A rectangular scrap falls as she does, but my eyes are fixed on her expression, waiting to see if it changes.

"Dear Ms. Treviño, We'd like to thank you for applying for the annual residency offered by our gallery…" Lourdes reads in a speedy monotone, and I feel like I'm going to throw up. "We believe this was our most competitive year with the level of talented applicants being of a caliber we've never seen…"

"I'm going to be sick…" My voice is quiet, my mouth dry.

"Oh no!" Valeria dashes to the bathroom and grabs the small trash can. "Don't get it on your dress."

"After much careful consideration and two rounds of voting…"

My mind is already finishing the sentence… I didn't get it…

"We're delighted to offer you this year's Arthaus residency!" Lourdes screams the final words, and I'm pretty sure my heart stops. "Please inform us whether you intend to accept this award by Monday, June…"

She continues reading, but I can't hear for the roaring in my ears. My eyes are flooded, and Lola is bouncing on the bed with Sofia beside me.

Valeria has her hand on her heart and tears in her eyes. "Your mother would be so proud."

Through all the commotion, I hear a soft tapping on the door, and I stand, moving my dress around my feet so I don't trip in my haste.

Deacon is on the other side of the patio door waiting. I can see his tall form and the darkness of his suit through the sheer curtain over the glass separating us. "Did you get it?"

"I got it!" I cry, my voice wavering as Lourdes hands me a tissue.

"Yeah, you did!" He laughs, and I want to rush into his arms.

"Deacon! What on Earth?" Winnie rushes up from the patio. "Shoo! You can't see the bride before the wedding."

"Then tell them to start it now. I need to hug my girl."

I'm behind the door with my eyes closed, laughing and holding my stomach, my face lifted to the ceiling in sheer gratitude. "I can't believe it."

"I can." Deacon's voice is warm. "Meet me at the arbor, and I'll show you how proud I am."

The music starts, and Winnie rushes into the room. She's the only one not dressed in pastel chiffon. Her dress is a straight, navy silk. "Everyone ready?"

"One last thing." Lourdes dots my face with powder as the other girls line up.

"My heart's beating so fast," I whisper.

Our eyes meet, and hers fill with tears. "It's all happening."

She gives me a quick hug then lowers my veil, arranging it around my shoulders before she goes to the door to walk down with Winnie, who we unconventionally put on Deacon's side.

Lola walks down with Sofia, who also sprinkles petals on the stone pavers.

I touch Valeria's arm before she steps out to meet Uncle Antonio. "See, we didn't even need decorations."

She gives me a squeeze. "Look what you did. You healed us."

"I'm glad I broke my promise."

"Me too." Shaking her head, she steps into the courtyard as the string quartet continues with Pachelbel's Canon.

Beto steps to the door, peeking in the room. He's dashing in a black tuxedo, his dark hair swept back from his intense face, dark scruff on his cheeks.

"Ready?" I turn, and his expression goes from startled to proud. He exhales a soft whistle. "You look beautiful, Sis."

Warmth settles in my chest as I reach for his arm. I'm no longer a child.

The sun is setting behind the mountains, and the sky is painted in the colors of twilight, the colors of my mother mixed with the colors of my soul.

We step out into the courtyard, and he looks up at the horizon. "Our mother's mountains."

"She's here with us." I whisper, tightening my hand in his arm as the music changes to the Bridal March.

Deacon turns to face me, and when our eyes meet, my head gets light.

He stands in front of the priest, blue eyes smoldering with love and lust and pride. My brother passes me to him, and he leans in whispering, "You take my breath away."

My hand is on his arm, and my body vibrates with so much happiness.

The priest guides us through our vows. We discussed writing our own, but in the end, we decided to go traditional. Everything else has been so untraditional, this felt like an easy choice.

We only omitted the part where the bride is given away. As hard as we worked bringing the family together, we decided to keep it that way.

With the vows recited, the priest holds his hands over our heads and pronounces us man and wife. Only one thing is left.

Deacon lifts the veil from my face, and cups my cheeks in his hands. His eyes glow with so much love, it radiates through my heart, down through my torso, into the heart of our baby.

"You have always been everything I've ever wanted."

Blinking fast, I can't stop the tears leaking from the corners of my eyes. "You've made all my dreams come true."

With that, full lips cover mine, soft and warm. The group bursts into applause, and I hug him closer. "We did it."

"I'm so proud of you."

We're still holding each other when two little arms wrap around my legs. "You did it, Cee-cee!"

I start to laugh, reaching down to place my hand on Sofia's little back. Suddenly another pair of arms, then more arms surround us. We're engulfed in a group hug of family, and the small audience of local friends starts to clap again.

Lifting my chin, I see the one holdout is Winnie. She's standing back beside the arch with her arms crossed. Her expression is a mixture of surprise and confusion... so stubborn. Still, I won't let her deter me. I stretch out my hand from the clump of my cousins.

Our eyes meet, and she glances down at my palm then to my eyes again. I give my hand an insistent shake, and after another second, she relents. Her arms drop, and she shakes her head, stepping forward to take my hand.

I give her a firm tug, and she stumbles forward—to be

immediately surrounded by the love of this expanded new family. *Mi familia…*

We feast on fresh local cuisine, tacos with red peppers and corn. Tortillas stuffed with chicken or fish and fresh guacamole. Sofia's favorite is the grilled Mac & Cheese a'la Carmen, which is, you guessed it, Deacon's special dish with my added spices.

The sun sets, and the arbor turns into a glowing yellow arch. The DJ plays a mixture of local music and pop tunes.

Deacon and I are dancing to Ed Sheeran's "Thinking Out Loud" when Winnie calls to the group. "It's time!"

Sofia runs through the crowd distributing paper lanterns with Lola following behind with lighters. The music stops, and we gather in a group while my aunt counts down to zero. We all light the small rings inside the lanterns—Deacon and I have the biggest one, which we light together. When she says zero, we release them, watching as the glowing beacons rise in the dark night, catching the breeze and turning into a swirling line drifting towards the mountains.

It's beautiful and hopeful, and as Deacon folds me in his arms, I relax into my happily ever after.

We healed our family.

We created a new path.

One vow we did add to our ceremony, and it drifts through my mind. No matter what, from this day to forever, without hesitation or pause, we choose each other, and we'll go on choosing each other, in a heartbeat, until death do us part.

Epilogue

Deacon
Six months later

"**M**I MAMÁ?" THE OLDER WOMAN HOLDS A PAIR OF GLASSES IN front of her eyes as she reads the card beside Angel's painting of the Sierra Madre at dusk.

We're at her showing in the Palladium, and the gallery is packed with business leaders, art collectors, students, and the generally curious. Angel is a pro. She's wearing a tight black dress that shows off her baby bump magnificently. It stops mid-thigh, and her toned legs are accentuated by tall, black heels.

Her hair is darker from being inside all winter, and she had it straightened. Although I prefer her crazy curls, she's very sophisticated with it shiny and smoothed into a bun at the nape of her neck. Oversized earrings are in her ears, and she is mouthwateringly gorgeous. She's a smart, professional artist I'd like to fuck. AILF…

I'm getting distracted.

"My late mother preferred a deep blue and green palette for her work." She gestures with her slim arms and elegant hands at the painting of the mountains. "I typically work in warmer, more vibrant tones."

"And the mountains?" The woman nods, stepping back to absorb the large work.

"The Sierra Madre. I grew up in the foothills living with her."

The woman's eyebrows rise, and she smiles, nodding as if she understands. Another work sold. Angel's premier showing to the Texas art world is a hit.

"I'm so nervous." She grabs my arm, speaking into my chest as the woman strolls down the line.

"You're amazing." My hands are on her waist, and I kiss her forehead, inhaling the jasmine in her hair. "You sound like you've been doing this all your life."

"Art, yes. Talking about it to super-rich, judgey, total strangers? No."

That makes me chuckle, and I lean down to kiss the side of her cheek. "You sound like a pro."

"Now, Mr. Dring, you can't monopolize your talented wife all evening." Her former professor walks up smiling, holding out her arms.

"Professor Roshay." Angel turns to give her a hug. "I'm so glad you made it."

"How could I not? You are one of the finest students I've taught. I wanted to tell you you'd get the residency, but how could I?"

"You're too kind."

"Farrell?" Winnie joins us, a glass of white wine in her hand. "Aren't you so proud of my niece?"

"Winnie, how very fortunate you are to have such a talent in the family."

"I have the privilege of saying I was one of her first portraits."
My aunt preens like a peacock, and I feel pretty proud of myself.

We built this bridge.

Angel looks up at me, her cheeks rosy pink, and I slide my
arm around her waist. "How are you feeling?"

We've been at this show for more than an hour, and the doctor is pretty sure Angel's about thirty-six weeks along. She could
go into labor any day now, which means we're staying at my penthouse for the duration.

"I'm tired, but I'm excited." I hand her a glass of punch. "I
think everybody likes what I've done."

Over the last six months, she's created several new pieces, but
the show also includes works she did before she received the prize.

"That one's getting a lot of attention."

I gesture to an oil painting of a male torso in blue and orange
with the face obscured and the waist covered by a small towel.
The gallery priced it at nine thousand dollars.

She gives me a sly grin. "A man walks into a bar?"

"What can I say? You gotta pay to have all this sexy on your
walls."

She leans into me, wrinkling her cute little nose. "I would
have marked it priceless."

I kiss the tip of her nose as a shrill voice cuts through the low
roar of voices.

"Who is the artist?" Looking up, I see Cecilia Westbrook making her way through the crowd of elegantly dressed patrons with
one of her little minions at her side. "Why, Winnie. I didn't expect
to see you here. Isn't this a fabulous exhibition?"

"Yes." My aunt crosses her arms, her answer clipped.

I haven't kept track, but my aunt has spent less time with her
former bestie since the Cattleman's Masque.

"I haven't seen works like this since they had the O'Keefe exhibit here." Cecilia places her hand on her chest. "I want to buy all

of them. Particularly that horse at the entrance. *Spirit*? It says *Not for sale*, but everything has a price, right?"

"You'll have to ask her." Winnie, gestures to where I'm standing with my hand on Angel's lower back.

"Why, Deacon…" Cecilia looks from me to my wife. "Is this—"

"The woman you disrespectfully called a little brown girl last year? Yes, it is."

"My goodness, that was a silly night." Cecilia blinks quickly shaking her head as if she's embarrassed. I hope she's embarrassed. "I think we'd all had a bit to drink."

"I hadn't." Angel smiles, holding out her hand. "It's nice to see you again, Mrs. Westbrook."

"My dear, you're very elegant. And who knew you had such a gift?"

"I knew." Winnie steps forward. "I agree with Deacon. I believe you owe Angelica an apology."

"Of all the things." Cecilia huffs. "People can't take a joke anymore. I'm certain I didn't mean to offend you, Miss Treviño."

"It's Mrs. Dring." My voice is firm as I set her straight.

"Mrs. Dring? I don't remember reading about a wedding."

"We were married at my family's estate in Mexico." Angel rests her hand on her bump, showing off her large diamond and the wedding band set around it.

I put my hands on the top of her shoulder so my band is visible as well.

"Your family's estate?" Cecilia's little minion finally pipes up. She's a birdlike woman peeking around her friend. "That sounds very refined."

"My mother was a well-loved artist. She owned a ranch house at the foot of the Sierra Madre mountains."

"Clearly we misjudged you, Angelica." Cecilia places her hand on Angel's arm. "You are a talented, smart young woman. Now about that horse at the entrance. *Spirit*, I believe?"

"It's not for sale." Angel smiles, tilting her head towards me. "*Spirit* is our painting. It represents a very special time in our lives."

"But surely—" Cecilia starts.

I interrupt her. "It belongs to me."

"Well…" She huffs, taking her friend's arm. "I'm sure you're very busy this evening. I'll let you get back to your exhibit. It was very nice meeting you. Winnie, Deacon, good to see you again."

She huffs away, into the crowd, and I look at my aunt.

Winnie grins and puts her hand on my forearm. "Hopefully that's the last we'll see of her. Now, have you tried this Gruyère cheese? It's delicious—sweet, but slightly salty."

"I'm not a big fan of the swiss cheeses." Angel walks with my aunt to the refreshments area, and I stand back, amazed at how close they've become.

Winnie takes her shopping all the time, she planned her shower. They have an entire wardrobe purchased for the baby already. Winnie goes to any doctor's appointment I can't attend, which are few. The very first time, they shared a moment I didn't completely understand. Now they're like partners in crime.

Another hour passes, Beto and Lourdes make an appearance, and Angel's brother purchases two of her sunset paintings. Both are dramatic mixtures of primary colors. Lourdes complains her bestie is too rich for her blood. Almost every painting is sold, except for the ones we're keeping for ourselves.

It's finally time to go, and I pick Angel up in front of the gallery.

Stretching back in the car, she slips off her shoes. "I think I'm walking on my ankles," she groans, rubbing her calves.

"Foot rub when we get home."

"Mm… And a snack. I'm starving." She slides her hand behind my neck, smiling over at me. "You're the best. Do you know that?"

"You've said it once or twice."

Back at the penthouse, she's showered and stretched out on

the couch in one of my sweatshirts with a bowl of watermelon cubes covered in red pepper on her lap. Her cute little feet are in my lap—which she keeps freshly pedicured for the delivery—chowing down.

"I don't know why I've been craving this so much." She slurps another piece, making it look so good, I steal one. "Hey!"

"You're really selling it."

"Speaking of selling, can you believe I sold every piece?" Her light brown eyes widen, and I answer without hesitation.

"Yes. Your work is brilliant."

"Even the newer ones… the ones with the angels?"

She included a few paintings she's done in a more classical style, featuring beefy men ravaging beautiful angels with round breasts straining in ecstasy. To the unsuspecting observer, they're interesting and imaginative. To me, knowing my nickname for her, they're incredibly erotic. Thinking about them has me growing a bit thirsty.

"We should have kept one for our bedroom." The tone in my voice has shifted, and she glances up at me from under her lashes. Sex kitten.

"I plan on doing more…" Her voice is sultry. "Maybe we should practice poses."

My hand stills on her foot, and I lift it to kiss the arch, the side of her ankle, running my nose along the soft skin of her lower leg. She exhales a sigh, and my cock stirs.

"Whenever you're ready."

She sets the bowl aside and stands, taking my hand. "Come with me."

Angel's back is against the headboard, and she's surrounded by pillows as I slowly remove my shirt, followed by my slacks. When we entered the bedroom, she took off the sweatshirt she was wearing, trailing it to the ground followed closely by her panties.

Now she's lying in bed in only a black lace bra, biting her bottom lip as I slowly disrobe.

My cock springs out and her eyes widen. "Sure you're not too tired for this?"

"Am I ever?"

That whole pregnancy makes you horny rumor? It's true.

Climbing on my knees onto the bed, I start at her ankle, tracing my lips up the inside of her thigh, watching her breasts rise and fall as her breath becomes shallow. I kiss the inside of her knee and she exhales a whimper.

Tracing my tongue along her inner thigh, I kiss, and pull the delicate skin as her fingers thread in my hair. Her back arches and her body sways like a dancer the closer I get to her bare pussy, and I'm doing my best to draw it out.

Apparently watermelon has the same effect on taste as pineapple, and I've been craving her as much as she's been craving it. Wrapping my arms around her thighs, I catch her heated eyes before lowering to slide my tongue around her slippery clit.

"Oh, Deacon!" She gasps, her fingers curling against my scalp.

I give her another long, slow figure eight, returning to focus rapid sweeps across that hot spot, and her back arches off the bed. I touch her lightly with my teeth and she cries out, tightening her thighs around my ears.

"That's it…" she gasps. "Keep doing that…"

She's bucking against my face, straining and moaning, and my cock is a rod of iron. I have her right on the edge when I quickly move around behind her, moving her leg forward and grasping my erection. As soon as I'm lined up, I thrust to the hilt, and we both exhale a groan.

I want to hold it, to make it last, but she's bouncing her ass against me, pumping my cock as I snake my hand around her waist, grasping her inner thighs, and trailing my fingers higher to her center. Our fingers entwine, stroking her clit as we move.

"Right there…" Her moans are feverish.

My forehead rests on her shoulder, and we move frantically, chasing the climax just within reach.

"Angel…" I groan, moving faster. "Angel, yes…"

Her moans grow more frantic, her movements desperate, and I know she's right at the edge. I move my fingers, circling faster, faster as I feel her shimmering around my cock. I'm right there, pleasure snaking up my thighs a bead of sweat trickling down my cheek, when she breaks into spasms.

"Ooh…" She jerks, placing her hand over mine to lighten my touch.

I close my eyes, ready to let go when something unexpected happens. A surge of liquid pushes me out.

"Holy shit!" I move back as Angel's face crumples.

"Deacon! Oh no… Oh, shit. I think my water broke!"

"What tha…" I'm out of the bed, confused and grabbing towels.

Angel crawls to the side, holding her stomach. "Oh, ow… It hurts…"

"We've got to get you to the hospital!" My heart rate kicks higher. Hell, I haven't come down from that shocking *coitus interruptus*. I jerk my slacks over my hips and grab the sweatshirt she discarded off the floor. "Can you walk?"

"Bring me a dress."

I run to her closet, ripping a black dress off a hanger and carrying it to her. It feels like I'm moving too slow but I'm moving as fast as I can. Angel lowers the dress over her head then puts both feet on the floor and tries to stand.

Immediately, she buckles over. Her head is bowed, and her shoulders shake. She makes a shrieking noise, and terror punches me in the chest.

"Angel?" I put my hand on her shoulder. "What's wrong, baby? What do you need me to do?"

Her chin lifts, and when our eyes meet I realize she's laughing. Loudly. "I shot your penis out like it was on a waterslide at an amusement park!"

My panic fades, and I'm about to laugh with her—it was pretty damn funny, after all—when she leans to the side and gasps loudly, "Oh, shit! Oh, shit... This hurts!"

Diving forward, I hold her arm, rubbing her shoulder and trying to remember what the hell I'm supposed to do to help her. I hold her hand and count... seven seconds...

She takes a few deep breaths, then she explodes again, laughing hysterically. "I can't believe my water broke... That's what I call coming."

I think my wife is losing her mind. "Honey... we need to get you to the hospital. Can you walk?"

"Yeah..." It's a high-pitched squeak through a peal of laughter.

I hold her under the arm, and we quickly make our way to my car, grabbing the hospital suitcase on the way.

"YOU'RE DOING GREAT, ANG!" ANGEL'S DOCTOR IS A WOMAN JUST A little older than my aunt, and I'm convinced she was a former cheerleader.

I keep waiting for her to start chanting "Push her out, push her out, waaaay out!"

Winnie, Lourdes, Beto, Valeria, and the girls are in that plush waiting room, and the perky male nurse peeps in every few minutes to get a status check.

"We're almost crowning," the doctor calls, and he holds up both hands doing a big nod, before heading out the door again to share the news with our family.

Angel's face is covered in sweat, and her cheeks are so red. Our hands are clasped, and she's squeezing the fuck out of my fingers. "I can't do it anymore."

"You've got this... You're almost there." I kiss her forehead, keeping my arm around her shoulder as she sits forward on the bed.

"This is it!" The doctor orders. "We're right there. Give me one more big push, and we'll have her."

Angel gasps again, looking up at me. I lower my face to hers. "You got this, babe. Ready? Let's meet our little girl."

She nods, closing her eyes, and with one last deep breath, she yells as she pushes with all her might.

The doctor reaches forward and grabs my wrist, dragging me down to the foot of the bed and putting my hand on something hot and wet. "Guide her out."

My heart drops to my feet, but I look down and realize... I'm touching our baby's head. "It's her!"

Angel pushes once more, and the doctor's hands are beside mine, guiding her into my arms. I'm holding her when she takes her first breath and starts to cry. My heart expands fifty times its normal size. Her hair is black and her skin is red and she's and covered in goo and screaming her little head off, and she's so gorgeous.

I wait as the doctor snips the cord, and the nurse guides me to the head of the bed, where I place our daughter on her mother's chest. I can't take my eyes off her.

"My baby..." Tears stream down Angel's cheeks, and I blink back my own tears as our daughter's little voice fills the room with strong cries.

A nurse joins us. "I'll take her for just a second."

Passing her for weighing and the rest, I gather Angel in my arms and kiss her on the mouth, long and full of love. Pulling back, our eyes meet. "You did it, Mamma."

"Oh, Deacon." She sniffs, dropping her head against my chest.

The nurse is back, and she places our daughter in her mother's arms, helping her latch onto Angel's breast.

After all the commotion, the craziness, and the noise, the room settles into peaceful quiet. The only sound is my precious daughter's little grunts as she has her first meal in the world.

I sit on the side of the bed, smoothing my palm over her little dark head. It fits perfectly in my palm.

"She's so beautiful," I whisper, my voice filled with awe. "I love her so much."

Our moment is short-lived as the crew files into the room. Valeria carries Sofia, who reaches for me and climbs over to look at the new baby.

"She's so tiny!" Sofia cries. "Look at her little fingers. Look at her little fingernails!"

We grin, watching her cousin.

"Great job, Sis." Beto, steps forward to kiss the top of Angel's head. "She's beautiful."

"Rockstar!" Lourdes holds up both fists. "First you slay the art world, then you slay the motherland… or something."

We all laugh, and Sofia climbs off my lap to get a better view of her new cousin. "What are you going to call her?"

Angel looks up at me, and I nod. We've discussed her name so many times, and we finally decided on just the right one.

"Heaven." Angel slides her palm behind the baby's head, positioning her so we can all admire her. "Heaven Valentina Dring."

"Heaven." Sofia repeats, nodding her head. "Hey, there, Heaven!" Her voice is quiet. "I'm your cousin Sofia. I'll teach you everything you need to know."

"She's a little piece of heaven." Winnie says, putting her hand on Angel's arm.

"Born from an angel." I add, and Angel wrinkles her nose at my corny joke.

"Carried in on a tidal wave of love," she snickers.

Our friends exchange a look, and I just shake my head.

I'm still amazed by all of us here together. All these people who hated each other not so long ago. Now we're laughing and hugging, surrounding my wife's bed and cooing over a tiny baby. Our valentine from heaven.

To think it all started in a park, on a warm spring day, when I crashed into a beautiful girl with the saddest eyes I'd ever seen.

Through all the bitterness and heartache, the violence and anger, we almost lost it all, but even in the darkest hour, I held onto my promise to her.

We chose love.

We chose each other.

From our first kiss to the vows we've exchanged, to our baby girl in our arms. Our love may be wild and free, but our family is united, stronger than ever, and choosing love over hate with every new heartbeat, with every reckless kiss, again and again, until death do us part.

The End.

Thank you for reading RECKLESS KISS!
I hope you loved Deacon and Angel and all the gang as much as I did.

Never Miss a New Release!
Sign up for my newsletter (http://smarturl.it/TLMnews) and get a
FREE 3-story book bundle.
And/or get a New Release Alert by messaging TIALOUISE to 64600
now!*
*Text service is U.S. only.

Loved Noel and Dove and the gang in Harristown?
Read Noel and Taron's angsty, small-town, brother's best friend
*romance **WAIT FOR ME** Today!*
It's FREE in Kindle Unlimited and available on audio.

Keep clicking for a short sneak peek…

OR!

*Mindy falls hard for Noel's older brother Sawyer in **HERE WITH ME**,*
a second-chance, military romance also available on audiobook!

Keep reading for a short sneak peek…

WAIT FOR

by Tia Louise

~~Dear Taron,~~
~~I should have told you this a long time ago...~~

~~Dear Taron,~~
~~Is there a time-limit on forgiveness?~~
~~If there is, I haven't reached it...~~

~~Dear Taron,~~
~~I still love you...~~

A letter never sent.
Heck, I never even finished it.
Taron Rhodes was my brother's best friend.
He was sexy as sin.
But he was more than that...
He was ponytail-pulling, ice down your shirt teasing, throw you in the lake screaming...
Strong, tanned arms and bright green eyes over a heart-stopping, naughty grin...
Did I mention his tight end?
I gave him my first real kiss, my heart, my everything.
I said I'd wait for him...
I'm still waiting, because Taron Rhodes is still the man of my dreams,
And I have a secret that has his bright green eyes.

Noel LaGrange stole my heart when she was only eighteen—
pushing me off a flatbed and calling me a city slicker.
Her brother Sawyer would kick my ass if he knew how many
times we made out that summer, how close we got.
Everything changed when Sawyer and I joined the military.
We were honorably discharged, but I didn't go to her.
Instead, I went back to the city… where no amount of money,
no amount of pills can heal this wound.
Only her whiskey eyes and dark hair, her slim arms and her sweet
scent, give me hope.
I broke her heart just as surely as I broke mine, but I'm going
back to make it right.
If she's still waiting…

(WAIT FOR ME is a STAND-ALONE small-town, second-chance romance. No cheating. No cliffhangers.)

Prologue

Noel

MY MOMMA WAS TOO BEAUTIFUL TO DIE.

At least, that's what everybody said.

Penelope Jean Harris was the scion of our town's founder and prettiest girl in three parishes. She was head majorette in high school and homecoming queen and prom queen and every other queen. She was Peach Princess, Teen Dixie Peach, and Miss Dixie Gem. She would've gone on to be Miss Louisiana if my daddy hadn't made her a Mrs.

I was eleven—that strange age between too big to play in the creek in only my panties and too little to sleep without the closet light on. I loved Dolly Parton and butterflies and picking peaches straight off my daddy's trees and eating them, jumping in the lake and running after jackrabbits with my little brother Leon.

In the summer the trees were rich green, and the sweet scent of peach juice filled the air. In the winter they were sparse, bony hands, reaching palms up to heaven. Branches like fingers spread, grasping for hope.

Momma's hazel eyes crinkled at the corners whenever she looked at me or my brothers or my daddy. Her sweet smile was warm sunshine when I got cold.

She would wrap me in her arms and sing an old sad song when I was sleepy or cranky or "out of sorts," which is how she'd put it. I pictured "sorts" as ivory dominoes I could line up and knock down or slap off the table, across the room. I'd pull her silky brown hair around me like a cape and close my eyes and breathe…

Then she was gone.

She went for a walk one crisp winter evening along the narrow, dirt road that runs past our orchard out to the old house on the hill. Frost was in the air; bonfires were burning. The man driving the truck said she came out of nowhere.

He never saw her.

She never saw him.

Six weeks later, in that same orchard with peach blossoms on the trees and dew tipping the grass, on the very spot she died, my daddy took his life with his own gun.

I guess sometimes love makes you forget things can get better.

I guess he didn't see a bend in the road up ahead.

I guess he only saw a straight line leading deeper and deeper into black.

My daddy was the star of his high school football team… but Life threw him a pass he couldn't catch with Momma's death.

Our world changed forever that winter.

Dolly says love is like a butterfly, soft and gentle as a sigh, but from what I've seen of love, I think it's more like a tornado, shocking and violent and so powerful it can rip your soul out of your mouth…

It's faster than you can run, and it blows one house away while leaving the next one peacefully standing.

I didn't know which way love would take me, quietly or with the roar of a freight train. I should've known. I should've realized the moment I saw him.

It was both. It was quiet as the brush of peach fuzz, but it left my insides in splinters. It twisted my lungs and lifted me up so high only to throw me down with a force that rang my ears and flooded my eyes.

It all started the summer before they left, a month before my brother was sent to fight in a war everybody said was over.

It all started in the kitchen of my momma's house...

Get WAIT FOR ME and fall in love with this brother's best friend, military romance today.
Also available on audiobook.

HERE WITH

Me

Sawyer LaGrange.
He's my best friend's older brother.
He's quiet, brooding, *sinfully sexy*…
Dark hair, a scruffy square jaw, and deep lines of muscle I trace
my fingers along slowly, followed by my lips…
He always does what's right.
Until me…
They say you get in life what you have the courage to ask for.
Well, I'm brave.
And I want him.

Secrets.
Everybody has them.
Big, small, innocent… *forbidden.*
Mindy was a line I should never have crossed.
But I did.
She was beautiful… sassy and tempting,
And rules were made to be broken.
We broke them all.

Now I'm home, released from service with hidden scars.
Now my secrets are the demons that grow stronger every day.
I try to send her away, but I can't let her go.
She's my reason to fight, and I'll walk through hell to be the man
she deserves.
To give her a reason to stay *here with me.*

**(HERE WITH ME is a STAND-ALONE best friend's older
brother, second-chance, military romance. No cheating. No
cliffhangers.)**

Prologue

Sawyer

LOVE WAS ALL AROUND ME WHEN I WAS A KID.

It was the twinkle in my mamma's eyes when my little sister Noel walked out on stage at the Princess Peach pageant. Even if she ducked her chin and wouldn't look at anybody, much less the judges.

It was in her full-body laugh the time my baby brother Leon ate cocoa powder and started crying because it was so bitter. We all laughed until he got mad and wouldn't speak to us for an hour. He said he wanted a new family.

It was walking with my daddy in the rows, listening to his thoughts on life. It was the warmth in his voice when he'd show me the green shoots of new growth on a peach tree. It was him calling me *son*.

One day, this will all be yours, son…

Sitting beside Hayes pond, I reach in a plastic box and pull out a brown cricket. Its spindly legs fan out as I thread the fish hook down its spine before tossing it onto the water. I don't like fishing with insects, but they're the best way to catch bass or perch, my daddy's favorite.

I watch as it bobs along the short waves, slowly getting water-logged, slowly sinking into the depths. The wind moves through the cold trees and the early-morning light is pale gray.

It's quiet.

I like the quiet. It helps my mind relax, and I can sort through my thoughts, straightening them out like playing cards dropped on the floor.

Fifty-two card pickup.

A dirty trick played on little kids.

Noel went fishing with us once. She was only five, and she chattered nonstop. Daddy didn't mind her flitting around, bouncing back and forth between us, but I was ten. I wanted her to sit down and shut up. Stop scaring away the fish.

When she saw us baiting our hooks with crickets, she fell back and got real quiet.

Finally, I thought, until I looked around and saw she'd opened the box and let all our bait hop away to freedom.

It was my mamma's favorite story.

She'd make Daddy or me tell it every time she wanted a good laugh. Her hazel eyes would crinkle at the corners, and she'd smile that pretty smile, lips parting over straight white teeth.

People say I've got my mamma's eyes...

Daddy and I used to go fishing every Sunday, but he hasn't left his room since Mamma died last month. He sits in a chair, not speaking, not eating, just staring out the window, like he's waiting for her to come back for him, waiting for her to tell him it's time to get up and eat something, start living again.

Mamma had gone for a walk that evening around twilight. She was just over the hill on the narrow dirt road when that truck came out of nowhere and killed her instantly.

The driver said he never saw her.

The coroner said she probably never saw him.

I hope she didn't.

I hope she was thinking about Noel freeing all our live bait that steamy summer morning. I hope she was laughing softly, thinking of her family, full of love as she slipped away to heaven.

When the sheriff told my daddy what happened, my daddy

fell to his knees. The noise that came from him was raw and wild, something I'd never heard before or since. Mr. Vincent looked at me like he didn't know what to do, so I went and carried my daddy inside to his room.

An ache lodged in the middle of my back that night, right between my shoulder blades.

I hope if I catch a mess of fish and cook them up how he likes, maybe Daddy will come back to us and stop sitting in that chair, silent and far away.

The line dips then a sharp tug almost pulls the pole out of my hand. My grip tightens, and I turn the spinner fast, reeling in a good-sized perch, a little bigger than my palm.

A few casts later, and I've caught enough to feed us all, once I clean them.

I'm walking back to my truck. At sixteen, I've been driving for about a year. It's close enough to walk home but cold as fuck, which is why I drove.

The last thing I expect to see is a girl sitting on the ground this side of the fence. It's Noel's friend Mindy Ray. She's wrapped in a thick, beige coat that looks like a teddy bear, and her frizzy, dark-brown head is pressed forward against her knees. She's crying. I can hear her sharp sniffles as I get closer.

"Hey." I put my hand on her shoulder, giving her a little shake. "You okay?"

She only pulls away from me, not lifting her head.

Frowning, I squint up to where my old red Chevy waits. I'm kind of maxed-out on the emotional front right now, but I can't leave her this way.

Ever since Mamma passed, the adults have been lost in their own heads. It's like they forgot about us kids, like they forgot we're suffering, too, and we still need them. It's made me feel like I need to step up and look out for us, and there's no way in hell I'm leaving her out here in the cold.

Reaching down, I catch her skinny arm and pull her to her feet. "Come on."

"Leave me alone!" She jerks her arm out of my grip and glares at me.

Mindy's only eleven, but she's got this look that kind of hits you right in the gut, bright green eyes, full lips, and all that thick, dark spirally-wild hair.

She's beautiful.

For a little girl.

"Fine." I start to go. I want to leave her after that outburst, but I only get a few steps before turning back. My jaw clenches, and my voice is more like a growl. "What's wrong with you?"

She answers sharp and fast. "Nothing's wrong with me."

"Why are you crying?"

"It's nothing you'd understand, Sawyer LaGrange. No one's ever made fun of you." She shoves a coiled lock of hair behind her ear. "Just forget you ever saw me here."

Little drama queen. Fat chance of that. "I got to get back to the house. Don't make me put you over my shoulder."

Her lips press together, and she glares daggers at me for the space of a few blinks. But when I start walking, I hear her following me. Reaching over the side, I put the bucket of fish and my rod in the bed of the truck while she climbs in on the passenger's side.

The engine is a low rumble in the quiet, and I shift it into gear before driving us slowly back toward my house. Mindy's arms are crossed. She's staring out the window, but her lower lip quivers. It makes me uncomfortable.

Still… "Want to tell me what happened?"

"No."

Suits me just fine. I direct my gaze out the windshield, thinking about what's waiting for me.

The sun rises slowly over the rows of peach trees that make up our family's 100-acre orchard. Golden light tips the frost on the dark green leaves. Frost is okay now with no buds on the trees, but frost in April can wipe out an entire crop, all our income for the year.

As the oldest son, Daddy's been grooming me to take over the place one day. Leon's only seven, and Noel's just a girl. I have mixed feelings about the idea.

Before Mamma died, I thought I might travel, maybe join the military. I've been in Harristown my whole life, and while it's my home, I want to do something, see the world before I settle down and take over.

Resting my elbow on the window, I rub my forehead wondering what's going to become of all that now. My mind's a million miles away when Mindy's voice pulls me back.

"Why do girls want to be in cliques?"

I look over at her. Her green eyes are red-rimmed, but she's stopped crying.

"Is that what this is about?"

"Elizabeth Haynes said I look like I stuck my finger in a socket." She tugs on the side of her hair. "Beth Hebert and everybody laughed. They said I must be adopted."

My hands tighten on the steering wheel. I don't know why girls do what they do. "Why don't you just hang out with Noel?"

Her chin drops, and she twists her fingers. "She's kind of... out of it." She quickly adds, "Which is understandable! I understand... I just get lonely."

My mind returns to that thought I was having earlier about the adults being out to lunch and leaving us to figure it out.

"Listen." Her green eyes fix on mine, and I've got her attention. I'm sixteen. I'm the oldest of all us kids, and they do what I say. "You're gonna be really pretty one day. Some girls have a problem with that."

Her slim brows furrow. "Gonna be? One day? Make me feel better next time."

This is why I don't say much. It always comes out all fucked up.

"I just mean people want to keep you in your place. You gotta blow that shit off and be yourself. Take the high road."

Daddy always said I'm "old for my age." I just keep my mouth shut and watch how people act. After a while, you start to notice patterns.

Mindy looks out the window again like she's thinking about what I said. We're pulling into my long driveway, and I see a few cars I wasn't expecting. One of them is the sheriff's, and my heart beats faster. *What now?*

The tightness in my shoulders moves around to the front of my neck, like somebody's strangling me.

"I guess I understand." Mindy's still thinking about her problem.

Reaching over, I pat her shoulder. "If you ever need somebody to talk to, just come to me. I'll take care of you."

She looks up at me, and her green eyes fill with an emotion I half recognize. *Trust.* I'd remember it better if I weren't doing my best to fight the panic settling on my skin like cold rain.

Sheriff Gautreaux stands on our front porch with Ed Daniels beside him. They both have that look on their faces—stony, preparing for what's about to happen.

The fish in the back of my truck are forgotten as I climb out of the cab. Whatever brought them here is like a bad storm rolling in. It's in the air around me, metallic on my tongue.

The sheriff is the first one to speak. "Sawyer, we need to talk to you, son."

Son.

My insides clench, and my breath gets tight. A small hand slips into mine, and I look down. Beside me, Mindy's brow is furrowed, her green eyes meet mine.

Somehow as small as she is, having her here beside me, holding my hand, I'm able to catch my breath. "Yes, sir?"

"It's your daddy." His voice is the same as the night he told us

Mamma died. The knot between my shoulder blades twists tighter with every word. "We found him up on the old dirt road... I'm sorry."

My daddy died from a self-inflicted gunshot wound. They found him in the same place they found my mamma.

I guess he got tired of waiting for her.

I guess he decided she was too much to lose.

I guess he forgot about us.

Roaring fills my ears like a hurricane, destroying everything, and sweeping it all away. My parents, my home...

No.

Not my home.

I won't let that happen.

Whatever it takes, I'll hold us together.

Mindy's small hand tightens around mine, and she holds me, an anchor in the middle of the storm.

I said I'd take care of her, and she's standing here trusting me—they all are.

Old for my age.

That day changed everything, but she stood beside me. A girl who turned out to be stronger than I knew, a girl who would hold my hand in the darkest hour.

A girl who would change my life.

It all started the day I thought I'd lost everything...

Get HERE WITH ME Today!
Also available on audiobook.

Books by
TIA LOUISE

BOOKS IN KINDLE UNLIMITED
STAND-ALONE ROMANCES
Reckless Kiss, 2020★
Here with Me, 2020★
Wait for Me, 2019★
Boss of Me, 2019★
Stay, 2019★
Make Me Yours, 2019★
Make You Mine, 2018
When We Kiss, 2018
Save Me, 2018
The Right Stud, 2018
When We Touch, 2017
The Last Guy, 2017★
(★Available on Audiobook.)

THE DIRTY PLAYERS SERIES
PRINCE (#1), 2016★
PLAYER (#2), 2016★
DEALER (#3), 2017
THIEF (#4), 2017
(★Available on Audiobook.)

THE BRIGHT LIGHTS SERIES
Under the Lights (#1), 2018
Under the Stars (#2), 2018
Hit Girl (#3), 2018

PARANORMAL ROMANCES
One Immortal (Derek & Melissa, vampires)
One Insatiable (Stitch & Mercy, shifters)

eBOOKS ON ALL RETAILERS
THE ONE TO HOLD SERIES
One to Hold (#1 - Derek & Melissa)★
One to Keep (#2 - Patrick & Elaine)★
One to Protect (#3 - Derek & Melissa)★
One to Love (#4 - Kenny & Slayde)
One to Leave (#5 - Stuart & Mariska)
One to Save (#6 - Derek & Melissa)★
One to Chase (#7 - Marcus & Amy)★
One to Take (#8 - Stuart & Mariska)
(★Available on Audiobook.)

Descriptions, teasers, excerpts and more are on my website
authortialouise.com

Never miss a new release!

Sign up for my New Release newsletter and get a FREE Tia
Louise Story Bundle!

ABOUT THE
Author

TIA LOUISE IS THE *USA TODAY* BESTSELLING, AWARD-WINNING AUTHOR of super hot and sexy romance.

WHETHER BILLIONAIRES, MARINES, FIGHTERS, COWBOYS, SINGLE DADS, OR CEOs, all her heroes are alphas with hearts of gold, and all her heroines are strong, sassy ladies who love them.

A FORMER TEACHER, JOURNALIST, AND BOOK EDITOR, LOUISE LIVES IN THE Midwest USA with her trophy husband and two teenage geniuses.

Signed Copies of all books online at:
http://smarturl.it/SignedPBs

Connect with Tia:

Website: www.authortialouise.com

Pinterest: pinterest.com/AuthorTiaLouise

Instagram (@AuthorTLouise)

Bookbub Author Page: www.bookbub.com/authors/tia-louise

Amazon Author Page: amzn.to/1jm2F2b

Goodreads: www.goodreads.com/author/show/7213961.Tia_
Louise

Snapchat: bit.ly/24kDboV

** On Facebook? **

Be a Mermaid! Join Tia's **Reader Group** at
"Tia's Books, Babes & Mermaids"!
www.facebook.com/groups/TiasBooksandBabes

www.AuthorTiaLouise.com
allnightreads@gmail.com

Made in the USA
Middletown, DE
20 October 2022